CLAUDIU MURGAN

CHAPTER 1

The recently reduced weekly water ration, the third one since the beginning of the year, still afforded Cherry the lavishness of a Starbucks-type mug of dark coffee once a day in the privacy of her home, and like everyone else hooked on java, once a week at any coffee shop that would scan the chip embedded in the back of her hand. It was almost ten o'clock and she had not yet finished with her usual schedule of a light breakfast of fruit and oatmeal soaked in coconut milk. She swallowed the last bit of food without being aware of its taste, grabbed the mug, and rushed to her office just in time to hear on the live broadcast of the *Water For All 2055* Conference, the UN-Water president, Geanine Botha announcing enthusiastically the next speaker.

"Now I have the honor of introducing the most enigmatic water activist out there, one that, most of the time, does what none of us can: uncover the atrocities water has endured at the hands of companies and governments that have lost their way in respecting the earth. Hayyin is once again with us, sparking the fight."

A copious round of applause and loud cheers followed immediately.

Quickly, Cherry pulled on an oversized jacket that hung on the back of her chair and in the process, her elbow hit the stack of her students' papers that were taking her limnology class at the University of Toronto. She picked up the mask that was leaning against one of the metal filing cabinets, and tied the straps behind her head. It had a long, oval shape, a wavy opening for the mouth, and two small cuts for the eyes under which marks had been made in red paint, signifying tears of blood for the injustice done to the African people by wave after wave of Europeans placing and keeping puppets as decision makers. This was the face of Hayyin, the fearless water activist who had kept her identity hidden for safety reasons. These were significant players she was going up against, unscrupulous men for which killing would bring no remorse. She put mittens on to hide any remaining exposed skin and to camouflage any hint of the speaker's gender before enabling the camera on her iPad.

The cameraman enlarged the view to capture the dimly lit room that had gone quiet. The thick carpet muffled the high-heels of late arrivals. The curves of the heavy curtains hung low, letting less light in.

"Hello, everyone. Peace be with you, Chief Landing Eagle and Kahuna Lapa'au. Your spiritual strength is the bond our weakened belief needs," she started by showing her respect to the elders invited to address the onsite participants and the online audience. She breathed deeply, trying to steady the nerves running through her legs, which had been bouncing in place. "Thank you, Geanine. Thank you all for allowing my presence at such a pivotal event held by our friends in Toronto.

"Let's be frank: as Geanine has mentioned, it was a real struggle bringing so many parties together by eliminating the distrust, the noise, and the rumors created by those that want us to stay divided. Even if there is reluctance about the honesty of our common goal, I assure you I've personally checked the funding sources of each of your organizations. We don't need tainted money. Throughout my investigation, I've identified people with good intentions, but a false idea about the origin of money for their projects. The enablers use multi-layer, shell corporations. In addition, they infiltrate the companies with low-ranking workers who leak information."

Cherry's voice came out distorted by the mask's narrow mouth-slit, but clear enough for the audience to hear her.

"Protecting the depletion of water resources, water remediation, and the prevention of water pollution are complex activities, and if not viewed from a holistic perspective, we'll just be 'treading water,' to use a figure of speech." Several giggles sounded at the remark.

"We can't afford to favor one over the other. There are priorities, but no exceptions. And while we all understand that the funding for water remediation is greater than that of a project related to pollution prevention, the latter is no less important."

Behind the mask, drops of sweat fell into her eyes, making her blink continuously, distracting her. "Excuse me for a second," she said. Cherry disabled the camera, lifted the mask, and wiped her face with the bottom of the extra-large t-shirt she was wearing. She tasted salt and felt thirsty. Cherry took a sip of her black coffee, slipped the mask back into place, and enabled the camera again. "I apologize. I needed a sip of water," she said, addressing the audience that had remained quiet during her short reprieve.

"I don't know how many of you have had the patience to read through the one-and-a-half terabyte of emails released by WikiLeaks last week, but the main stories are about US congressmen who have done the same as any other senator or congressman does on a regular basis: they used their positions for human trafficking, influence and corruption.

"There was also a story about polarized energy and clean food conglomerates' stock manipulation, known in the circles of power, yet no one lifted a finger to sanction them.

"And let's not forget about diplomatic embarrassments in Asian countries, and the number of CIA cover-up activities 'that never happened'," she said sarcastically. "But that's just the fluff.

"Usually, WikiLeaks is searched using a name as a starting point. From there, one connects the dots to get the whole story. My search was a bit different: I used nouns. A query on the word, water, returned some interesting results. Names, too, but not the ones I expected. Private security companies with international offices have developed profitable subsidiaries staging freshwater resource takeovers, either from governments or rightful, private owners. Then, they stay put, protecting newly-acquired assets on behalf of their masters. They are official mercenaries, used even by governments when they want off-the-book initiatives.

"Is anyone in the room from either South America or Europe?" she asked. Five hands rose upward. "Ecuador, Brazil,

Romania?" she said. Representatives from these countries were not shy to identify their place of origin.

"You guys should be on the watch in these countries," Cherry said, empowered. Once more, she felt drops run down her skin. "South America, Africa, and several European countries are their main targets, with easy to manipulate governments and relaxed laws regarding ownership of local water resources and how they should be used. This creates opportunities for international players to take advantage. As I've said so many times before: access to water is a birthright, not a privilege, but this statement has been twisted until it's lost all meaning. Peoples' short-term attention has been even further distracted by the next fake news or fad."

She felt the mittens stick to her sweaty palms, and the weight of her mask pushing against her nose, forcing her to breathe heavily. Acknowledging the difficulty of attacking so many challenges at once choked her. Cherry clenched her teeth, swallowed to push the knot in her dry throat down, and continued. "When, fifteen years ago, laws forbidding the use of paper in day-to-day life as a measure to stop both legal and illegal tree cutting were implemented, the companies affected by it switched their attention to other commodities, water included. On the black market, water sells for gold or Bitcoin. The latest satellite images show no improvement in deforested areas undergoing recent, significant, forestation programs. It's as if without any trees to support, the water has moved somewhere else, and can't be convinced to come back. Is this our punishment? If so, it's an intelligent one, and we deserve it."

Cherry had to move her legs and get some air beneath her disguise. The wood of the mask warmed by the heat of her burning face released a soft, oily scent that cleared her throat for several long moments. She regained her thoughts, lost in the depths of slashing plastic debris and dead mammals and images recently gathered by the Greenpeace incursion in the North Pacific only two weeks before which had stuck in her active subconscious. Cherry straightened her back before delivering the last part of her message, pain stabbing at her shoulder blades.

"We shouldn't end this conference without a unanimous decision as to which short- and long-term projects we are going to fund; what the emergency procedure for unforeseen events is, when even government intervention teams cannot react in time; and what the approach for the 'path of least resistance' to change the media's persistent narrative that the 'brink of disaster is not here yet' will be. Having all of this accomplished will strengthen our position and attract volunteers from communities of every size. One person per community as a catalyst will be the spark. We have to identify that person and provide all means for the spark to ignite organically."

Cherry leaned over to grab her coffee mug, forgetting, for a second, that she was wearing a mask. She smiled at her silly gesture, then continued. "I'll be checking the live webcast and the information published on the projects that will make it onto the shortlist.

"Goodbye, and thank you again."

She disabled the video connection, muted the microphone, pulled the mask off, and gulped a mouthful of coffee that satiated her burning thirst. She used her blue t-shirt to wipe the perspiration from her face and looked amused at the wet marks left on the white logo—large parentheses—, a bold "W" whose sides curved on the way up, signifying an embrace or an invitation for all interested and concerned to join the cause. Wearing Hayyin's persona hadn't gotten any easier over the last five years. She didn't like hiding; not taking responsibility was the action of an immature person. The alternative, however, was much worse.

Cherry missed Geanine Botha's opening remarks, but she was planning on watching the recording later that day. She picked up the iPad and the coffee mug and moved to the living room.

"Connect to the TV," she commanded and the wireless feed appeared on the larger screen.

She made herself confortable on the couch and blew several times into the mug of steaming coffee before taking a couple of sips. Her mind was deeply plugged into the charged atmosphere of the *Water For All 2055* Conference, hosted in Toronto, her city, over the next few days. Cherry felt energized after talking in front of the crowd of NGO representatives, carefully selected CEOs of companies, environmentalists, activists, and any other parties thinking that they could make a difference and were willing to pay the entry fee to the most anticipated water-related event of the year.

For a moment, the live feed switched to the Royal York's elegant ballroom dotted with round tables covered in white sparkling tablecloth, then the camera angle cut to the impromptu podium where a long table had name labels for seven individuals on display, some of the most trusted leaders of the water movement, there to enforce the idea of unity for the greater good.

She knew most of them personally. Sunil Samaradinghan, an older Indian man whose relentless belief in the power of one had gathered an entire village around his efforts to clean a dirty river venerated by the community for centuries; Martin Cousteau, great-great-great grandson of the unforgettable Jacques Cousteau, who had also pledged his life to saving the oceans; Geanine Botha, UN-Water chair and *Water For All*'s president whose presence was required to bring legitimacy and structure not only to the present event but to any future program run under the WFA umbrella; Mark Watershed, actor turned humanitarian who lived by example, keeping bare necessities to a minimum and shedding the aura and the ostentatiousness of the celebrity lifestyle; Chief Landing Eagle, speaking on behalf of Native Americans who, even to that day, stood as the most reputable water defenders against the destruction oil pipelines had on pristine ecosystems that were an integral part of all tribes and their only known way of living; Kahuna Hualani Lapa'au, one of the last spiritual leaders of Hawaii and herbal healer; and Nancy Grotenberg, the president of Clean Water Funding Association.

They were all representing organizations or communities making a stand against those denying climate change and environmental pollution.

Cherry would meet them later on at one of the panels she was chairing.

Kahuna Hualani Lapa'au spoke next. Even when sitting, his stature was a foot taller than that of his colleagues at the presiding table. Only his wide nose and the area around his cheekbones were free of tattoos. Hawaiian symbols ran from his forehead to the sides of his shaved head and down over his jaw and chin, symbols of an ancient language, there for everyone to see, but few to understand. The only remaining hair on the top of his head was gathered in a long ponytail down his back. Leather bracelets circled his thick wrists, and a blue, triangular crystal the size of a chicken egg hung at his neck.

"My people have always had a special connection with all of God's creations: the mountains, the ocean, the crawlers, and the flyers. We don't discriminate between them, but instead, treat them with respect. Our survival depends on their survival. We still bow to Pele, the mighty spirit of the volcano that birthed our islands and sing praises to every creature that breathes around us. Hawaiian people never thought of themselves as being separated from nature—it's unthinkable. But when white men arrived, destruction followed. Balance was disrupted and never returned. We've been fighting since with prayers, songs, love, forgiveness, and through legal means, but white men are more powerful, sneakier," he thundered, fists closed in front of him. "Even to his day, our land is the playground for big corporations preferring to pollute remote locations, far away from their homes. Instead of acknowledging their mistakes and leaving, they sue us, claiming we have interrupted their operations.

"How to fight such lies? Our children are sick, our elders die before their time. The ocean is angry with us. The catch is scarce and tastes rotten. Our forefathers warned us that such times might come. Why are we being punished for someone else's mistakes?" Kahuna Lapa'au stood up, his enormous chest filling the entire screen. The view quickly scaled back.

Cherry felt his pain, the sum not only of the Hawaiian community but of humanity suffering at the hands of a few, fortunate groups, thrilled with their access to power, money, and the thought that the sublime conditions would last forever. A knot tangled her stomach and a light nausea tried her.

Still standing, Kahuna continued addressing the invisible enemy. "I'm saddened by my choice of words as love, hope, and cooperation is what our ancestors have passed from one generation to the next. Our written records abound with joyful colors and positive wisdom. For the young people joining this crusade, I tell you that Mother Earth speaks to us. We feel her pain, see her deep scars that only get deeper while the greedy chase her for resources, and we understand her defense system. Wake up, you lost sons of Pure Energy, and protect your mother." Kahuna's warning seemed to explode from the screen, his eyes squinting fiercely and directly into the camera. His words carried no hatred or venom, only the soft disappointment of the powerless situation in which the leader had found himself.

"The fight of the Hawaiian people goes beyond water protection. We are trying to save an entire ecosystem that has survived for billions of years." He sat down, covered the blue crystal with his right palm, and began a low-voiced prayer lasting no more than several seconds; a moment of gratitude to the higher spirits.

Cherry's heart, sensible to the pain endured by the Hawaiian people at the hands of those corporations disrespecting sacred beliefs, poured out tears through her blue eyes. She stared intently at the TV screen to check her reflection, the reflection of Cherry Mortinger, a forty-two-year-old limnologist, and also the one representing Hayyin, a radical water activist that had successfully kept his real identity hidden. Hayyin meant water in Aramaic, Jesus's tribe's language, also considered humanity's primordial spoken language. As Hayyin, she usually delivered incendiary facts about the atrocious behavior of major worldwide corporations on carefully selected blogs and websites that stood at arm's length from the subject of her investigations. Each time she spoke as Hayyin, she required extra measures of security. It wasn't fear of death that had forced her into a secondary identity, as she was well aware that her soul would live forever, but the fear of not doing enough for the cause. Her physical elimination at this late stage in the water salvation fight was not a chance she was willing to take. Though everyone in that ballroom had exposed their identities, her investigative work uncovering mind-boggling scenarios as to how corporations kept securing freshwater resources had made her a desirable target.

Chief Landing Eagle stood up next. His even tone was equally as firm as Kahuna's, and it penetrated to the back of the frozen room. He wasn't wearing his customary headdress, but all of the other markings of his tribal heritage were on display. Stone beads of various colors and a wind chime hung from his neck. Light brown leather pants and a jacket covered his frail body. His long hair floated freely over his shoulders, like a layer of virgin foam released from the heavens.

"We stand by our Hawaiian brothers and sisters in our sorrow for the disastrous times we are living in. We've been uprooted, slaughtered, humiliated, and forgotten to the point of extermination. The 'white man' has respected none of our treaties. Few can recognize evil when looking at it, and we are among those few. Fear the day when water remembers what we have done to her. Only then will you recall my words."

He gestured to the gathering like a father teaching his son an essential lesson and continued. "The spirits of our ancestors still watch over us, and they will lend a hand during Mother Earth's healing process, but the destruction must first come to a halt. The awakening Mrs. Botha mentioned has a double meaning. Spiritual awakening is what we lack. We have all lost our sense of attunement with our ancestral Mother. Until that vibrational field matches again, we should still consider ourselves lost." The old Cherokee leader sat down, grabbed the jug of water closest to him, poured a glass, and said a short blessing before taking a sip.

The remaining speakers said their parts, focused more on actual facts and figures as opposed to the spiritual aspect with which many were uncomfortable. "Let's discuss, for a moment, the decades of useless efforts to clean the North Pacific garbage patch," Mark Watershed explained during his presentation. "No one can sail into that area anymore, no matter how they try. This is because we are working on one side of the problem: cleaning it, without considering the root cause. Now, we have a better understanding of the tributaries and main dumping areas. The cleanup could never keep up with the pollution caused upstream."

Cherry remembered the initial discussion, dismissing the education of communities dotting the shores and offering them alternatives to their discarding, without which they would always be at square one.

"Using this two-pronged approach is the only solution we should consider. Businesses along main waterways that have been exposed as heavy polluters should be engaged and given the carrot, not the stick. I have spoken with several of them in Uttar Pradesh in India, and there is no doubt in my mind that if given the funds and the opportunity, they wouldn't say no to making their operations clean. But they don't have enough profit to reinvest in filtration, renewable energy sources, and training for workers." The young-looking actor brushed aside a lock of blond hair covering one of his blue eyes and shuffled the stack of paper he was holding, giving the impression he'd found an important piece of information that someone had tried to hide from him. "The money invested in downstream cleanup could be redirected to the activities I've just mentioned. With no pollution upstream, the water and self-sufficient balance of nature will bring back the nutrients, the plants, and the fish and rebuild the eco-system," Watershed concluded.

A new round of applause marked the ending of all the introductory speeches. Geanine Botha used her microphone once again.

"Panels and workshops are being held on this floor and on the one above. Ushers are available in case you don't find certain rooms. Have a productive day," she said and turned towards Kahuna Lapa'au to her right for a hushed conversation.

Now, that the opening remarks were done, Cherry walked to the bathroom to wash her face and get ready to leave for the conference. The unbearable heat inside the house formed droplets of sweat that followed the gravitational pull from her face to the sink, some of them finding their way down the curve of her chin and neck. The fine recesses in her forehead, giving the impression she was deep in thought all of the time, even when she was smiling, retained some water. She grabbed a towel hanging by the sink, dried her face, fixed her boyish hair-cut, and moved to the bedroom to get dressed for the afternoon sessions in which she would participate as Cherry Mortinger.

Cherry took her t-shirt off and glimpsed at her body reflected on the vertical mirror facing the bed. It was slim and without any voluptuous feminine shapes. She normally didn't bother wearing a bra as she enjoyed the feel of the light gusts of air that found the openings of her blouse and played on her unencumbered, upper body. A pair of striped, light blue pants, a white top, and blue, low-heeled shoes made up her outfit. Cherry didn't wear make-up, lipstick, or fancy earrings. She embodied the standard of a simple, high-impact lifestyle. Her DNA had positioned her low on the scale of beautiful women physically, but high on intelligence, grace, and inner beauty, qualities for which she had much more appreciation.

She went to the living room, connected to *Water For All* website and downloaded on her phone the recording of the just finished remarks. Then, she picked up a yellow, imitation leather bag and left the house, a tiny, detached, two-bedroom in Toronto's Danforth area. She had inherited the property after the death of her father who'd been unable to endure the emotional divide created by the passing of his wife two summers before. Cherry's bi-weekly visits hadn't brought relief to his silent suffering. Somehow, a portion of his soul had left when he'd lost the love of his life, if something like that were possible.

The lack of a stable romantic relationship didn't bother Cherry at all. Her gut kept reminding her she wasn't meant to follow in the footsteps of the long-lasting connection her parents had had for almost fifty years. Moving into the mortgage-free property had cut her expenses in half and had given her entertainment budget more flexibility when it came to books, the opera, and taking exotic trips. And, of course, the contributions to the water movement which had slowly become the pivotal activity of her existence.

She turned left onto Coxwell Avenue, entering the subway at a saunter. After a three-minute wait, she boarded the Bloor westbound train, intending to switch to the south line at Yonge and Bloor. The Toronto Transit Commission hadn't significantly improved its underground transportation over the last thirty years, other than ordering driverless cars, capable of higher speeds, free Wi-Fi connectivity, and heated tracks for outdoor exposed segments. This hadn't stopped them from increasing the fare price tenfold.

She arrived at her stop, got off, and caught her train south just before the doors had closed. The fifteen-minute ride allowed Cherry to watch the beginning of the conference.

"Good morning, everyone," Geanine Botha spoke into the microphone. Cherry adjusted the volume not to miss a word. "Please be seated as we'd like to start. I hope you've had the chance to browse the schedule, which is packed with panels, video conferences and working sessions. But most importantly, I look forward to the decisions we must come to an agreement on."

The African woman's voice demanded reverence. The rustle of paper, side discussions, and phone conversations died down, allowing her to continue. "Everyone at this table and many more have worked extremely hard over the last two years. We've had to harass, twist arms, beg, and prove our sincere intentions through small gestures of goodwill. Decades of mistrust fueled by benefits foreign to humanity's betterment have laced a distorted sheen over actual water interests, blinding us and diverting our attention from what was happening. On behalf of UN-Water, I firmly endorse the saying, 'We are awake now'." Botha kept her full, dark lips together, lest a smile interrupt the message she had just delivered. Her unruly curls formed a free-flowing halo, almost doubling the size of her head. During her five trips to UN HQ, Cherry hadn't seen the African woman without her traditional head wrap hiding the beautiful entanglement.

"We are awake and ready," she repeated, looking left and right along the table to her colleagues who nodded in support. "Over the next three days, we'll all share our experiences. We'll discuss projects worth joint-funding, drawing a line of action without overturning existing cleanup initiatives. My UN colleagues have compiled the lists you all sent us, mapped locations, cross-checked names, and further investigated online and print stories corroborating the facts."

Geanine Botha glanced at the projector screen to her left, displaying her enlarged features—her round but firm cheeks, high forehead, and bushy eyebrows—the temporary focus of the broadcast. A vertical pane on one side of the screen displayed the number of viewers, countries they logged in from, and an uninterrupted flow of countless questions as they were posted.

Cherry broke a shy smile, capturing the meaning of that brief affirmation from the UN official. *Water For All* was a transparent, public event encouraging crowd-funding and voting rights from areas with high numbers of donors. The counter indicated 57,633 viewers at present, and the conference had barely started. Hayyin's speech was eagerly anticipated by her regular followers, a sentiment enhanced, no doubt, by the exposure and magnitude of such a gathering. Allowing an unidentified activist uncensored access to a UN-sanctioned event was like bringing an Anonymous Group member to speak at a now-defunct Federal Reserve board meeting.

"One more thing," Botha said. "For those watching us online, I have a simple request: please check the FAQs posted on the conference's website before asking your question. I've already seen multiple inquiries about why we're holding this conference in Toronto and not at the UN in New York. This has been answered on the website, but just to clarify before we move on, I'll say it again: Canada owns ten percent of the world's fresh water resources. This is even lower than the seventeen percent it had only three decades ago. Its government has voted in the most restrictive usage laws of such resources. Cleanup technologies are significantly developed and implemented, especially in Sub-Saharan countries where the ratio of oil spills seems to be much higher than anywhere else. Last but not least, Toronto is the hub of an extremely effective group of water activists, some of which will be moderating panels throughout the conference," she concluded.

"Union Station next; Union Station," a pre-recorded, female voice announced, and Cherry paused the recording and bagged her earbuds. The tunnel seemed to swallow up the train. She stood by the glass doors watching as the emergency lights zipped by outside her car when there was the sound of a loud explosion. It drowned out the roar of the moving train. An abrupt jerk took everyone by surprise. Cherry's head hit a metal bar behind her. Warm blood spilled onto her left arm.

She dropped the bag, trying to maintain her balance and fell to the floor. A teenager wearing a Roots hat and listening to music from oversized headphones tumbled on top of her, inadvertently kneeing her in her calf. Cherry felt a sharp pain, followed by a cramp causing her to fold forward. She avoided smashing her mouth into his head by centimeters. Several others also lay on the floor, swearing and looking to collect their books, bags, or eyeglasses that had fallen with them. Those still in their seats pressed tightly against each other. A tiny, old woman screamed stridently, having took on the full weight of the oversized man next to her. She looked oddly deflated, beneath him. A stroller carrying an infant boy tilted precariously on two wheels as it rolled away from the mother who had landed on her knees, one hand glued to the edge of the seat, the other desperately trying to grab the handle.

It was less than a minute before a real voice, rather than a recording, announced in a tone belying any panic, "Hold on tight. The train is moving again and won't stop at Union Station. There was an explosion at street level." The train gathered speed, jarring everyone with a brusque shake.

The backpacks, fruit, books, and contents of opened purses were strewn about in piles throughout the car.

Still dizzy from the bump on her head, Cherry looked through the window to see the blur of a dim light as the train passed through the station without stopping. Inside the train, the crying and groaning around her grew in intensity. The teenager that had slammed into her had a cracked lip; his headphones were twisted around his neck.

Three stations later, at St. Patrick, they disembarked. Paramedics were on site, waiting to treat the seriously injured and transport them to a nearby hospital.

"What happened?" Cherry asked a female paramedic who hurried to help a disheveled, old woman carried by two men with dark bruises on their foreheads. The paramedic didn't seem to have heard her question. Rather than answer, she pointed to the stretcher, indicating where the men should take the woman and asked her if she felt any pain.

Cherry went up the stairs to get closer to the surface for better Wi-Fi connection—for some reason, the underground connection wasn't working. Security guards were stopping people from entering at the main entrance. Those that had travelled in the same train as her were allowed to leave as long as medical attention was not required.

The CBC was already broadcasting live from outside of Union Station. The Augmented Reality device was on by the ticket booth. The sound was off, but the captions were on. Smoke billowed from street level, where the conference had been taking place. She cringed and dropped her bag. Her legs softened beneath her. The gray wall behind her accepted her weight and stood firm as she slid down the grimy tiles.

She looked at the monitor. The caption indicated *Water For All* had been deemed the primary target, since no other floor had suffered similar damage. Cherry watched as more people streamed out from underground, scared, hurt, and trying to make sense of what had just happened to them.

There were only two ambulances waiting for the injured outside. All other medical resources had been directed to the Royal York Hotel, or so Cherry had assumed by looking at the live images. The anchor mentioned there was not evidence yet to call the incident an act of terrorism and the victims had yet to be identified. Firefighters had been sent inside the hotel along with RCMP officers to secure the perimeter.

Cherry felt the dried blood tightening her skin. She tried to stand up, but her right calf was numb from the earlier impact. Cherry got to her knees and crawled to a nearby service door whose handle she'd intended to use as support. She was sobbing, involuntarily, as if it were her body's defense mechanism. She wanted to believe there was a less horrifying side to the story, that the explosion had been an unintended incident—an overheated boiler, a gas leak—any cause unrelated to the water gathering. There had been so many good people in attendance.

She reflected that whatever had happened was an exercise in decapitating an efficient organization.

She struggled to pull herself up using only her left leg. Limping badly, she started toward the automatic doors in search of fresh air. Outside, she took a deep breath only to discover the air wasn't fresh anymore but humid, tinged with burning asphalt, exhaust fumes, and heated by the midday sun.

The driverless taxi she hailed hadn't bothered to stop, probably having been locked online by another customer, so she limped closer to the curb to catch the next available one. She asked Siri to send a request with her coordinates and leaned against a pole, waiting. Going back home was the only sensible thing to do. Her swollen calf and jarred skull both needed attention, and cable news would serve as a reliable news source until proven wrong by Internet feeds and Twitter posts.

The subway traffic south of Bloor had been stopped both ways, creating havoc and adding to the sound pollution Toronto didn't need, especially on a summer day. The vehicle arrived shortly, and forty minutes later, she was home. After cleaning the crusted blood from her head, spreading a layer of tea tree oil on the cut, and wrapping ice around her throbbing leg, she dropped onto the couch and turned on the TV.

"Here at CBC we are on high-alert and the building has been locked down until further notice," the anchor announced. The national television outlet's HQ was only half a kilometer away from the hotel. "We still have no indication as to what happened to our crew who had been broadcasting from inside of the ballroom." He looked down at his notes for a moment, then continued. "I'm told that the mayor is addressing Torontonians from inside Union Station. Let's listen to what he has to say."

The image of the immense marble hall of the railway station appeared on the screen. Surrounded by a wave of reporters and by-standers, the mayor kept a poker face and looked straight into the cameras.

"In concurrence with the RCMP Chief, I've ordered the immediate evacuation of downtown Toronto. Most of the high-rises have been emptied using the PATH and GO Transit has provided supplementary trains in all directions. Please remain indoors and stay calm. We'll provide updates every hour. Thank you."

Even to this day Cherry was impressed with Toronto's well-designed, underground pedestrian tunnel system, an entire, functional city with all of the necessary amenities, offering relief from both the heat and the cold. This time, however, the PATH's purpose had changed.

Firefighters rushed out of the hotel and cameras focused on the first stretchers loaded onto the ambulances lining the street and wrapping around the corner, lights strobing, sirens on mute so they wouldn't add to the existing panic.

After three hours of analysis by security experts, politicians, journalists, and behavioral specialists, a statement was issued: a list of the injured and dead was published on the city's website, to be updated hourly. Cherry grabbed her iPad to check it out.

CHAPTER 2

Cherry's mind, still shaken by the explosion targeting the *Water For All* Conference, was trying to cluster her thoughts into intelligible actions. She'd been bothered by headaches since, translating to mild migraines, throwing her daily schedule off most days.

Ingesting painkillers or another chemical substitute was a non-starter, preferring, instead, to endure the surplice. She was able to walk normally now; only a fist-sized, violet mark on her calf remained to remind her of the incident. Her physical pain wasn't of much concern—she could handle that—but the heaviness of her soul and the loss of the friends who had died in the explosion was burned into her psyche. Her mind simply refused to accept it as fact.

She cried continuously for days after receiving confirmation that Geanine Botha, Mark Watershed, and Sunil Samaradingan had perished. Martin Cousteau, Chief Landing Eagle, and Kahuna Lapa'au were in intensive care, their third degree burns having turned them into unrecognizable mounds of flesh.

"How do you feel?" Marinka, Kahuna's older daughter asked her while nibbling on a energy bar inside the hospital's cafeteria two weeks after the explosion.

Cherry's interaction with Kahuna's extended kinfolk, who had considered themselves water caretakers, created a bond immensely deepening her soul and opening her mind to a new meaning behind water, not the practical one discussed repeatedly in the media but of one with a significance subtler than any major civilization was aware. The discussions in which Cherry engaged with Kahuna and Chief Landing Eagle's children and grand-children left her thinking without a doubt that the last two thousand years had been humanity's most irresponsible in the way it had treated and dealt with water. From clean, fresh, and plenty, humankind had ended up with squalid, fetid, and scarce water resources, endangering humans and animals equally.

Cherry appreciated the question, knowing how much Marinka was hurting inside seeing her father unconscious.

To complicate the survival of the wounded, shattered glass from crystal chandeliers hanging from the ballroom's ceiling had cut deep into their bodies, like shrapnel from a loose AK-47. The damage to Kahuna's skull had been extensive, with shards of glass protruding from his wounds, penetrating his frontal lobe and his cerebellum in the back. MRIs taken over consecutive days revealed blood clots had formed near the impact zones, even after the razor-thin glass had been removed, or so Ilanda Mazandir, a neurosurgeon, had explained to Kahuna's family. She checked her patient daily, refusing to operate until his vitals had stabilized.

"I still have headaches early in the morning and my skull res-onates strangely from time to time like an echo from the metal handle I hit. I've become a human echo chamber," she said and cupped her thin neck while leaning her elbows on the table.

Cherry was a regular at St. Michael's Hospital, visiting them every other day, watching as their bodies struggled to break free of their comas from behind the ICU's protective glass bar-rier. She believed the spirits the leaders had mentioned during the opening speeches were present in the pristine and odorless room, performing an invisible ceremony of dancing, singing, and incense burning that would force the souls of the great men back to their physical forms.

The time of their passing had yet to come. The water move-ment needed them. The water itself needed them. The memory of the water recorded the history of all tribes, washing their naked bodies clean. The water remembered every deed, every flaw, and every strength that had turned them into the human beings they were today.

Cherry prayed fervently, leaning her narrow forehead against the coldness of the windowpane, trusting her sincere thoughts to increase the potency of the already vigorous healing taking place beneath an invisible layer of energy. Her prayer encompassed the spirit of water, too, though she wasn't certain whether each stream, rivulet, lake, sea, or ocean had its own protective spirit. *Was there a hierarchy of spirits, or a unilateral, omnipresent force safeguarding all?* She often thought to herself.

Not all of her visits to the hospital were depressing. The tragedy had brought families together, giving everyone the chance to share venerable stories tribal elders would have heard from their fathers and grandfathers, stories meant to enrich an existence too altered by the modern way of life.

Moving the injured to a medical facility in the U.S. was out of the question since their frail bodies wouldn't survive the strenuous trip. St. Michael's in Toronto was the logical choice and accommodations for family members had been made at nearby hotels.

Eighty-eight good people had died on that summer day, and one hundred and twenty-two more had been injured. Lost limbs and fingers, partial burns, and psychological trauma would forever mark most of them as victims, but the cause was worth fighting for. Cherry understood that the momentum of what had been achieved up to the conference couldn't be allowed to die, but rather, had to be built upon. She remembered the number of viewers who had logged onto the website just before she'd left home that day—11,744,231—and acknowledged that a way to turn them into dedicated, active, water supporters had to be identified.

Hayyin had become even more crucial in the conflict that had turned unexpectedly bloody. Her digging and exposing of corrupt businesses working to monopolize wild water for the profit of a few had a meaning that only Hayyin could expose in the guise of her secret identity.

Cherry also had the chance to share her story when the question was asked.

"How did you become a water activist?" Marinka wanted to know.

The limnologist bite once more on the energy bar, her thoughts reaching as far back in the past as possible for an honest answer.

"It took over my life seamlessly in 2035. As a gleaming limnology graduate, I understood society had reached the point of no return regarding freshwater resources and water pollution, with the former being depleted at an unbelievable rate, the latter increasing at a similar percentage," Cherry explained. She gathered her thoughts not sure if she should mention her frustration with the projects that had provided her previous income: occasional consulting jobs offered by the water conservation folks, and the work for real estate developers who thought that a rivulet of water large enough to host two frogs and a water snake was an inconvenient obstacle to their tens of millions of dollar subdivisions and that they could deal with it by dumping dirt on top of it.

She hated those jobs. Her activist side always seemed to break through her otherwise calm attitude. Those were the moments when she would lecture everyone within earshot as to how we, as a species, cared less and less about nature, which was the other fundamental component God had created so we could keep our emotional, spiritual, and physical balance intact. Her light blue eyes would take on a darker cast as fury at the immoral thought of money being the most important goal in one's existence clouded her judgment. Cherry decided to keep all that frustration to herself.

"I had to get involved somehow and make more than a symbolic difference." She cleared her throat with three consecutive sounds. "I didn't know where to start, what organization or NGO to join—there were so many—, or who to trust. I delved into my own research and the results of five weeks of hard work revealed thousands of worldwide water initiatives run by local groups, powerful NGOs funded by shady interests, personalities looking for more media exposure and publicity, and many more acting as money-laundering façades for shell corporations. Known to play a cunning game when it came to protecting their turf and profits, oil and gas giants had declared their unwavering commitment to maintaining pristine operations, reporting and containing leaks and spills, and participating financially to develop renewable and clean technologies. They were playing the millennia-old game of moving money from the left pocket to the right. It wasn't encouraging at all." She tried a wry smile at Marinka who was waiting for more.

"How did you end up choosing WFA?"

Cherry sensed a real interest in the Hawaiian woman's question.

"My intuition told me that WFA could become the adhesive between the mosaic of players that claimed to be water protectors, and eliminate the dissension between them. This state of things kept the water movement fragmented and incapable of piloting tangible, long-term projects with explicit results. It was that moment of realization that had given even further purpose to my life. My search had ended with the realization of a firm path not walked by many, as such crisis never reached similar disconcerting heights." Cherry paused for a moment to take a sip of coffee and think about what else could she reveal to Marinka and what she should keep to herself.

The shimmering energy that had brought awareness of her future meaning had carved time for a split second, revealed hurdles, small triumphs, and significant milestones that would dot the pathway she had chosen ... or rather, that had been chosen for her. She wasn't sure anymore, but she had surrendered to the theory of a greater plan that would be divulged to her when necessary. Adding to all that was her first anonymous posting about the shady dealings of Jinghua Shui, a Chinese water-bottling company claiming to be using an aquifer for which proper rights had been obtained, generated a viral outcry movement, a vortex of political and grassroots implications that sunk the company and landed its management in jail for a substantial numbers of years. The company had signed a baseless understanding with the corrupt local water municipality body, consenting to let potable water flow directly from the tap into Jinghua Shui bottles without spending a dime on its extraction. The agreement seemed to keep the officials happy. Further investigation through satellite images and geologic maps proved there was no significant aquifer in the area, only a trickle of water that couldn't have sustained the company's business model. The ripple effect of the news had put her on the radar of the Anonymous Group, the reputable hackers that had survived despite numerous attempts by various governments, to shut them down, and who, later on, became her online guardian angels. The group had provided her not only with numerous tips that furthered her research into international chemical and pharmaceutical companies without self-regulating pollution guidelines, but secured communication channels through VPN software and additional encryption layers.

"Listening to the stories told by your elders, I learned new angles with which I might appreciate water—not as a commodity, but as a living, mystical being that pulses within and without the earth; not as her blood, but as the heart of the Divine Mother, as she was called in the old scriptures," Cherry continued her confession.

"Water has always been special in our culture. Since I was a little girl I was taught that water could mimic human feelings and health states understood by only a few," Marinka shared a piece of her own experience with water.

It nudged Cherry to make a mental note to go back to Dr. Masaru Emoto's books, forgotten in a plastic box in the basement of her house, and review the images of frozen water crystals exposed to various types of music, thoughts, and emotions. One need not look further than those beautiful hexagons to comprehend that water was alive, that it could be happy and sad, structured and non-structured, healthy and sick. This was a side of water not taught at universities. It reminded Cherry of a similar scenario, regarding medical students not being required to take any courses on nutrition.

"We are water," Marinka explained next. "The same way we are energy…what do people think we are?" she asked rhetorically, combing her long, black locks with her chocolate-milk-colored fingers.

"That we are matter," Cherry replied, more guessing than convinced of the correctness of her answer.

Marinka nodded and continued her rationalization. "Take the water away and we'll be nothing but bones and perish. Remove the energy that keeps our cells together and the particles of our bodies would spread apart as fast as wild bees chasing a honey thief, but our understanding of such subtleties are still a foreign concept, even if we claim that we are in the process of a spiritual awakening."

The woman wasn't young anymore. Creases around her eyes were heavy with the worries that had grabbed her life of late. She was also the one set to inherit the knowledge of their Hawaiian ancestors, but her training, for obvious reasons, had been cut short.

Cherry changed the subject. "How we are going to patch what was broken two weeks ago?" She had several ideas. She knew the movement couldn't rely on the ones who had died or been injured, but she wanted validation.

Marinka extended her long legs and crossed them. She leaned back in her chair and yawned.

"People are afraid to get together again," she said.

Cherry had already known that from the comments posted on the *Water For All* website. Bravery and defiance punctuated the crowd's reaction now and again as if the common consciousness had awoken for brief moments to speak against an injustice that had gone under the radar for too long. Nevertheless, the overall message was one of hope and desire to continue the initiatives identified as critical.

"Why don't we expand the website's functionalities to a voting platform for all the projects that still need funding approval?" Marinka said. She took a sip of coffee from the paper cup in front of her.

"How would we do that?" Cherry enquired, pushing her chair back to make room for her extended legs, too.

The Hawaiian pulled out a small pad of paper and a pen from the purse hanging on the back of her chair and drew Cherry a visual explanation. "We've created a form for project submission, including location, category, affected areas—in square kilometers, if applicable, type of contamination, numbers of years since the incident occurred, and several more, with the aim of centralizing them and identifying the most affected regions to estimate budgets and timeframes. The bulk of assessment and voting was supposed to have been done in person at the conference."

Marinka enclosed the small rectangles with the names of the projects she'd mentioned into a bigger one. "All clear so far?" Marinka asked. She looked at Cherry, who nodded.

"Considering that we are hunted by unidentified entities, we upload all the info we have on each project and let the crowd vote. The chip embedded on the back of one's hand is the identifier we need to confirm their uniqueness. We make our recommendations for the top twenty projects in each category and justify them. A live crowd conference will help us to answer any questions," the Hawaiian woman continued, drawing two more boxes, labeling them "VOL"—for voting online—and "LCC"—for live crowd conference.

"Would the hosting crystal support the additional data load and streaming?" Cherry asked.

"I was told it's a semi-transparent, yellowish stone of second-grade quality, able to handle a minimum of 1,000,000 TB of data and millions of connections at the same time. And it's a dedicated crystal," Marinka said, weight and conviction in her statement. "It's like in the old days, when DSL and phone lines were assigned to a specific person or business, but there are no more wires anymore and no more power outages." She smiled, reflecting her happiness in her eyes.

Cherry tried her coffee, biting delicately on the peppermint stick that came with it. She brushed some crumbs off of the table and looked at the rough drawing once again.

Marinka crossed her hands behind her head, her sight lost in the ripple of white clouds visible through the cafeteria's large windows.

"I agree," Cherry said. "It could help us make a faster decision.

"Have you heard from the RCMP[1] on their investigation?" Cherry asked, knowing the information, if available, would have already been mentioned by Marinka, but she asked anyway.

The Hawaiian shook her head. "No other developments since the initial declaration. No suspects, no new leads. They recited

---

[1] **Royal Canadian Mounted Police**

the usual script: we do everything in our power to blah, blah, blah."

"So the water-intensive industries had covered their tracks pretty well. They'll get away with it. Darn it!"

"It could be any of them: the water bottling companies or the mining ones," Marinka replied in a resigned tone.

Cherry touched Marinka's hand and squeezed it lightly, showing her support. They both let their thoughts wander for several moments, forgetting the unfortunate circumstances that had brought them so close together.

CHAPTER 3

"You came back early today!"

Ilanda Mazandir welcomed her husband, Maahes, sarcastically. She was holding a glass of red wine, swirling the liquid around as if to settle its taste. Ilanda was sitting on the side of the kitchen island, facing the door.

She addressed him nonchalantly, trying to hide the irritation of having had to eat by herself. "I thought that we could have dinner together at least once a week." In a way, the silence in the luxury condo calmed her, making her mindful of her actions, the food, and random thoughts she had to push out of her mind to keep it clear. She could barely impose a similar, serene attitude on herself during hospital hours where, as a neurosurgeon, she had to make quick decisions while having a steady hand, unaffected by wandering contemplations. Ilanda watched as Maahes poured himself half a glass of wine.

"Cheers," he said.

Ilanda still loved his Egyptian features, taken from his mother: dark, smooth skin, wavy, shoulder-length hair, and tall enough to match her own height. Age had necessitated the addition of a pair of square, wood frame eyeglasses to adjust the vision of his dark green eyes. It had also increased the volume of his belly, for which shy attempts at shaving it with weekly gym sessions hadn't made a difference.

"How was your week?" she asked to make conversation. "How is the water business doing these days?" She was aware she'd said it without much interest in the tone of her voice.

Ilanda sipped her wine, pushed her empty plate aside, and leaned forward on her elbows.

"Sorry I didn't let you know that I couldn't make it on time," Maahes said, his tone less derisive than hers. "The flight back from Europe arrived as scheduled, but the board wanted a report on my trip. It couldn't wait until Monday."

He sat on the opposite side of the table, pulled the salad bowl closer, and munched on the remaining greens and tomatoes.

"Are they worried that Vivus Water Inc. is going out of business?" Ilanda asked, more conciliatory this time.

The man swallowed, sipped the wine, and removed his black and white tie before answering. "It won't happen any time soon. We still own considerable assets around the world with more to be secured. And don't forget about the desalination division." He finished the salad and moved on to a piece of white fish garnished with herbs and lemon.

"Ah, I forgot this was the ticket you ran on for the CEO position. 'The oceans will never run out of water. With the right technology—and there is plenty to choose from—we'll continue to maintain our leadership position as a water bottling company,' or something along those lines. Am I correct?" the woman enquired as she poured herself more wine.

Ilanda felt as if in a daze. The pressure of the last couple of days of complex surgeries had driven her beyond her comfort zone. Cases of crystal implant attempts had increased tenfold lately, not only in Toronto, but across Canada. All of them had been failures. They were cruel surgeries, attempting to connect the crystal hardware to the area surrounding the pineal gland. The price of fake pieces of finely cut quartz had been boosted on the black market as the demand from less discriminating buyers grew exponentially. Fictitious origin certificates for each stone served to deceive the unwitting purchasers even more, contributing to the flood of deaths as a result of people's desire to have the artificial brain enhancement. Ilanda could only describe those who forged their vast experience as neurosurgeons as butchers or as leeches attaching themselves to a juicy piece of meat

The victims—most of them part of the higher middle class—who had still been breathing when brought to the hospital, had their heads opened up like ripe melons, the quartz crystals hanging on the outside, looking like an umbilical cord attached to the wrong place. All Ilanda had to do was detach the wires, stop any bleeding, cauterize the ends, and run an MRI with the skull still exposed to assess the real damage. In most cases, the injury was irreparable, something that would leave the patients impaired for the rest of their days, a burden to their families and social insurance.

"Yes, the oceans will never run out of water," Maahes repeated the slogan and strategy that had, indeed, put him ahead of his competitors three years prior when the sudden death of the previous CEO—who happened to have been his mentor—had made the position available.

He stared at his wife intensely as she spoke. "Even the oceans have become polluted beyond repair. I read yesterday on the *Globe and Mail*'s website that the garbage slush is already ten meters deep not only in the North Pacific, but also in the Atlantic, close to the coastal areas. The undercurrents are changing fast." She looked at the wet trace left inside the glass as she swirled the liquid inside.

"That's what we pay the media to report. Who would go and check the depth of the plastic patch? There are restrictions in place. Even Greenpeace needs a permit to venture into those waters, and they aren't issued easily. Our consortium keeps tight control of it," Maahes replied, a confident smirk on his face.

Ilanda felt her eyebrows knit together as if frowning at the insensitive remark. Their views on the earth's health and actions that might save it were on parallel paths. She didn't want to rewind the yelling session that had taken place before his last trip, but many of the daily dramas she experienced at the hospital were the result of macro-level actions of companies similar to the one Maahes led. Ilanda often felt as if she were a contestant in a game show called "Who can bring the earth to the ground first".

"In fact, our pipes have to go down around three times that depth," he continued. "Our specialists tell me the marine life has adapted amazingly fast to the surface slush, avoiding it completely. Very rare are there instances when a turtle or a dolphin comes near enough to get caught in the plastic shit." He was still smiling, somehow content the loss of wildlife wasn't as bad as everyone had thought.

"You have influence, why not ask your powerful consortium to initiate a cleanup?" she persisted.

He huffed as if ineptitude had come out of her mouth. "Why throw good money after bad? I think you get it—it's a waste of time," Maahes confirmed. He had the mindset of a corporate CEO, interested only in how long he could hold his position by making the shareholders happy at any cost.

"Did your people have anything to do with the attack on *Water For All*?"

The question seemed to stun the man, and he almost choked on his sip of wine. He used a paper napkin to wipe the red drops dotting his chin, looking like a sudden eruption of chicken pox. His green eyes expressed sincere surprise at the blame that had been put on him and his peers.

"Why would we commit such a pointless crime? It took all of them what…two, maybe three years to finally agree on a handful of terms? Most of them weren't a danger to our business activities. We have a healthy percentage of the media on our side, and weak governments in areas where the pollution is high are also in our pocket. Why would we do it now?"

Maahes shrugged his wide shoulders, his locks of curly hair dancing back and forth with the gesture. "If things get out of hand and business is impacted, I'd understand calling for radical measures, but not now," he reassured Ilanda who squinted her eyes inquisitively, still trying to identify any trace of insincerity on his features. "The scarce land-based water sources have nothing to do with the activists going against us. It's nothing more than another natural cycle earth is going through."

"WFA was looking at forcing firm legislation on numerous multi-nationals. And not only in the third-world countries, but here, and in Europe as well," the woman pointed out. "UN-Water is on their side and that's a significant player."

"Don't forget that a high percentage of the funding for UN bodies comes from private sources, though distilled through several layers, so in the end, their money's clean. There are instances where we are those sources," he replied. His smirk widened on his face.

Ilanda read Maahes' grin as sincere. He truly believed money controlled everything and everyone. "I hope that one day water will refuse to be treated as a commodity and punish those that take advantage of her." The statement had burst from her subconscious past her parted lips, surprising even her.

Maahes laughed. "You're hilarious. That's why I fell in love with you the moment we met in that refugee camp in Egypt. You looked exhausted, dirty, everyone trying to get you to attend their wounds, but you cracked jokes like nothing out of the ordinary was happening."

They kept silent as their minds went back in time, reviving those dear moments when, as part of Doctors Without Borders, Ilanda had traveled the world, trying to make a difference. Youth made people insanely idealistic, she reflected. There were no insurmountable boundaries or hurdles, only a deep sense that they were doing marvelous work for the benefit of humanity. The organized life she'd had in Toronto back then shattered in comparison to the primitive conditions of the refugee camp, spawned by local, inter-ethnic wars. Maahes, whose mother had immigrated to Canada and married outside the Egyptian culture, was also trying to bring some normality to uprooted lives.

Water had linked them together, roaring through their veins like lava blazing into the open air, etching love on their innocent hearts. Maahes had provided the water needed by Ilanda's patients as humanitarian aid from the US-based companies he represented. They both understood what the lack of water had meant in a bone-dry zone, and their working relationship—that became personal shortly thereafter—had saved many a poor soul.

"I read your latest article in the *Journal of Neurosurgery*," Maahes said, changing the focus of the discussion to Ilanda. "It's very compelling. Do you really think people would actually embed crystals to enhance their brains?"

Now, it was her turn to smile condescendingly. "Haven't you been watching the news lately?"

"Nope. It gives me a lousy energy," the man replied, followed by jeering laughter.

"Inadequate procedures are killing people every day. Shabby doctors pretend the crystal assimilation is safe, but such a thing can't be guaranteed. They run no compatibility tests and no previous health checks on the patients. They just cut them open, wire them up, and power the stone to assess its vibration. An experienced neurosurgeon starts with that last step," she clarified. Her chest heaved and swelled, outraged at the onerous business that had flourished over the last five years.

"Why doesn't the government make it legal as a medical procedure?" Maahes asked hands crossed over his ample belly.

Ilanda gauged her husband. They were estranged now, due to their hectic schedules and shifting priorities, but mainly due to their different views as to how capitalism should treat the world. He had become very wealthy by manipulating the water supply, taming it and selling it for profit, refusing to accept the fact that access to water was a human right. Their clash of opinion had persisted over years.

"It has to do with a lack of control over the population," she answered. "WikiLeaks revealed documents about government-led initiatives identifying the group of hackers by the name of Anonymous' crystal-based hosting locations."

Maahes shrugged his shoulders again, indicating he had no idea what she was referring to.

"Crowd computing served us well until government-related agencies started poking around in people's personal information under the guise of ferreting out possible terrorist threats and identifying money launderers. Hosting companies couldn't control the legalities when it came to the prevention of sharing what they considered private data. So Anonymous, which went slowly underground to protect its members, came up with an innovative concept: hook crystals together, power them wirelessly, and turn them into storage devices. They last forever," Ilanda explained in plain terms.

Maahes didn't react, waiting for more.

"Crystals can't be hacked. An algorithm similar to the blockchain created for cryptocurrencies reaches a staging area where the vibration of the sender, embedded into his fingerprint, and the desired destination is checked. If the frequency matches, the results are 'written' into the cloud-crystal. Anonymous claims these crystal-based clouds can also act as telecommunication boosters, rendering existing providers obsolete. It's an interesting concept, but it's still in its incipient phase."

"Are you saying that our mobile phones will use crystals one day?" Maahes asked. Ilanda wondered if he was trying to goad her by asking silly questions.

"A tiny crystal embedded into an AR—or augmented reality—the device will deactivate its regular roaming connection and automatically switch to a nearby crystal generator, making it impossible to be traced by a communication company or government entity. At least, this is what the experts are saying. If we decide to go that path, we'll be exposed to less harmful electromagnetic waves and a more beneficial crystal influence. It's a battle in which the government and the monopolies are taking a similar stance, losing their levers of manipulating us, making them desperate."

"Any successful attempts to graft the crystal onto humans yet? How is Anonymous doing it?" the man inquired, a flicker of interest in his eyes.

"I'm not aware of any yet. Anonymous won't publish any material on the subject for now. I assume they have their own research lab well-hidden. The equipment needs adaptation. And to get back to your question, there is no health insurance that would pay for the operation. Hospitals—St. Michael's included—are reticent to tread on the unbeaten path."

"But it's doable, right? This is what you're hinting at, correct?" Maahes pushed away from the table and went to grab another bottle of wine from countertop rack.

"I have no doubts there are 'entrepreneurs'," she said in a derogatory tone, "ready to fill in the void. The investment is high, and there's always the risk of being caught. The punishment could triple if there are fatalities as the result of such actions."

He popped the cork and poured wine for both of them.

"Would you go for it if the procedure proves to be safe?" Maahes asked, his eyes locked onto Ilanda's reaction.

She thought for a long moment, then answered, "I don't know what's cooking in your excited neural network, but it can't be good. Stay out of trouble," she added, concerned that if he did something stupid it might affect her as well.

"It's a simple question. You're a highly-skilled neurosurgeon who's aware of any possible secondary effects—who else would I ask? If you're confident of the benefits of such enhancements, I would do it when the time is right," the man admitted. He was fiddling with his glass.

Ilanda pushed her chair back enough to cross her legs and replied, "I think we, as humans, are fine the way we are at this point in our evolution. They say—and research proves it as well—that we use only five to ten percent of our brains. We lack the determination to find within ourselves the mechanism to unlock the remaining potential. We prefer the easy way out, artificially attaching external stimuli."

"I'd take it. Why waste time on this 'mechanism within our-selves' when the end result will be the same? It's like walking when I could have taken a private jet," Maahes replied.

Ilanda mused at how the appearance he'd affected of an older Casanova, with his long hair and sheepish smile didn't fit Maahes, given his age. "Nevertheless, I do agree there might be instances where grafting a crystal for brain stimulation might be the only alternative in extreme cases of long-term care for comatose patients. I could do such work and still keep my con-science intact," the woman said. She scratched the back of her thick neck. "It's a direction that will require consistent effort and funding. My findings, as mentioned, are based on only two years of working with mice."

"Have they learned how to count to ten yet?" Maahes asked sarcastically. He dodged the cork his wife threw at him.

She countered with, "Yes, they did. They also asked when the big corporations are going to stop destroying the planet. Now you have the world's rodent population against you." She smiled, enjoying the verbal tussling. "Seriously, it has changed them. I'm a bit taken aback by the findings, so I've asked my interns to re-do certain tests. They have no expectations of the results in order to influence them," she further explained.

"What do you mean when you say, 'influence'? Are you saying the interns' predetermined mindset might impact the work at hand?" he asked.

The woman knew science always fell short on Maahes' comprehension list, way below business concepts, termsheets, and financial numbers. She didn't want to sound superior, but she couldn't help giving him an innocent verbal sting.

"That's why I've been encouraging you to read more scientific books for years. You might also read up on water. It *is* the object of your daily occupation, after all."

Maahes slanted his head to the right as if looking at her from a different angle would help him to avoid addressing the statement. Instead, he waited for her to continue her technical mentoring.

"Water is sensitive to our emotions, thoughts, and feelings. If my interns visualize a specific intention in their minds, it would affect the results. For once, I need them void of any thoughts." She felt warm to his appreciation for what she was saying.

"I've only published a fraction of my research, and believe me: it's fascinating. I've exposed the mice to classical music and frozen a blood cell, and the shape of it was a perfectly-formed hexagon, which is nothing new. Oh, I almost forgot to mention that we monitored the little buggers' brains during their musical education period," she said, her round cheeks pushing up into a large smile.

"What do the hexagon blood cells mean?" Maahes interrupted her.

She sighed, exasperated he wasn't able to recollect any knowledge on water she'd shared with him previously. "Don't you remember those books written by Japanese scientist Masaru Emoto I showed you years ago when you admitted you knew nothing about water despite being in the business?" she said, trying to rekindle his memories.

"Oh, those images I remember. Structured and non-structured water was what they were called, weren't they?" he asked, illuminated.

"Yes. Everything positive turns water molecules into structured molecules and have the opposite effect for everything negative. We injected this type of blood into a crystal-grafted mouse. Molecular changes appeared two days later with minimal impact on its overall health and brainwaves. It's not bad, but it's not world-shattering either," she said. She moved her hands a gesture better suited to a dissertation in front of a larger crowd. "The next logical step, and the last one we'd planned, was to drop the blood sample directly onto the crystal."

"And?" Maahes leaned forward in his chair.

"The mouse's brainwaves spiked as if spooked by a sudden threat, identical to the ones from the initial, sample mouse. Molecular transformations took effect within minutes, and…*la piece de resistance*, the frozen impression of the blood cell matched the one the crystal had come into contact with."

"I'll be damned," the man said, impressed.

Ilanda nodded her head several times, acknowledging the importance of this discovery.

"Just to be sure there's no misunderstanding between what you're explaining to me and what I really understand: the crystal absorbed the information from the blood cell exposed to the music and mysteriously transferred it to its host?"

"That's exactly what I mean. Not only that, but the similarity between the brain waves made us believe the host 'felt' the music," she clarified. "The vibration of the crystal resonates with the liquid, enhancing its qualities."

"There's no one else doing similar research?"

Ilanda swallowed her sip of wine, then replied, "The special healing properties of crystals have been known and used for hundreds of years. Lasers were created using quartz. There's only one company that's developed a crude technology similar to what I'm trying to achieve and it's in Toronto."

"Really?" the man exclaimed, his eyes growing wide behind his square-rimmed glasses. "Have you tried it?"

She smiled but said nothing, teasing him like she had in the games they used to play many years ago.

"C'mon," he insisted, anxious to hear about her experience.

"Yes, I did. It's not bad for someone who has low expectations. I'm aiming for a more realistic result. What this guy, Ojani, offers are shallow images and feelings processed by oval-cut lapis lazuli attached to a mesh similar to the ones that check for brain activity. It takes the special water specimens they use a long time to filter through the crystals to make them vibrate properly to release the encoded message."

"Their technology's a good start, but I'm looking at it from a different angle, one in which the crystal has to be directly connected to the pineal gland or to a conduit that touches the pineal gland."

"Unbelievable!" Maahes agreed. "Memories conveyed through liquid? Why attach the crystal to the pineal gland? What's so special about it?" he asked innocently.

"I figured it out pretty quickly. The pineal gland's embedded with crystalline structures made of calcite. They act as a cosmic antenna, capable of connecting us to realms of light and other dimensions of consciousness," she explained.

Maahes remained slack-jawed as she spoke. When she was done, he said, "I thought you're supposed to be a scientist and not some spiritual weirdo." He'd said this without a trace of amusement in his green eyes.

"That's why I can't risk my career and reputation divulging more until the documentation, the results, and the quality of those doing the tests is impeccable. That's why I've been telling you for years that water is more than a simple liquid, a commodity. It's the primordial element of survival. The bottled water your company sells is dead water, nothing more. Crystals are nature's creation: beautiful, pure, perfect models of divine design, representing water in solid form," she said, circling back to the point that had started their discussion."

"Yes. Water, again and again." He blew out air in exasperation.

Ilanda extended her arm, picked up the tablet left on the counter by the sink, opened it, entered her password, and searched for the *Water For All* website. "Have you seen their numbers lately?" she asked Maahes. Her determination to change his perception of water had no limits.

She turned the screen toward him and pointed to the top right corner where the live counter indicated 533,288 users from forty-three countries. "The organization's visibility has increased a hundredfold since the tragedy. Those sitting on the sides undecided about their stance on climate change and environment pollution shifted within days."

Maahes took a closer look at the screen as if to pacify Ilanda, his face void of any recognition of the evidence that the world's water situation was everyone's concern she was showing him. "This number doesn't change what I said earlier about not being involved in any retaliatory action against them."

She believed him. There was no hint of sarcasm or psychological craftiness behind his statement, no tremble or shrill voice, just a plain rebuke of her accusation.

"How many wounded have you operated on from the explosion?" he asked, staring at the screen as comments scrolled quickly by.

"Only six needed me. Two I couldn't save. They looked like porcupines, the glass shards sticking out of them like needles. I had to cut deep. The other four still aren't out of their comas yet. Big Kahuna's family will bring their healers and water from ancestral places in Hawaii."

"Big Kahuna's your patient?" Maahes exclaimed.

Ilanda nodded.

"Wow! I've heard of him. Freakishly big guy."

She smiled at his unexpected reaction. "Yes, and he hasn't shrunken a bit over the last two weeks. I marvel at the history of his people etched into his body, which is strong as a lava-stone sculpture. His daughter's convinced the spirits of the island are keeping him alive, that they're healing him in the astral plane so he'll be able to return and lead the tribes again."

"Really!" Maahes blurted, the smirk returning to his face.

"His whole family wept when we shaved his head. It took him twenty-five years to grow those locks. They plan to keep it as a talisman," she said with reverence as if spirits protecting Kahuna had materialized in the apartment at the mentioning of his name.

"What are his chances of survival?" he asked, moving his empty glass from one hand to the other.

"I really don't know. Any built-up pressure from the unexpected swelling in his brain could burst blood vessels or pinch the nerves at the base of his cranium. If they go undetected, over time it could paralyze his motor or speech functions or push him beyond the possibility of coming back as a whole man." Ilanda felt saddened by her inability to do more. "I'll have to operate on him again as soon as his brainwaves begin to follow a well-behaved pattern."

She paused for a moment, mentally evaluating her patient's condition as result of the conversation she was having with her husband. "A healer from Hawaii will arrive soon, I was told," Ilanda confessed to a puzzled Maahes. "I'm not sure if a ceremony will be allowed on the premises since it could become noisy and turn the ICU into a circus."

The man cracked a large smile and said, "Do what I usually do when things don't go my way: find a loophole. A legal one."

"Loopholes are non-existent in the medical field. There are twenty pages of rules and clauses for every potential circumstance from a simple slip on a wet floor to the most complex interventions I perform," she reassured him.

"Just go with the simplest justification: the healer's a priest summoned to offer the last religious rites to his flock. It's common practice in any denomination. Keep the door locked and the blinds down."

She looked at him admiringly beaming warmly.

Maahes unbuttoned his shirt to reveal his hairy chest. "I'm hot. It must be the wine." He checked the label and whistled. "Sauvignon: 2025, Italy. I won't ask how much you paid for it, but it's worth every penny. I think 2025 was the last year before water rationing for irrigation was enforced in Europe, after erratic and low rain levels couldn't support what was needed for a healthy crop. We won a couple of significant contracts that year in both Italy and Croatia with our desalinization plants," he recounted.

"Listening to you, I've decided that from now on I'll ask for my salary in refined wine. There'll always be a cask stashed in an aged countryside winery in Portugal, Spain, or maybe even Romania." Ilanda burst into laughter.

Maahes also let out a laugh. The sound seemed to resonate off the kitchen cabinets and wooden floor.

"Have you ever tasted grapes irrigated with desalinated water?" she asked.

Maahes regained his breath, wiped a tear from his cheek, and replied, "Sometimes I believe all these stories about water memory. Our treated water has no salty taste. Chemical analysis shows no trace of salt either, but when used for agriculture, and especially on grapes, the salt resurfaces, taking over the sweetness of the grape, though no one can figure out why." Maahes continued on a serious note, "This is what affects my business, not the tree-huggers and the water caretakers that meet to sing Kumbaya. The only reason we haven't been sued by our customers yet is because of the undisputed tests their own chemists have performed."

Ilanda noticed his frustration as his fingers raked nervously through his hair. The second bottle of wine was still half full, having remained untouched since their discussion of the wineries had begun. "It's not the chemical composition that's important, but the structure of the water molecule. Check it out and show me your findings," she said.

"I think I'll go to sleep," Maahes declared. He stood up, pushed his chair back, and walked toward his bedroom.

Ilanda listened to the muffled sounds coming from the bathroom, the shower, the hairdryer, then the deep silence. She was alone again with her own professional and personal challenges and no one with which to share them. Ilanda put her empty plate and cutlery in the dishwasher and sat on the couch, blindly contemplating the lights of the building across from her dotting the darkness. It seemed as if the sky had shifted downward just to please her, playing with the stars and arranging them into new and ephemeral constellations that would dissolve as soon as she refocused her attention. These moments of heavy loneliness always gave her the shiver of regret for not having children. The prospect of upward career-mobility for both of them had soothed their egos, blinding them from experiencing the outright joy of tiny fingers hungrily grabbing the air to sense the new environment, the outrage of smelly, newborn poo, or the ups and downs of a toddler's first steps. Hectic travel schedules had kept them apart for weeks on end at times, weighing considerably on their decision to stay childless.

As a successful neurosurgeon, Ilanda enjoyed interacting with her younger patients, the brief moment of supervising their health satisfying the resurfaced longing for warm hugs and innocent kisses, fueled by the gratitude of having been saved. Sometimes, if her attachment to them was too great to warrant their imminent discharge, then against her better judgment, she'd extend their stays for a day or two. It was a selfish way to diminish the gap until the next child needing her would check in.

Nowadays, fewer children needed her. The water restrictions that had been imposed twenty years prior had triggered unforeseen societal changes, including fewer births in general and healthy ones in particular. The water ration per newborn was a mere five liters per week. The government had justified this dumb decision by the fact that newborns drank mainly mothers' milk, but the tasteless and unhealthy food had weakened everyone's immune system. Internal transformations at the cellular level had impeded the thyroid's function of balancing the metabolism. Mothers' milk had dried out, forcing infants to drink the dubious liquids the government provided as a substitute for the water quota.

Ilanda had witnessed the worldwide depravation of the human and natural lifecycle. Whole areas had died due to water starvation, forcing migrations to zones that still had resources enough to rely upon if managed realistically.

The staggering number of inept laws following the restrictions had marked unexplored boundaries of friction between government-controlled military forces and the general population who was once more paying for accumulated bureaucratic mistakes that had negatively affected the planet. Being a high-priority environment, hospitals were somehow shielded from many recent regulations and were the first to benefit from the latest technologies: waterless toilets, waterless hand and surgical instrument sterilization, waterless everything one could think of.

Ilanda leaned on her side and rested her head on a pillow, incapable of taking the few steps to the bedroom. Aware of her steady breathing, she switched her thoughts to the magnificent universe of crystals and water, the subject of research that had captivated her imagination for so long.

"It's a pure and perfect world that we just couldn't match," she whispered to herself, "yet we try so hard to destroy it."

She flashed a sad smile at her own inability to make an impact. Her senses numbed by a thick tiredness, she wondered if her findings would ever become breaking news.

CHAPTER 4

Egypt drew Maahes back again, justified by the worsening situation of water quality at the desalinization plant run by his company. He found the time not to only visit his cousins, but also to pick up his new Egyptian identity that would help him settle in Costa Rica incognito. Bribes in that part of the world were still an efficient way of dealing with certain government officials.

He was sitting in the kitchen of his mother's childhood house, a two-story brick enclosure that used to host a family that had once been large but was reduced now to three members. He'd accepted the overnight invitation reluctantly, instructing the driver to pick him up the next day around noon.

Ilanda's accusations about the water consortium having blown up the *Water For All* conference had bothered him tremendously. He didn't like being lumped in with potential criminals and associated with acts of terrorism. It was one thing to joke about it to come off with the attitude of a tough guy, but it was another to acknowledge his participation. Maahes reached out to his confidants with quiet inquiries about the incident. The feedback was one of total outrage for the lives lost along with smoldering fury at the negative perception attached to the heavyweight water corporations whose unlimited financial means was more than enough to have banked the operation.

No terrorist group had claimed the atrocity, so it was generally perceived as a sign that business and political interests had firmly joined hands to extinguish the movement that had gone against their wishes.

International power had shifted in the last twenty-five years since the US, in spite of their enormous military budget, was silently annihilated by a unified front of countries calling for their debts to be paid off simultaneously. The usual blackmail strategy every US government had used in the past, halted it, and the war mongering factions within the CIA and the military agreed to stand down. Even they realized that starting a war on multiple fronts would lose the few remaining allies they still had, creating a level of chaos beyond control.

For him, the CEO of the third largest water-bottling company in the world, the accusation was a wakeup call, meaning that a different approach to valuing water should be implemented. He considered stepping down a couple of times in an attempt to simplify his life, never to even entertain future, similar offers in the corporate world. The joy and satisfaction of his job's perks had left him a while back, forcing a false, impertinent rictus to mask his discontent and misery. With Ilanda, he'd played the role of an insensitive, ignorant CEO. None of his peers could sniff out the real reasons behind his dropping—out of the blue—the reins of a winning horse in a race of a few, pure-breed contenders. Even Ilanda would hear the same health-related story to explain his early retirement or sudden death, as he wasn't yet sure of the level of drama required for his story to sound truthful. No gaps or doubts would crack the polished veneer of the scenario he'd worked so hard on. She would be worried and try to convince him take additional tests and to get a second opinion, but his usual stubbornness meant suspicion wouldn't be raised when he'd declined the offer. Stringent water restrictions and regulations hadn't stopped him or any of his competitors from enduring, but it had forced them into the loophole scenario he'd mentioned to Ilanda, which had always proven to be in the multinational corporations' favor.

His wife's comments about the position of strength he was in, along with the uncountable missed opportunities to learn about water, quickened his exit decision.

"Maahes, are you all right?"

He came back from his reverie, feeling the light touch of his cousin, Ramira's, hand. She was the daughter of his mother's sister that had never left Egypt. Every other year, he fulfilled his mother's last wish: to visit his remaining relatives in the country. Over time, they had grown closer for the visits.

The town of no more than two thousand people, mainly elders, had been forgotten by their children who had left to find a better life in Cairo or even further away. It was close to the Syrian border and a hundred miles from the nearest city. Pesky dust, thrust about by persistent winds, laid a thin coat over the low houses and items left outside in the scorching weather. The asphalt of the desolate streets without sidewalks had vanished under a crust of sand that, over time, had melted into the softened tar.

"I'm fine. A bit tired. I hope to get some rest before my flight tonight." He dipped a piece of pita into the bowl of hummus in front of him.

"Has anything changed at the camps?" Ramira poured turbid water into his glass and gave him time to swallow. Only three years younger than him, the woman's face and posture displayed all the signs of a harsh life: wrinkled eyelids hung over colorless eyes lacking any spark of energy, her shoulders seemed overly hunched, and tangled locks of mainly white hair hid under a plain bandana tied at the back of her head. The grayish dress covering her feminine form was made from a thin fabric. Maahes knew how grateful his extended family was for the additional gallons he'd arranged for them on a weekly basis, delivered from the local subsidiary of his company. No other gift held a similar value or appreciation, so, over time, he stopped bringing anything else.

The monthly water-trucks supplying the area were less reliable, and most of the time the cherished liquid could not be protected from the sand infiltrating through cracks and rusty openings which turned it into a barely usable product. Medical necessities and staple foods were also provided by the government, but with the political situation worsening every day, Maahes couldn't predict how much longer the people would benefit from such generosity. The government made it sound as if they were doing them a favor, even if the retirees had been forced to forfeit their pensions in favor of food and water at inflated prices.

"It's like I never left. It all looks the same, but worse. Power is failing daily, and the maintenance crew left two months ago due to owed salaries. There were no pumps pulling the water and no power with which to pump it. Every two or three months they had to go deeper to look for new veins. The latest geological maps indicated a thick layer of rock only two hundred meters lower than the existing depth, but there is no backup plan for when that point will be reached," he said.

Maahes picked his glass up hesitantly and glanced at his cousin who was attentively measuring his words and actions. When he sipped, his lips touched the water delicately, as if he'd expected it to be hot.

"Will your company be able to supply them after the pumps go dry?" Ramira asked, her shoulders hunched even more at the anticipated challenges the people would have to endure.

"Existing contracts have to be fulfilled and the demand will only increase. The humanitarian allocation has shrunken considerably. Not even the UN can dictate who should get water first since they don't have the money anymore," Maahes said, repeating the excuse he'd prepared for that very question. "The migration to other camps in Syria has already started, but there is no guarantee the newcomers will be allowed in without proper military protection. If rejected, they'll fight for a place behind the fence out of desperation. The alternative of moving to the next camp deprived of water and food means a slow death in the desert." He'd kept his voice mellow in an effort to ease his harsh but true statement.

This last trip to the region was part of his departure plan, an initiative under the legitimate disguise of inspecting the facilities. Quietly trusting the people who led water-related NGOs and other water defending activities, he'd signed legal documents, effective immediately, to return exploration and usage land rights to their rightful owners, which would have given them more negotiating power with corporations like his. He knew that legal actions would commence and injunctions would be issued, only to slow or block the usage of remaining wells. His actions followed the pattern of asset nationalization, not engaged by a hostile and populist government, but from inside a private company whose management was suddenly struck by the remorse of its previous ill decisions.

Maahes had no doubt he'd be declared an enemy as soon as the news became public. Synchronizing the release with the timing of his resignation or sudden death had required considerable energy and finesse. A large acreage he'd acquired in a Costa Rican mountain forest upon which he'd built a self-sufficient house, would make a safe refuge, at least until the informational tsunami holding the world's attention died down. His financial freedom and lifestyle had to be maintained, which is why, for the last twelve months, his stockbroker had been selling his company's shares in small chunks so as not to draw attention. Funds were converted into bitcoin and similar cryptocurrencies to diversify. Worthy projects and people in need would benefit from his stash, which was too much for him to spend by himself over ten lifetimes.

He smiled at the thought of having a bounty on his head, either dead or alive. Ilanda's remaining affection for him might swell to increased admiration for the insane stunt or shift to acidic hate, given the unnecessary spotlight the media cast on her while trying to find out how exposed she'd been to his plan.

"When will we see you next?" Ramira enquired, her left hand playing with the rough and wrinkly skin on her opposite palm. It was a question that stirred up emotional butterflies in his belly, their invisible flapping warming him from the inside out.

He thought about saying, "Never," but erased the thought immediately, as if afraid she would read his mind. Maahes held her gaze, knowing that no feature on his face would betray him.

"Not for the next six or eight months at least. The subsidiaries are being faced with new challenges every day. I have to travel, asses the local situation, advise, and see it implemented, if possible. Don't worry—the rations will keep coming, I've made all the arrangements," he confirmed and forced a smile as encouragement.

The woman continued manipulating the skin on her palm as if looking for messages hidden there. "I'm not worried," Ramira assured him. "We survived similar harsh times when the military took our water resources over three decades ago. I'll never forget that panic—the skirmishes, the fear ingrained by the thought we would die of thirst…God had mercy on us then, and He will save us again."

Maahes kept quiet, looking beyond his cousin at the framed photographs hanging on the kitchen wall; black and white, sepia and color—they were snippets of the history of an Egyptian household that was barely thriving in a world preoccupied with its own survival. He loved the ones in which his mother, then ten years old, looked happy as she played with her siblings on the beach. He moved his scrutiny along the timeline of prints to more recent events: the same person, now an older woman wearing eyeglasses and leaning on a cane, surrounded by her two surviving brothers and their children and grandchildren, all of them smiling but her. Maahes instinctively knew she was expressing her disappointment with him for not being there and for not fathering kids. After his father had passed, there was no motivation for her to live in Canada, and she needed the love, attention, and warmth of the family she'd left behind for a better opportunity ages before. At first, Maahes had resented her decision. It was a selfish reaction that he'd regretted tremendously. He'd accompanied her to the town of her birth, knowing the barren land would soon become the place of her burial.

"What happened to the water?" the woman asked. "It's grayish and tastes salty."

For an inexplicable reason, the water purification process hadn't produced the same quality results recently. The result was a tasteless and colorless liquid, sold mainly to North African and Gulf countries. Industrial filters had been changed, chemicals had been checked, and employees had been supervised for foul play—all conducted in his presence—but none of these variables had identified a plausible cause. What puzzled him the most was one of Ilanda's statements regarding the structure of the water molecule that had stuck with him on his way to

Egypt. He'd ordered multiple molecular structure tests before and after desalinization. The expected structural shape of the ocean water was a fuzzy hexagon. Oil and gas pollution spills from the increased number of ships transporting goods between continents and the effects of climate change that had dramatically impacted the oceans had broken apart the crisp, crystal shape of the salty water from thirty years ago. The molecule of the treated water had a visibly improved hexagonal form, even though the chemical composition displayed no traces of salt and its taste said otherwise.

Maahes remembered another of Ilanda's comments: *Water has memory.*

"I don't know yet," he said, frustrated at being unable to identify the malfunction causing it. "Our treatment steps haven't changed. We've increased the number of supervisors and ninety percent of the process is automated, so getting water of this poor quality doesn't make sense," he clarified.

It was pointless to explain to Ramira that his company was supposed to have generated dead water void of any minerals, water stripped of life, of decency, of pride. It was nothing more than a simple, amorphous liquid for which many parties would pay a significant amount of bitcoin. Instead, the new version had a better molecular structure, showing its character through its odd taste. It seemed the water had used the destructive chemical process in its favor, fought the dissolution of its identity, and come out alive and aware of what had happened.

"We boiled it to get rid of the taste, but it didn't go away," the woman confessed. "The gas is rationed, too, so we gave up after a couple of attempts. I'm afraid the children may get sick."

She looked away from Maahes as if she wasn't sure whether she should to trust him or not.

"What?" he encouraged her.

Ramira exhaled slowly as if preparing to make an important declaration. "We asked the town's healer to pray on the water. That's why we haven't gotten sick yet."

He stayed still, processing this outrageous statement, aware his body language might offend his cousin. "Is that the water I'm drinking?" he nodded at the glass on the table.

"Yes," she confirmed. She reached up to arrange the bandana on her head.

Maahes felt a sense of surrender enter her tone, to an intangible force and energy represented by the healer who hadn't explained himself in any way. It had been implicitly accepted, believed in as the law of the land that had survived natural cataclysms and strife, one of the last vestiges of what the Egyptian ancestors had left to posterity.

He'd heard of these healers in his mother's childhood stories, humble people requesting favors from the invisible realm on behalf of those in need, which had been ingrained in his pristine mind as a youngster. He'd never actually met one in his many visits to the region. The memory hadn't ever resurfaced until now.

"May I take a sample with me?" he asked, hoping that testing its molecule structure wouldn't prove the healer's impact.

Ramira stood up, walked to one of the cupboards, and got a small, glass jar into which she poured some of the liquid.

He took the jar silently, considering it an idiotic idea, stirred by another of Ilanda's comments: *Would the structure of the water molecule change again, influenced by his existing thoughts and predisposition?* How could he empty his mind of so many unnecessary worries, baggage created by restlessness and life's complexities?

Maahes held the container high in the dim afternoon light coming through the window, examining its contents for visible indications confirming his wife's theory but saw nothing. Involuntary respect surged through his body, a protective gesture triggered by what the tiny pool of water might do to him.

"Does quantum entanglement work for water?" he asked out loud. He hadn't heard the term before. "There's so much quantum entanglement in nature, shouldn't water obey the same universal rules?" he answered his own rhetorical question.

Ramira seemed puzzled by his behavior though she didn't react.

"Say goodbye to everyone. I have to leave now, but I'll call you soon. Don't forget that no one but Sameer should fix the solar panels if something goes wrong. I won't trust anyone else," Maahes warned her.

He kissed her left cheek, went to the bedroom to pick up his bags, and then walked out to the driver waiting for him.

"God help these people survive and strengthen my resolve," he mumbled to himself while getting into the car. "This is penance for what I've done wrong. Forgive me!"

CHAPTER 5

"Dr. Mazandir!" Cherry yelled. She quickened her step to catch up with the neurosurgeon leaving Kahuna's room. "Sorry to bother you," the younger woman said. "I'm a limnologist, interested in crystals like you."

They had a similar height, though while Cherry was thin and fragile, Ilanda was well-built, her thick waistline hidden under her white coat.

"How can I help you?" the doctor asked. "Are you a member of Kahuna's family? I've seen you in his room before."

"Just close friends. We're involved in the *Water For All* movement. I missed the explosion by minutes—or should I say, the explosion missed me," Cherry clarified in a hushed tone as if embarrassed by her luck.

Ilanda gave her an understanding smile.

"Aside from being a limnologist, water activism is a part of who I am," Cherry continued.

"I assume that's the reason you're part of the WFA," the neurosurgeon said, stating the obvious.

"I've watched several videos of your scientific approach to water and crystals, and I was impressed by the depth of knowledge and novel ideas you have," Cherry said. She moved aside to let a child in a wheelchair pushed by a nurse pass.

"Yes, I dabble a bit in the field. It's fascinating," Ilanda replied without much enthusiasm. "It's mostly at a theory level right now."

Her enthusiasm—or lack thereof—didn't prevent Cherry from pushing forward. "You're too humble for a specialist of your stature. Believe me, I did my research: no one's died on your surgery table in the last fifteen years, and the one remote death wasn't your fault, but an equipment malfunction that displayed incorrect readings. There's no similar research on crystals. If there is, it's being kept hidden. Most probably—"

Cherry saw Ilanda stiffen and her smile vanish.

"Sorry," Cherry said quickly. "I was just trying to point out how skillful you are and how appreciative the entire family is that you're the one taking care of Kahuna. His survival's in your hands." She hoped her gratitude was enough to have diverted Ilanda's focus from the bad memory she'd unceremoniously brought up.

"How can I help you? I've already shared why I'm still delaying the surgery with his kin. Do you want me to repeat it for you?" the doctor asked, turning her body in the direction she had to go.

"Dr. Mazandir, your incipient research on crystals could be a pivotal step in Kahuna's healing."

Ilanda's brow furrowed.

"Maybe I'm too optimistic when I say healed. A conscious recovery is what all of us hope for, regardless of his loco-motor functions. His mind and spirit is what needs to be saved, the knowledge that's been accumulated over centuries through word of mouth and needs to be transferred to Marinka, his daughter." Cherry maintained a low tone. "Their healer will be here tomorrow, and while I think the purification ceremony will help, in my opinion, his brain requires a sensorial shake, a brain resuscitation, if you will, similar to what we do to the heart."

Ilanda took her hands out of her coat pockets and crossed her arms over her chest showing no imminent intention of leaving.

"And how do you expect me to jolt his brain?" she asked. "First off, there's no safe procedure I'm aware of, and second, the hospital's board would never agree to it. They measure benefits against liability, and in this case, as a neurosurgeon, I agree the liability's not worth the attempt."

Cherry sensed Dr. Mazandir was expecting more of an explanation from her since the tone of her voice didn't scorch her high expectations. She continued, "You are well aware that our bodies are made of structured water that dilutes and becomes non-structured with age. Diet, physical exercise, and positive thinking are factors that contribute to the overall health. They also implicitly impact our levels of structured water. In fact, our cells could live forever if the concentration of the liquid they float in is of pristine quality."

"So?" Ilanda asked impatiently.

"I've tested Kahuna's blood's molecular structure, and he's in amazing shape. Nevertheless, the accident's put him in a 'frozen' state that won't maintain the same level of cell consistency. The healers, through their chanting, will replace Kahuna's daily meditation session, generating beneficial vibrations as a temporary solution. From the MRI scans you shared yesterday, his brain activity is minimal but broken by random spikes. Very soon, we need the brain to take over the functions that are now on cruise control." Cherry drew her finger from her mid-section to her head as if to show the direction things should flow in Kahuna's body. "The captain is asleep and the passengers will panic if there's no communication."

"When do you get to the part where you ask me to do something illegal?" Ilanda shot back. She sounded amused and more than a little intrigued.

"Please don't be presumptuous," Cherry replied. She took the doctor gently by the elbow and pulled her closer to the windows in the hallway for more privacy.

"If your research is correct," she said, "Kahuna's brain could be excited in a non-invasive and safe way through the power of the crystal as it translates the 'memory of water.' The information we'll encode in the water molecule should seamlessly filter into his blood. His brain is conditioned to react to such stimuli."

"Wow! Your confidence in my results exceeds mine. This has been trial and error so far. I always start and end my presentations with the disclaimer that my work is still at the trial level and joke, saying 'Don't try this at home,'" Ilanda replied.

Cherry noticed the neurosurgeon's reaction to her statement. Her pupils had dilated as satisfaction engulfed her, she dropped her crossed arms and put her hands back into her pockets, and even leaned one shoulder against the window, expecting their discussion to continue. Cherry had to push forward and break her reticence.

"I would like to remind you that the concepts, forms, and structures you're working with have been divinely created. They're part of nature. Follow nature's rules, respect them, and nothing will deter your goal. But as you stated briefly in one of your published papers," Cherry continued, "the right mindset is paramount. You have to obey your own rules, too, otherwise, the results will be impacted."

Dr. Mazandir turned her back to the distraction created by the continuous back and forth of the nurses, patients, and visitors in the hallway, forcing herself into a bubble of quietness. "So, you weren't teasing me about doing in-depth research," the doctor remarked. She kept staring at the traffic outside, ambulances bringing in emergency cases like bees dropping nectar into a hive before hurrying out again to collect more for the common cause. Police drones, equipped with sensors to identify the illegal possession of guns and water containers that didn't conform to the strict regulations, hummed meters above the crowd's heads.

Cherry didn't want to hurry Ilanda, and she waited patiently before continuing with what she assumed would be an outrageous and somewhat illegal request. The doctor hadn't been far off in her assumption, Cherry thought. The neurosurgeon would have to walk a thin line and maybe adopt a duplicitous life, as she had done with Hayyin.

Still fixated on the chaotic movement of passersby and cars outside, Ilanda asked for more information. Cherry obliged.

"The research you've achieved so far has had funding, equipment, and personal limitations, let alone legalities tied to potential liabilities that the university had you sign for. Would these ties be broken if you continued your research in a private lab?"

Ilanda looked at Cherry with incandescent eyes. "Are you teasing me?" she inquired, her face reddened by the emotional effect of such a possibility.

The limnologist was ready with more details. "The WFA has access to independent funding sources, all clean and willing to participate. Some of them won't come out publicly so they won't become targets of those opposing us. I might be able to convince the board that what you are doing is complementary to our work and shouldn't be discounted."

"I still don't see the connection," Ilanda insisted.

"Saving Kahuna's a gesture of defiance for us. His recovery will mobilize additional members and imbue them with new, untapped energy. There are medical benefits in which water could play a primary role, replacing a significant chunk of Big Pharma's output of useless and harmful drugs. What if Kahuna's memory could be saved on a crystal and be downloaded to Marinka through a water imprint?"

"You want to start a war with the pharmaceutical companies now? The one with the water industry isn't enough?" the doctor exclaimed, surprised at how the discussion had turned.

"They started the war on regular citizens a long time ago. Do I have to remind you of the milestones they're so proud of? In 2024, cancer was eradicated with a concoction attacking any form of the disease. Further investigation revealed that the removal of certain hazardous ingredients from the food and beverage manufacturing process significantly diminished cancer cases. With people tired of donating money to a cause without a resolution in sight, those geniuses that created the problem in the first place decided to end the charade by reversing the process and still make a killing. They just had to undo what they did decades ago before cancer became deadly."

Ilanda shrugged her shoulders in agreement and let Cherry continue.

"In 2031, enforced legislation lobbied by the same companies about the so-called 'medical chip' came to the forefront. It turned out to be another scam involving the insurance companies. I would have opted out along with the millions of other citizens like me who were awake enough to see through their lies, but the politicians were paid handsomely, laws were passed, and we all ended up with it." She tapped the back of her hand where her chip had been implanted.

Ilanda pulled out her AR device when it buzzed in her pocket. She glanced quickly at the message on the screen. "I'll have to go soon," she announced, but she showed no sign of impatience.

"Let's not forget 2036," Cherry continued, "when another man-made disease burst onto the world's firmament as the next deadly threat we had to fight against. The dry macrophage virus, or DMP, obliterated macrophage cells as a method of weakening the immune system before drying the cells of vital organs such as the liver and the kidney.

"Where did it first appear? On East-Africa, their preferred playground. So, the cycle of research, testing, trial, and cure got a new name. Nineteen years later, no one knows the cause, let alone how to treat it. Without enough water available to maintain normal body hydration, the insides of the people affected evaporated it as if exposed to an internal heating source. It's a sham rubbed into our faces over and over again." Cherry was unable to contain her frustration with this leech-like infection that was almost impossible to cure.

Ilanda stepped closer to Cherry until she was almost touching her and said, "Follow me." They walked toward the end of the corridor, down a flight of stairs, turned right twice, and then the doctor placed her thumb on the lock of her office door. "It's safer to talk in here."

It was an austere space with nothing more in it than a glass-topped desk, two chairs, and a three-seat couch for furniture. Two framed posters of the CN Tower—one black and white and one in color at night depicting the building illuminated by colorful beams of light—hung on one wall. The opposite wall had multiple diplomas and photos. There were no specialty books—all had been taken and locked in the hospital's library, the one place they would be studied. The ban on paper printing had turned all physical books into electronic formats, their value having skyrocketed faster than that of the cryptocurrencies on their heyday. Inventories of both brick-and-mortar and online stores had been cleaned out overnight by massive purchases before sales had depleted to a trickle. Now they happened only out of necessity for cash, water, and other bartered products.

"It's a shady system," Mazandir agreed. "Every doctor is forced to prescribe drugs for a minimum monthly amount and over the last three years, that amount has only gone up. The thin line of deontology had been crossed a long time ago and everyone is either too complacent or too embarrassed to check their conscience and admit malpractice. When a doctor recommends medication for various symptoms without examining potential side effects that could screw the patient up even more, that's malpractice, but it's a sure way to generate revenue for the hospital. The more people are messed up, the more they'll come back."

Cherry understood how difficult the confession she'd gotten from Ilanda had been, even though she'd maintained her composure and even tone throughout. "What do you need in order to develop a crystal-based technology that will use water as a healing medium?" the limnologist asked.

Mazandir looked down at the transparent AR device she was holding, then at the walls filled with framed diplomas and photographs depicting important milestones in her career, as if searching for a sign that might influence her decision.

"I'm risking everything," she said, still avoiding Cherry's gaze. "I'll give you a list of equipment that's required. It should be enough to start with. This discussion never took place… understood?" Mazandir firmly concluded while fixating on the woman seated across from her.

Cherry nodded. "On the list, add the size of the lab and the kind of helpers do you need."

"Do you mean lab assistants?"

"Yes."

"I'll bring my own from the university," the doctor replied.

"No one connected to you from the hospital or the university can participate in your future research. Until you have firm evidence, your work will be kept incognito as you could easily become a target," Cherry said, telling her the rules attached to the project. "They must all sign confidentiality agreements, and their chips will be tagged for additional supervision. No phones or documents will get in or out of the lab."

"Are you trying to scare me before we even start?" Mazandir asked, seemingly amused.

Cherry returned the smile and clarified. "I don't make the rules. The funders want to secure and protect the outcome of your work. I was told that one of the clauses stipulates your right to sign any published paper, prototype, or finished product. There is also a mechanism in place on how they'll recuperate their investments if that stage is reached."

"Understood. Let's deal with it when the time comes. But I also have one condition."

"What's that?" Cherry asked.

"There's one company in Toronto which has developed a crystal-based technology that mimics what I have in mind. It's very basic—a mesh of low-grade crystals—but using water as a medium that sparks the crystal's vibration. I've tried it myself and it didn't meet my expectations."

"So?"

"I want to engage the owner of the company, Ojani, to provide the water samples he's gathered over time. He might perceive me as competition, so I have to be honest with him. I don't see him spreading the word about the lab," Ilanda explained. "If, in the end, we have to share the material benefits of the results, so be it. Accelerating the research is more important for me."

"I'll ask if that's allowed. It might be a risk you'll have to take." Cherry paused for a moment, then asked another question: "How long will you be able to keep Kahuna checked in?"

The doctor swiveled on her chair, opened a drawer of a plastic cabinet that had been painted light brown, and took out a box of biscuits. "My comfort food. They're salty, in case you want one."

Cherry took one and nibbled at it slowly, still waiting for an answer.

"I'll keep him in as long as necessary. The government pays for it, and they can't force my hand in any way. It would be bad PR. He has to stay alive by whatever means possible. Healers, structured water, singing, prayer…I don't care, but I need that lab ASAP otherwise there's no point going through the hassle."

Cherry displayed a blithe smile; it was the answer she'd expected.

"If his family agrees, we'll have him moved somewhere else," the younger woman said, detailing a potential strategy. "Maybe where the lab will be so he'll be under permanent care," she added.

It was Ilanda's turn to nod in agreement while munching on a biscuit.

"I have to admit that I didn't understand all of the medical jargon and terms used in your presentations," Cherry said, debating whether she should take another tempting biscuit to snack on.

Ilanda's AR device rang again, this time with a different tonality, announcing a text message from another sender. She swiped the screen, read it, then closed it. "My interns just let me know that some strange results came out of the tests between water and crystals. The reaction of these two mediums in our trials has only gotten faster. It gives one the impression they learn together to process the gained knowledge and adapt through changes in structural behavior. The lab you build should speed our findings up exponentially."

Cherry agreed. "I really hope so, too. You mentioned the pineal gland as the switchboard controlling the informational flow to other major areas of the brain, and that's why it should become the primary connector for the embedded crystal. I've always believed the thalamus to be the switchboard—are you going to take the same approach with Kahuna?"

Ilanda's face lit up. "You're the second person to ask that same question in less than a week. I'll give you the more in-depth version, only because you have a better understanding of the subject.

You're right about the thalamus being the junction point connecting brain and body, but mainly to external stimuli. We're using the pineal gland as a shortcut. There's a certain enigmatic aura regarding this pinecone-shaped structure in our brain above the cerebellum. The pineal gland chemically regulates the level of sleep and wakefulness through neurotransmitters that are influenced by the amount of light the eyes receive."

"But Kahuna's eyes are closed," Cherry said, interrupting her, suddenly doubtful about the strategy.

Ilanda didn't seem to mind. "That's true, however, in his case, I'm not only considering jittering his brain with active thoughts but charging the water molecules with sunlight that will simulate regular daytime. It should send the right stimuli through the crystal structure to the cerebellum and hypothalamus. The former will generate a signal mimicking what should be a proper balance, posture, and body position, while the latter, based on the same message, should regulate internal body functions by spawning neuropeptides. We'll fake it until his brain is 'convinced' of the normality of each organ and brings its consciousness back."

The neurosurgeon threw the empty biscuit box into the recycling bin and looked at the limnologist with a serious demeanor. "The equipment I need for the lab should cost a minimum of four bitcoins, maybe more. It's enough for the WFA to clean up a couple of river communities."

"It's worth it. At least, in the long-term, crystal technology could save many lives. In the meanwhile, I'll plant the seed in Marinka's mind about what we've discussed, and yes, she will be discreet," Cherry added when she saw Ilanda's intention to object. "I'll share only what's necessary and your name won't be mentioned yet. At least, not until the lab and Kahuna's accommodations are ready."

"Thank you," Ilanda replied. She seemed relieved her confidentiality would be respected.

"Do you have a trusted and reliable source of crystals?" the water activist asked.

"So far I've purchased them through the university account, low quality to fit the budget. Your fund allocation should allow for above-average crystals, even some rare ones. Laser cut pieces will give us more efficiency of use and allow us to test for various vibration ranges."

Ilanda crossed her legs and dropped her chin into the cups of her palms. "I'll take time off from the university as soon as you confirm the location and arrival of the equipment. Arrange for the vendor's technicians to be on site for a full week. Everything should be tested and signed off."

"Understood," Cherry said and stood up. There was nothing else to discuss for the time being. The amount Ilanda had mentioned, four bitcoins—the equivalent of four million dollars in old currency—was a hefty number. Her easy acceptance, Cherry thought, had come from Ilanda's assumption the WFA would never agree with her pitch—she had been so wrong.

"Tell Marinka I'll be witnessing tomorrow's ceremony. Oh, and I need a sample of the water the healer's bringing from Hawaii. I want to test its structure and determine how it affects Kahuna," the neurosurgeon said.

"I'll take care of it," Cherry confirmed, and she walked out, closing the door behind her.

CHAPTER 6

Maahes knew he was about to break protocol. He took off his shoes, jacket, shirt, and tie, then put on a hospital gown, which he didn't bother to tie at the back.

He made his mind up as to what his next step would be. The degrading, scarce water resources along with the even more complex political- and geo-strategic games had eliminated the small and medium players in the industry. The five companies leading the pack had been given the opportunity to gobble up the existing infrastructure and natural assets at blowout prices, turning them into a water monopoly. Strategy, market updates, challenges, and next steps would be discussed quarterly when the CEOs of each of the companies met in secret and in person. They always met in person, as they had learned that even when hiding behind the most secure firewalls, they could not stop a determined hacker from eavesdropping on their private conversations.

"I'm ready," he said, addressing the young woman waiting by the door, holding a make-up bag. She came closer, opened her kit, and with quick motions, applied a white powder to his cheeks and neck with a sponge. Next, she drew a couple of dark lines under his eyes, creating the illusion he'd been suffering from insomnia. Light brown lipstick dimmed the color of his lips, helping with the overall cadaveric impression. When she was done, she handed him a mirror.

"I feel amazing," Maahes joked and looked at the doctor sitting on the other side of the bed, enjoying the charade.

The woman stepped outside so she wouldn't appear in the augmented reality conversation.

"You have to be concise," the doctor told Maahes. "I might not be able to keep a serious face for long."

"One minute, tops. My friends don't expect me to excuse my absence anyway. Just intervene after we exchange pleasantries," the CEO reminded him.

Maahes slipped between the bed sheets.

The doctor applied several sensors to his chest, taped a needle to his arm to make it seem as if it were a real transfusion dripping essential liquids into his veins, and turned the monitoring equipment on.

"Make the call," Maahes said, giving his AR device to the doctor. "Video: on," he added.

"Maahes, where the hell are you? We're all waiting," the respondent—who had obviously recognized Maahes' number before answering—said. He paused when he saw the doctor's face. "Who are you?"

"I'm Dr. Noni Timberlane at Princess Margaret Hospital in Toronto. Mr. Mazandir is my patient. He asked me to call you." The doctor changed the direction of the camera so the speaker could see Maahes.

"Hi, Derek," Maahes whispered, barely moving his bloodless lips.

"Oh, my God, man—what happened to you?"

Maahes closed his eyes for a moment, upping his theatrical performance. "Sorry I couldn't make it to the meeting. Next time."

"Doctor, what's wrong with him?" Derek yelled, forcing Dr. Timberlane to come into view again.

"His annual check-up found heart complications, nodules on his thyroid, high levels of heavy metals, and increased acidity in his blood. We're trying to determine the cause. It could be something he drank, his diet, or…who knows? If not treated in time, we expect kidney failure. We're running some tests. He needs an extended stress-free period, healthy food, and proper rest."

"Are you serious? He's supposed to be here, in Kuala Lumpur," Derek exclaimed, showing no empathy.

"Sorry, but he's not transportable and won't be for a while. I can't imagine what could be more important than keeping him alive," Timberlane replied morosely.

"Yes, of course. I'll let everyone here know about his condition. Take good care of him and thank you," Derek said before hanging up.

"He bought it." The doctor cracked a large smile and gave the device back to his friend who was already sitting on the edge of the bed waiting for the wires to be removed.

"You guys were very convincing, given the makeup and medical assistance. This prank will buy me some time. Thank you."

The doctor let the young woman in again, and Maahes waited patiently for the layers of makeup to be removed. Five minutes later, she packed up and left.

"Please keep my medical record up to date in case anyone pokes around," the CEO suggested. "I also don't want you to get into trouble—be sure to cover your ass."

• • •

Wealth, especially in a time of crisis, had raised Maahes to a social status only a few enjoyed. The endless opportunities with which one might live one's life cluttered his judgment initially, hiding any conscious thought of bad behavior under a rug of cheap excuses and baseless justification. His honesty, trustworthiness, and principled nature as a company man, both before and after becoming CEO, had gaps that no good deed done over the course of his lifetime would remedy. The army of highly motivated lawyers without which a multi-national couldn't survive had helped him keep the pretense that his decisions were always backed by the legality of the situation. Responsibility for the implementation of whatever strategy he or the board had voted on was, most of the time, a remote afterthought. The buffer imposed between the decision maker and the implementer conferred Maahes confidence that the curses, the fury, and the frustration of those affected by projects he'd greenlit couldn't touch him in any way. He had a false impression that his personalized natural filter would let only positive vibrations and beneficial wishes pass.

When politicians and ruling personalities from countries of interest didn't succumb to the company's requests due to unexplained nationalistic pride, Maahes would personally intervene in the process, minimizing the number of the people involved and decreasing the risk of leaked information. He would meet the hacker, the private investigator, or whatever other instrumental player was involved in his choreographed drama and eliminate, frame, or blackmail those who opposed his company's water-related acquisitions. Over time, as technology evolved and planting deceitful information in less invasive ways proved much easier, he only kept in close contact with Marian, a hacker.

Now, he was in need of him again. Maahes briefed Marian of his goal to reach out to his wife, Ilanda, through a third party while maintaining total anonymity. He offered several key details, such as her place of work, the WFA, and Kahuna as a potential link to one of its members. Two days later, Marian came back yielding concrete results. A cross-referenced search between the names of Toronto-based members listed on the NGO's website and those that had visited the huge Hawaiian had produced only five identities, and two of them were women.

"I've focused on the women because it would be much easier for one of them to have approached your wife. Out of the two, only one goes there three to four times a week. There's a high chance Ilanda has already met her, so whatever you have in mind for her to do shouldn't be a cold call," the hacker said, explaining his logic over a cup of coffee at one of the few Starbucks still open in the Financial District. "I am, however, intrigued by Cherry Mortinger—that's her name, by the way—and the additional layer of security on her AR device. I can usually crack into any off-the-shelf application, but not so with this one. It's very unusual."

Marian's head resembled a bowling ball with the trio of holes into which you jam your fingers replaced with deep eye sockets and a tiny, sunken mouth that barely moved when he spoke. His knees touched the underside of the table while his hands were large enough to completely cover his venti-sized paper cup.

Maahes arched his eyebrows waiting for the man to suggest another solution.

"It's not a problem, though. I've created a fake WhatsApp ID connected to an AR burner so you can use it. I just wanted to scan her device for more data before you contacted her," Marian said, removing the top of the cup. He took big gulps from it as if drinking water. This is his weekly ration, Maahes thought.

"So, is she the right messenger?" he asked.

"Hmm," the hacker acknowledged before swallowing the hot liquid. "Let me know when you're ready. Here's the burner. It's set up to call her directly without my involvement." He dropped what appeared to be a regular AR device on the table. "The augmentation component is disabled," he told Maahes. "I'm still available if you need any help. It might take a bit of convincing before she replies to an anonymous contact, so be patient. On the forums, people are still bringing up the explosion and how some of the WFA members have been hunted."

"This is bull," the CEO reacted, annoyed. "No one gives a shit about this movement. It's all paranoia so more sympathizers will join the cause."

Marian ran his left palm over his skull as if to check that it remained shiny. "You might be right. I've looked into the names you gave me of your CEO buddies. Couldn't find any incriminatory text, email, or document pointing to the explosion. I've downloaded their company's development strategy for the next ten years, though. All yours, free of charge," the hacker said. He knit his eyebrows together, waiting for a reaction.

Maahes focused on the steam coming out of the tea on the table. His actions were about to inflict chaos on the industry, and he wasn't sure if, after reading how his colleagues planned to pillage the earth for another decade, he would publicly reveal their identities. It was tempting and dangerous at the same time. "I'm too weak to refuse such a gift," Maahes said. He grabbed his cup with both of his hands and took a sip.

"Happy to oblige," Marian replied. He pulled a small USB device from an inside jacket pocket and pressed his thumb on its top surface until a green light appeared on the side. "Change security locks," the hacker said. The light turned red. "Your turn. Right thumb. Don't attach it to anything connected to the Internet. I couldn't find an electronic signature that triggers when the docs get opened, but there are smarter people than me out there," he said candidly.

"Can I be traced through the WhatsApp account?" Maahes asked, a bit concerned at the thought of handling the communication with Cherry Mortinger on his own.

"She doesn't have the means to track it back to you," Marian said in an attempt to reassure his client of the secured connection. "At least, I don't expect her to be a highly versatile hacker with access to tools that even few on the black market have. The number I used jumps two networks and is linked to another burner sitting behind various firewalls."

Maahes made the USB vanish into his breast pocket and looked at the AR device resting on the table.

"Having second thoughts?"

"No. No way. It's moving along as planned," the CEO replied. "Did I consider all the possible scenarios?" he said out loud. Reflective talking always helped him identify gaps in business strategies and ad-hoc solutions for his company, and now, Marian was a part of the process.

"I guarantee you didn't, be sure of that. It happens all the time. There's no reason to sweat over it."

The hacker gulped the coffee remaining in his cup and pushed his chair backward, indicating he was ready to leave.

"Anything else that needs to be addressed?"

Maahes shook his head. "No, we're all good."

"Then you shouldn't need me until it comes to the payment."

"Thank you," Maahes said, but Marian was already on his way out.

CHAPTER 7

"The prognosis shows sunny weather next week," Cherry said, addressing the twenty-five students registered in her limnology course at University of Toronto. "Check your inboxes for details on Wednesday's field trip. Let me know if you can come by this Thursday in order to make transportation arrangements. We'll visit the shore of Lake Ontario at the mouth of Humber River for water samples and collect immersed rocks that look like they might host micro-organisms and algae before heading upstream. We want to find the difference between the samples taken close to the water source and those along the settlements and how it impacts the water structure," she explained further. "Next, we'll drive to Lake Simcoe."

The room could have hosted a larger number of students but still had an intimate feel to it. Its large windows faced an indoor, dry garden arranged in the Japanese tradition after the person who had donated the funds. Benches made out of recovered wood had been positioned on the outer rim of a circle of white sand dotted with rough stones partially covered with moss of different colors.

There was a constant influx of students to her course, given the increased interest in what was happening with the world's water resources. Teaching young people with a high civic awareness about nature's broken balance kept her engaged and inspired to impart a positive message. The gloom and doom scenarios were on full display for everyone to see, but with her students, she applied a problem-solving approach.

Cherry would let Hayyin, under the protection of her anonymity, dismantle the barrage of fake, public relations news distributed by the main players in the water industry. Even so, as a limnologist, she had to have an opinion. Staying completely neutral in debates about WFA actions and daily news regarding "too little, too late" initiatives might raise some unwanted questions.

"Georgian Bay will be our last stop."

"Will we investigate the water structure there, as well?" a round-faced, head shaven girl in the second row asked. The dark contour of her lips and eyelids gave the impression she was wearing a mask.

"Yes, Zanice. I'll prepare checklists for on-site and off-site activities. We want to identify property correlations between samples from both lakes and the river, water structure differences, and as discussed three weeks ago, how we're going to influence the samples that we'll be carrying with us for the rest of the day," Cherry said. "On the bus, each group will focus on contrasting thoughts and feelings which should visibly influence the water's structure. I'm already biased as to the outcome."

"Are you referring to the ancient practice of native caretakers who prayed for the health of rivers and lakes?" Zanice asked.

"Precisely. Forty years ago, Native American tribes initiated an annual walk around the Great Lakes not only to raise awareness as to the devastating effects of pollution and indifference to water, but also to offer a collective cleansing through an invocation of love and gratefulness. It brought forward the profound connection these people had with what they believe is the infinite and undisturbed memory of the earth. There are little to no written records during the Native American's existence on what is today the US and Canada. All of their beautiful stories of origin and evolution were transferred orally so the wind could take it to the nearest river and etch it in the memory of water. Their conviction that water, which preceded humanity and could survive any extinction, was a collective and atemporal memory that couldn't be shaken."

Twenty-five young faces voraciously inhaled her enthusiasm, getting drunk off the vapors of their future, successfully implemented water initiatives.

Cherry took pride in teaching them, instilling a sense of duty toward fixing what others had destroyed. She'd always openly admitted to being an active WFA member, and after the explosion that had killed so many, eleven of her students had joined the organization. Action suddenly became important. The other students cared as well, but complacency weighed more on their scale of priorities.

The limnologist grabbed a thick metal pen and wrote the word 'water' on the digital board, then circled it. She drew several lines out from the circle and wrote words on the end of each line: alive, memory, survival, ancient, life-giving, warm, loving, protector.

"This is how I characterize water," she explained. "Just a few significant properties. Create your own list and generate your own point-of-view."

A hand raised at the back of the room.

"Yes, Opanah?"

The mahogany-skinned man had dense curls flowing over his shoulders to the top of his wide chest. Full, dark red lips covered crooked, pearly-white teeth with spaces in between his front four. His nose seemed smashed onto a rectangular face, and his brown eyes were a bit too far apart to maintain physical equilibrium.

"We all understand the motivation behind the WFA's existence and you joining them like most of my colleagues, but we never brought Hayyin up as an enigmatic ally in our discussion. Hayyin's like a modern-day Robin Hood who fights with information on behalf of the people. How's the WFA helping him unravel the illegal activities of corporations?"

Cherry thought for a moment. She had to choose her words carefully. *I'm Cherry Mortinger...I'm Cherry Mortinger...* The words rang loudly in her mind, dissipating any remaining threads tied to Hayyin's personality. She refrained from smiling. I'm not bipolar, she thought. I'm just an activist with an acute sense of self-preservation.

"Other than providing a free platform from time-to-time at WFA events, there's no close collaboration with Hayyin that I know of. As a public entity that could be easily dragged into a lawsuit, the WFA stays away from hacking or actively engaging in operations that border on irresponsibility. There are internal rules preventing such deviations. Also, having UN-Water as a reliable partner increases the threshold of an audit on how the WFA operates," Cherry answered.

"What can we do to help his stand?" Opanah asked. "What can we say that would convince our friends to get involved?"

She knew a blunt, abrasive answer.

"This always works for me: I'd ask them, 'Will you be drinking water today or tomorrow or the day after? What happens if the water ration is halved overnight? Could you live without water? How long would you be able to live breathing the thick smog others inhale as normal air in other countries?' These are rhetorical questions that can only be answered by their consciences. Next, I'd tell them: 'If you don't give a squirrel's fart about future generations,'" she continued in a raised voice, "'then do nothing. Sleep well, party hard, numb your senses with any substance you can get your hands on and thank the government for all the perks they offer as bribes to keep you quiet.'"

Her fingers were void of blood from grabbing the edge of the desk in order to hide her anger. The question got to her every time, like a pre-conditioned password implanted in her subconscious against her will. She browsed the frozen faces painted with dark spots bred by the combination of natural and artificial light in the room.

"That's a pretty intense answer." Opanah sounded amused. "If you don't mind, I'll use it, too."

"You have my verbal approval," Cherry replied, less tense.

She put the marker cap back on and sat behind her desk. The 2D aerial map of Lake Simcoe was still open on the iPad screen. Her fingers tapped to an inaudible music she didn't recognize. Her mind shifted outside the immediate reality as if a parallel track of her life had just overlapped with the existing one. A low-toned whistle initiated in her right ear and grew in intensity, joined by the whisper of trickling water as it forced its way through the cracks of the land. For a moment, she had the impression of hushed words echoing from the liquid's surface, a story released in the ether while the stream was still capturing new memories delivered on the wind.

"Let's try a different type of assignment for next class. We've just talked about the ancient beliefs of Native Americans—write a short story on the subject. Whatever crosses your mind. I'll penalize only those who don't participate," she said, enchanted by sudden inspiration. "Minimum two thousand words. The plot can happen anywhere in the world. The first and only prize is a free ticket to accompany me to the opera, so do your best."

Everyone packed their things. Animated by the discussion and perspective of an exciting field trip, their chatter moved to the corridor and died down behind the elevator doors.

Left alone in the classroom, Cherry didn't rush to gather her belongings. Rather, she touched the spot where she'd banged her head on the subway. Three weeks had passed, but she could still feel a small scab hanging onto her scalp. The pain hadn't bothered her lately; the frenzy of her schedule had pushed the tendrils of unpleasant memories away. The absence of memories included those of Hayyin, too. Even if Anonymous Group provided a couple of leads on Mosamoni and Narankama, she wouldn't find the disposition for in-depth research. Emails of highly-classified documents had been placed on the network where she could download them, followed by a note sent to her inbox which read, "Track the security companies." But Ilanda was in an idle mood, not yet ready to put the mask back on to publicly announce further shady water dealings in unprotected corners of the world. People liked an aggressive Hayyin, one that didn't shy away from calculated danger and just then, she was probably disappointing her followers all over the world.

She might jump on the situation later that evening.

Outside of the classroom, dusk settled on the late summer day, and she felt the urge to be outdoors, taking in the heat and humidity, but firm fingers of laziness kept her glued to her chair, melting her will. Random thoughts exploded inside her skull, a clatter intentionally distracting her from birthing a potentially significant idea. Various crystal shapes and colors, frozen water structures, and the sound of ocean waves agitated by astral rumors collided in her consciousness, making her groan. Energy and vibrations fought for the same territory, unaware or oblivious to the pain they caused to their host.

She shook her head in an attempt to rearrange her troubled neural networks. Bits of pain still nipped at her frontal lobe, though reduced significantly from before. Only the image of the crystals remained on her mental retina, oozing a sap-like liquid running down its smooth surface in perfect droplets, falling off in slow motion.

Cherry focused on what she was seeing. The drops were jumping off the edge, not falling, as if their density contained innate energy pushing them on a pre-determined trajectory. She followed the calculated aerial dance to its destination and gasped at the view: people lined up like ants waiting to pick up their load and return to the anthill along a pheromoned path. Adults and children alike, their mouths wide open, moved forward one at a time to receive the nectar of the crystal, one drop for each of them at set intervals. No one pushed, shoved, or jostled for a better place in line. There was an eerie calmness about them, a conviction the elixir wouldn't run out.

She gazed further, assessing the size of the crowd. On the barren land, broken by the mild hills and valleys, the multitude stretched to the horizon. She smiled at the idea she might also be down there, obediently expecting her turn. Colorless, emotionless faces characterized the wait, leading to the glowing aura and animated gestures of the bodies that had been touched by the blessed water. They were positively transformed, younger, and revitalized.

Cherry rarely daydreamed and never in such vivid detail with such an obvious message. Puzzlement stuck to her like gum to the sole of a shoe. She had the impression of wearing virtual reality glasses, but there was no physical device able to encrypt the message into her awareness.

Amused, she turned her head gently, enjoying the elevated view. In the distance, a frightening shadow appeared, a moving wall, dark with grayish fringes on top that she couldn't identify. It took several moments before she realized the tsunami, swelling from nowhere, was aimed at the people who were oblivious to the imminent danger. Panic strangled her throat, and she was able to utter no more than a squeak from her dry mouth. Even so, she understood that not even a lion's roar would have reached those hypnotized by the prospect of renewed health and energy. They would be washed away and discarded on foreign shores when the strength of the wave finally diluted to a meager swell. An impressive force pushed the water forward, making their escape impossible.

Cherry's body tensed, bracing for impact.

The strident ring of a new text message disrupted her nightmarish vision. She cursed herself once again for forgetting to mute the AR device. Her mental image had collapsed before she'd been able to envision the horrible ending. Cherry looked at her phone to see a WhatsApp message blinking on the transparent screen. She confirmed her fingerprint.

The sender was unknown.

Cherry Mortinger—my sincere congratulations for your WFA involvement. I'd like to help fund some of the initiatives, but in return, I have to ask you for a small favor. Why you? I'll explain later. Condition: my donation, two bitcoins to WFA, will stay anonymous.

"Two bitcoins," Cherry exclaimed. "A lot can be achieved with a donation like that. I hope you aren't going to ask me to kill anyone," she said, addressing the invisible donor. "Probably a bad joke, more than likely."

The message concluded: *Reply to this message if you're interested.*

She deleted the message, intrigued by the amount promised and the request to have the donor's identity remain anonymous.

Who in the world would lack vision not to spin such a magnanimous gesture into a public relations campaign?

The question was rhetorical.

She put her iPad in her backpack, erased the notes she'd made on the digital board and left the room, still thinking about Anonymous' emails and how she might approach the research.

• • •

The hacked letters contained inoffensive remarks about future development plans in Asia and a Memorandum of Understanding (MOU) between Narankama and Mosamoni, two conglomerates. For the past sixty years, they'd behaved as savages for whom the concept of cutting the branch beneath one's feet and falling himself was inconceivable. They'd agreed to pull in resources from Kazakhstan, Mongolia, and North Korea—target countries—and through intimidation and bribery, purchase land rights on plots known for having high-depth aquifers in the past. The Gobi Desert, close to the south-eastern Chinese border was as dry as a bowl of milk after a handful of kittens had had their meal, but it hid an important vein of untapped, fresh water. Previous readings from twenty-five years ago, before the water crisis had hit its exponential curve, displayed no such findings. Similar cases in other parts of the world revealed a definitive pattern of water having disappeared from one location only to magically appear in another. No one could tell if it was the same source of water or if the liquid had played hide-and-seek with an innate intelligence that would gear the stream to safer places outside of human reach.

Cherry wanted that elusive water source to stay pristine and deepen its flow to preserve its primordial memory and structure. There was no mention in the MOU about a security company, and she wondered why she'd been given the lead to a potential dead end. Anonymous always liked to plant clues for her to pursue, and she did, with the tenacity of a bloodhound.

She'd asked Siri to check the corporations' websites where she found mention of a different business strategy they'd used for markets in the Far East. The press release had been diluted with a lot of meaningless, hollow-sounding words and no definitive steps with which to enlighten the reader. It was done this way to withstand a SEC audit and at the same time, tell nothing to potential, nosy reporters, at least, not until the action had been set and near impossible to undo. HQ had issued it without specifying where the signing of the MOU would take place.

Cherry widened her search of the CEOs' schedules to include the previous week, hoping to find their trajectories intersect to connect more dots. And she did. Narankama' CEO was in Mongolia, visiting the region bordering Kazakhstan, while Mosamoni's had spent the past three days in Kazakhstan on a leisure trip, but still taking on discussions with local entrepreneurs and landowners enchanted by the prospect of meeting with such a powerful man. Local and international reporters had been offered crumbs of information that in no way would insinuate a synchronized visit to cover up a much more sinister purpose.

"Siri, find references to any new reports on water resources in Mongolia or Kazakhstan," Cherry said.

"No reports found." Siri's answer had come back within seconds.

"Enlarge the search to all countries in the Asia-Pacific region," she instructed.

"Found one entry in the issue of *Communism Rebirthed* from June 14, 2045 in North Korea."

"Display."

The limnologist tapped the air to enlarge the fonts and read the article out loud. "Two underground rivers discovered using sonic waves were proven to be muddy waters of high temperature, moving with unusual elevated speed on ruts angled downward from the surface. Samples were taken, and the results exhibited a radioactive composition that was maintained after existing water filtration technologies were employed."

She inhaled noisily, exasperated by the lack of useful nuggets. "That can't be it or the media all over the world would have picked it up."

Cherry caressed her chin with a slight movement of her fingers, thinking of new ways of to hone Siri's search ability. "Look into the annual reports of Narankama and Mosamoni for any investments or buy-outs of engineering companies, vertically integrated and offering geo services such as surface and underground imaging, marine geophysics, and seismic surveys," she tried again. "Let's see if they suppressed publicity on subterranean rivers by taking control of the company that discovered it."

A new window popped up on the screen.

"Both annual reports list only one entry under 'Other Investments,' with no clear specification of its purpose. For Narankama, it's called the Asia-Pacific Fund, an investment vehicle that assesses opportunities in the region outside of the company's core activities as a way of creating new revenue streams," Siri said, reading the description.

"Track any such investments of the funds," Cherry told the AI.

The results came back moments later. "Both funds placed contributions in similar companies, one in Mongolia and one in Kazakhstan."

"Great job, Siri," the woman said, praising her artificial helper. "Find any reference to these companies: articles, websites, anything." Her fevered imagination was already running allegoric scenarios of designs the conglomerates might have implemented.

"No recent information is available."

"They don't have websites?" Cherry said, fully aware that something wasn't right. "Expand your search to caching servers or personal computers that have accessed the sites and still maintain the source files on the browser's cache. If necessary, go back five to ten years."

Intrigue permeated her thoughts. Cherry walked to the kitchen looking for a mug and a tea bag. She picked up the kettle, turned on the faucet, and a trickle of water came out. It dried up after several seconds.

Your daily ration has been used, the digital display announced to her.

"Fuck you!" she said in frustration. She waited for the meager amount of water to boil, poured it over the tea bag, and returned to her office.

Siri had done her best. Cherry opened the first link on the screen. All of the icons were missing, and the text displayed in a language she didn't recognize. "Siri: translate."

"'Kangali Earth Service is a company specializing in infrastructure projects that serve communities and conserve the environment through thorough assessment studies. The company also evaluates water and hydrocarbon reservoirs, optimizes field exploration, and has built an extensive database of geo maps. Kangali has heavily invested in a proprietary technology that identifies underground water streams. For more information, click this link.'"

When she tried the link, the browser returned a blank page.

"So, these nasty guys were busy covering up any mention of Kangali. I'm pretty sure Mosamoni did the same with their acquisition on the other side of the border," she said to herself. "They hedged their bets in case only one of them succeeded in buying a similar company and the land necessary to tap into the hidden source of wealth and control leverage."

Cherry sipped from the half-full, hot tea cup, glancing at the links she hadn't opened yet.

"They've found important veins of underground water and they want to keep the news bottled up," she muttered.

"Siri: display legislation, old and recent, passed by the governments of these two countries, especially those forbidding water exports, if any."

"Six new articles and four changes to existing articles in Kazakhstan, and only two changes to existing articles in Mongolia," Siri announced.

"Compare the content and analyze which country's restrictions are more stringent on water exports."

Cherry was slowly identifying more to the scenario with each new search. The swarthy tactic applied by such corporations still kept the citizens in a permanent vise of fear and uncertainty, allowing the CEOs to remain, unchallenged, in the background.

"Through its latest laws, Kazakhstan has completely forbidden foreign companies' expatriation of newly-discovered water resources, either fresh or those that require processing. Local entities reporting new veins have to hand extraction rights over to the government who is the only deciding factor as to how the water should be used. The initial owner receives twenty percent from the proceeds and can barter products for up to another thirty percent," Siri read her partial conclusion with a steady, and in several instances, a high-pitched voice, mimicking human tonality.

"And it remains in the good grace of the government," Cherry commented, interrupting the AI.

"I didn't understand the request," Siri said. "Please repeat."

"Don't mind me. Continue the analysis."

"These laws were implemented shortly after an economic agreement was signed with Russia in December 2054. A one-way trade of cereals and oil from Russia is to be sold to Kazakhstan. Comments on several blogs mention that, in return, the exporter expects significant water quantities. The former chief scientist of a geo-planning Russian company who now lives in the US has spread the rumor that the water crisis situation in Russia is kept confidential at the upper-levels of government so it won't hinder next year's elections. President Ranchucik is on a mission to rally allies that might help add to his water achievements."

"What about Mongolia's laws?" the limnologist inquired.

"Similar laws in Mongolia are much more relaxed. Foreign investors need to have a local partnership and can export up to fifty percent of their water reserves. Restrictions apply only to European countries and the US, destination countries who are not allowed to import Mongolian water."

"Any violations found?"

"Two in the last ten years. The entities that didn't comply were shell companies funded with US money through Guatemala and Ghana. Their local partners pleaded guilty, their assets were frozen, and the foreign partners declared persona non-grata. These harsh measures proved effective," Siri said. Cherry read a sentiment of satisfaction into her artificial voice.

"Determine the land holdings of the companies owned by Mosamoni and Narankama at their common border, superimpose them on the map, and based on known soil composition, determine the most likely direction of an underground water source."

Cherry glanced at the time on her cell: 2:00 a.m. Ideas continued to inundate her mind, maintaining her aroused state of consciousness. Working at odd hours came naturally to her. The reverence of silence conceived by the night's darkness discarded other daily worries, allowing Hayyin to focus on the burning issues.

"Four thousand, seven hundred acres in Kazakhstan and twenty-three hundred acres in Mongolia. There are no known underground water resources, but if any, they would flow west to east, toward Mongolia," Siri said, displaying an enlarged map of the region on which both lands had dotted contours.

"So, the companies used a proprietary technology developed in Kazakhstan to identify water and secure enough land to prevent competitors from extracting from the same spring while capturing the flow on the Mongolian side," Cherry murmured.

She remembered Anonymous' guidance about the security companies.

"Is there any mention regarding security organizations mandated with the protection of the land?" she wanted to know.

It took Siri several seconds to load new maps displaying the capitals of both countries and two other remote towns closer to the borders.

"Vontechum is a Swiss-based company with subsidiaries in this region. Recently, permanent training camps have been established on the lands previously mentioned. The company's elite team was part of the security detail for both CEOs." Siri brought forward an image taken in Ulan Bator. In the background were heavily-built men, head shaved, wearing shirts displaying an embossed blue Z, crossed in the middle with a gun.

"Thank you, Siri. Create a new folder on the desktop and upload all the information accessed today, then duplicate and upload that to the staging server. Allow access to Anonymous only."

She wanted Anonymous to hack into the companies for more information. Anything about undeclared water reserves and law avoidance depriving locals of their right to water. That way, when Hayyin distributed the news, given the amount of overwhelming evidence, she couldn't be dismissed by the PR machine.

Cherry turned off the lights and retired for the day.

• • •

She received the second text message from the secretive sender three days later with an added enticement: *I will offer an additional bitcoin if I get an affirmative answer within twenty-four hours.*

Amused, Cherry decided to play along and reply, confirming her interest. She also forwarded the message to her Anonymous contact, convinced the hackers would be able to track the sender's identity.

The troubling news was conveyed on all major online channels along with live reports about sizeable crowds gathering at the banks of the Ganges and Jordan River, which were considered sacred water flows. Indians taught their children the meaning of the Ganges before they were able to walk, and so its purification powers, having been designated by their Gods, was ingrained in their religious beliefs. The river never failed the nation—it irrigated fields, provided water for livestock, generously received the ashes of the physical bodies of the departed, and without exception, cleansed the sins of believers immersing themselves in its squalid content daily. For the Christians, the Jordan River carried a similar significance, except taking a dip in it was a costly task. One had to follow certain rules overseen by the clergy on site. One couldn't jump in for a quick swim or quench the burning heat of his body without starting an uproar in the omnipresent crowd that wanted an unaltered image of the sacred river in which they were about to immerse themselves and say a prayer of thanks.

Livestreams broadcasted by younger devotees, more attuned to the opportunistic side of their character than keeping an even, internal state of contemplation, depicted the instantaneous color changes of the flowing water, first of the Jordan River, and then, two hours later, of the Ganges at Varanasi. It looked like a delayed communication between the two rivers, or a quantum entanglement, conveying a message of importance to the world. The rivers' new, reddish nuance forced false and real prophets and spiritual and political leaders to come out of hiding and share their views. They sermonized aged messages about the end of the world, the punishment for people's irresponsible treatment of the earth, in addition to the mention of our carnal sins.

"Pray harder to God as only He can erase our misdeeds. Repent honestly and we'll be forgiven," was the message replayed by the clergy with the hope of regaining parishioners that had strayed from the flock.

"It's just another cycle in Earth's evolution. Don't worry too much—it isn't good for your health," the sarcastic, faithless business leaders said in an attempt to further confuse the crowd. "If the rich and spoiled are calm why shouldn't everyone else behave the same way," was the message they tried to impose on the masses, but when asked for scientific proof of similar events that had taken place in recent history, they couldn't provide any.

An ad-hoc interactive augmented reality invitation from the WFA's executive committee to discuss the latest events buried all the thoughts Cherry had deemed important at the beginning of the day.

"Has the water's chemical composition and structure changed?" and "How is it going to affect the WFA projects in those areas?" were the burning questions; the answers were ambiguous.

"Our local contact in Varanasi collected water samples, and we are waiting for the results," confirmed one of the scientists present on the call. "I can tell you now that the color alteration comes from a chemical reaction. As far as the nature of such a reaction, I don't know what that it is yet. The molecular structure might still be the same."

"Are there any tanneries upstream? Any reported spills?" Romana Pilb, the new WFA president asked.

"There is no such thing along the Jordan River," said a man Cherry recognized as Pat Boulanjois, the Montrealer in charge of collecting all information on projects considered for WFA funding. "They've been celebrating Diwali in India since yesterday, so many businesses are closed. In Varanasi, the tanneries are south of the ghats, while the pigmentation happened further north. There is no logical explanation thus far," he concluded.

"I've just received a message: determined crowds from all over the world are gathering along the banks of major waterways to witness the strange behavior first hand," Romana Pilb read. Then she continued, explaining her personal position: "These two cases aren't enough to draw conclusive results. The only commonality I can think of is that both rivers are considered sacred, holding a lot of religious and spiritual meaning."

Cherry intervened. "India has multiple rivers that carry a similar significance: Yamuna, Sarasvati, Narmada, Kshipra, just to name a few. We should dispatch teams to areas where water changes are most likely to occur."

Romana Pilb made several notes on a pad in front of her, then asked.

"And how are we going to determine these spots?"

"Tourist areas," Cherry specified. "I think this is why it happened in Jordan and India, places with high visibility in case this is a message addressed to us."

"Still having doubts about that?" interjected the scientist who had spoken first.

No one commented. The virtual room was full of worried faces, some of them wearing signs of having been abruptly woken from a sweet dream. The committee had members in every time zone and the call of duty required their presence.

"Are we going to freeze any of our projects until we get clarification on the nature of this incident?" Boulanjois asked.

Pilb and Cherry started speaking at the same time generating smiles from everyone involved.

"You first," the limnologist conceded her turn.

"I suggest that in India and the Middle East, all initiatives related to raising awareness about the water. situation and the available options should stay their course. It's a project component that has to be completed anyway. When it comes to spending actual cleanup funds, we should halt our efforts until, as Pat said, we understand the nature of such a disturbing transformation," the WFA president shared. "Cherry, anything to add?"

"The WFA's expected to come forward with a statement based on facts and data. You've heard the declarations of the leaders that would try to benefit from such hysteria. Neither political nor religious figures can be allowed to misinterpret the WFA's message. Those who pilgrimage to these sacred places are not regular tourists," Cherry said, explaining her major concern.

It was morning on the east coast and she hadn't had the chance to finish her coffee yet. The top of her pajamas, a plain, gray t-shirt with four blue, wavy lines going across it could be taken for outside clothing, and she hadn't bothered to change it. "Ninety percent of them have strong faith and they live their lives according to the Ten Commandments. For them, experiencing the Jordan River or the Ganges at Varanasi is the trip of a lifetime. Their hearts are filled with awe and reverence, but also with the undeclared desire for Krishna or Jesus to appear in front of them out of thin air or walk on water on his way to blessing the masses. In other words, a miracle is what they expect."

"You're right, but what does that have to do with the WFA?" Romana Pilb questioned. "As long as we keep the message clean and bipartisan, we should avoid any backlash. You suggested that only minutes ago."

Cherry pushed herself up on her couch and replied, "Based on the religious crowd's behavior, it's very likely those already on site will hold their position in case additional phenomena occur. Anything out of the ordinary could become the tipping point for believers to grow blind. Our field teams should be careful— no comments, no visible WFA logos. They need to keep a low profile and collect samples as far downstream from the crowd as possible."

"That's good thinking," the president agreed. "Let's reconvene in twelve hours so we get some rest. In the meantime, the press release will come out and the results—or partial results, at least—will reach us," she concluded. Remembering an item she'd lost track of, she added, "Cherry, several days ago, the WFA received a substantial donation, and your name was listed as the reference. Great work! Do you know who the donor was?"

The limnologist's eyebrows raised as if pulled by an invisible force and her mouth formed a perfect "O." She couldn't believe the anonymous stalker had already transferred the funds.

"How much, if I may ask."

"Three bitcoins. We'll slash the funds next week at the monthly meeting. By then, the worldwide tension should settle and let us continue our work," Pilb replied.

"And to answer your question," Cherry said, " I communicated with the donor by text only. I don't know his identity."

The slits on Pilb's stretched face that were his brown eyes squeezed briefly, and then her features relaxed into a stern face.

"We should ask Hayyin to poke around for his identity and the source of the funds. It's a nice gift, but we can't afford to have any strings attached, not now, not ever," she suggested, rubbing her palm-wide forehead.

"There isn't much to work with—just a text from a fake account. Nevertheless, I'll send it to him," she said, duality tugging at itself inside her.

"How's Kahuna doing?" Pat Boulanjois asked. The question was on everyone's mind. No recent updates from the family meant no significant improvement in his condition.

"He was visited by a Hawaiian healer last week. Against medical advice and hospital policy, a healing ceremony was performed and water from a pristine rivulet known for its quality replaced the vitamins in the perfusion. His brain activity surged a bit, but it dropped again soon after the perfusion drained. They need to keep it going continuously for it to make a difference, but that's impractical," Cherry said, providing the information she had.

"And how will this process help him recover?" Boulanjois asked.

She didn't want to dwell on unnecessary details. "It maintains his body's water structure which, in turn, simulates the normal functioning of his internal organs. It's a temporary solution until the neurosurgeon decides he's stable enough for another surgery. As for Landing Eagle, the situation's not as optimistic. His body's weakened from the trauma, and I'm afraid his family members are about to sign his release to transport him back to the reserve. The other elders are making preparations for his soul to join his clan's ancestors."

Cherry remembered the chief's speech during the conference in which he'd mentioned the elders were dying before their time. Now, it was his soul's time to light up the sky's firmament as a bright, new star, watching over his clan's members and guiding them in keeping their customs unaltered by the surrounding craziness.

"Landing Eagle used to say that after his body returned to dust, his soul would continue to paint the canvas above our heads with marks and signs for those of us connected to the earth's vibration. Very soon, the elder will, indeed, from his celestial place, create masterpieces of meaning as a way of presenting his unconditional love for us," the limnologist said, offering a passionate view of the end drawing near. "This is why we shouldn't surrender to torment and anguish, but instead, celebrate his imminent passing and join our energy in saving Kahuna."

Several people on the call mumbled "yes" or "of course" or "whatever it takes."

Sadness struck Cherry during this last remark. The reason for their fight went beyond martyrdom, and the determination of many would ensure the message was carried forward.

CHAPTER 8

"We need to download certain log files off of your AR device," Anonymous told her after investigating the online electronic signature left by the text message she'd received from the mysterious donor. She unlocked it and let them do as they pleased. To them she was an open book with nothing to fear, someone trusted and reliable in her daunting role as Hayyin.

"The additional firewall we installed has light, nearly imperceptible fingerprints that are only visible to us. We've integrated a nano-tracer in the reply to the sender, a 'thank you' for his donation. Even if the message is scanned in traffic on multiple hop-servers, our tool is seamlessly integrated. It will wait patiently until the receiver hits reply, after having taken all precautions. Using the same text thread is paramount as it closes the loop and provides a complete trace," Anonymous said, explaining what had been done.

Even if she was protected online by powerful and skilled allies, in real life, Cherry felt exposed to the potentially crazy actions of those monitoring her from behind the shadow of their anonymity. Thoughts ruminated through her mind raising pensive questions as to how much Anonymous already knew about Hayyin or if picking her for the secretive job had just been a coincidence. The basic meditation classes she'd taken during her university years came in handy from time-to-time, somehow settling her swirling thoughts. Humility, love, and empathy intertwined into a crown of serenity she imagined sitting atop her head, which had a metaphorical calming power. Suppressing fear and conveying strength was the attitude that Cherry and everyone else involved with the WFA had to radiate.

Being chosen for the enigmatic activity that had yet to be revealed proved once again how fate had disregarded her decision to live simply, insisting on dishing out unexpected assignments, chores, and responsibilities that only added pressure and worry to her fragile balance of existence. The explosion's repercussions had dragged Cherry's psyche to somber depths, the likes of which she hadn't experienced before. Only recently had she been able to bring herself back within bearable limits. And now another twist had hurled her thinking process off, making her the messenger of a generous, but probably deranged donor.

Cherry opened the living room windows to let the breeze of the balmy fall day in, bloating the transparent curtain into playful, round forms. After she'd moved into the house, she hadn't attended to renovations other than replacing the beat-up carpet with laminate boards and a fresh coat of paint. It was enough to enhance the feeling she was taking good care of her parents' most valuable possession. Several antique pieces of furniture had been sold during a Sunday garage sale to make room for their modern equivalent: a round, glass kitchen table, two curved, red leather armchairs with stunted black legs, and an Indian-made, woolen carpet with a large Aum sign weaved into its center. It never failed to attract the immediate attention from the few visitors she had. Four original, abstract paintings had found their place on the light gray walls, bringing her joy and calmness at the end of hectic days. The dated couch had a cover matching the armchairs, which completed her bare necessities. She sat down on the couch, holding a tiny, shiny apple resembling the plastic replicas of fruit, which adorn the glass saucers used in interior design set-ups in furniture stores. The bite she took from it had no flavor. For the last three years, she'd noticed labels no longer mentioned the products' origins, as if they had grown in a place too shameful to name.

The apple and cherry trees her father had planted in the backyard when she was still a baby had provided shade and sweet fruit during her childhood. She'd hung from their branches like a monkey. It was there she'd discovered that swinging her body's weight back and forth built momentum. Enthralled by the ease with which she'd climbed to its top, Cherry had spent countless hours observing the neighbors' roofs and the ever-changing blue canopy overhead while munching on the plump, dark cherries. When she grew tired of watching the sky, she'd would play a game in which the pits, when spit from her mouth, became circus acrobats. The hard, little spheres would drop, finding their way to the ground without hitting any obstacles. Cherry celebrated each successful attempt by putting another fruit into her mouth. Simple games like that served to enrich her days of solitude.

Water rationing and its usage ban on anything except personal consumption had turned the once flourishing speck of green into a desolate landscape as if a voracious evil had sucked the nutrients from the ground. Occasional rainfall wasn't enough to satisfy the insidious thirst of the scorched dirt. Grass and beds of dried geranium and peoni perished leaving behind rough earth, bitten by gusts of wind and stuck under the unforgiving sun during the extended summer months and frigid cold winters. A pair of maples stood their ground but life left them, too. Death grabbed onto their lower branches first and then, like a plague teasing its host, slowly advanced to the top. The dead wood, twisted, cracked and hollow, when looked at from the living room, gave the impression of a man kneeling with raised hands, asking for mercy. To Cherry, it was another sign depicting the tenuous relationship humans had with the environment.

Her iPad signaled that the augmented reality WFA evening meeting was about to start on schedule. She accepted the call and several familiar faces appeared in her living room, projected from the waist up, fifty percent smaller than in reality.

"Hello everyone," Romana Pilb addressed Pat Boulanjois, Ikiku Asu—Japanese, geo-physicist, Josephine—an intern with the WFA, and five other people Cherry recognized as members from the USA, China, Brazil, and Russia. "Srinitham Maghatham from India, the latest addition to our team, will be joining us shortly from Varanasi. What updates do we have? Pat? Cherry?" Pilb said, a stern look on her face. The scar on her upper lip twitched a couple of times.

"In the short time we've had, we've been able to determine the chemical changes to the water in the Jordan and Ganges Rivers were not caused by man artificially." Pat's elongated head appeared even larger due to the flaccid skin hanging under his neck like the pouch on the throat of a pelican. "However, it seems the molecular structure of the water was also affected, and the usual, hexagonal patterns are fuzzy or muddy in appearance, rather than crisp, as they once were. The disturbing part is that the samples we took from each river are perfect molecular matches, which is a mystery to us. The Varanasi sample has traces of Palmaria Palmata, a harmless red alga found in the northern Atlantic and Pacific. So there is no explanation how a saltwater alga has ended up in a freshwater location. It's simply implausible these algae could have migrated to the Ganges without leaving a trail for us to follow."

"Didn't we recently hear in the news about a new strain of Palmaria Palmata that displayed a level of toxicity when in bloom?" Pilb asked, almost hinting at another question. She was a hydrologist who specialized in underground water but had spent most of the last twenty-five years of her career in business.

"Yeah, you're right. Massive areas turned red along maritime routes. Samples extracted from the Atlantic proved toxic. It can kill fish and make the surrounding air difficult to breathe," Boulanjois explained in a rapid-fire assertion.

"Are we confident that this is the harmful algae we are dealing with at Varanasi? And is there any opinion on what caused the extreme mutation in Palmaria Palmata?" Pilb asked.

"There is no scientific explanation for it yet. And because it's a recent discovery, we didn't check if there were signs of a toxic strain at Varanasi or in the Jordan," Pat replied. "Earlier today, Cherry suggested this could be a warning, but one without repercussions as of yet. Next time could be different. I personally have a difficult time believing in this theory, Cherry—no offense," Boulanjois continued, almost laughing at the thought that water could be capable of taking intelligent action against humans.

"None taken, Pat," the limnologist assured him in a calm voice. The light of her blue eyes confirmed she maintained composure. Even in the scientific community there were few bold enough to comprehend and accept water's perceptive properties. "Water anomalies are being reported all over the world, but in many cases, such incidents come to us from online posts. Preoccupied with the latest events, we completely ignored a crucial section of the WFA's website which is my responsibility, too, and I have to take the blame for it. I spent a good chunk of time today filtering through several hundred emails received in the last week alone. Ten percent of them came from oil rig workers in the Atlantic, the Pacific, and the Northern Sea. Deep sea oil extraction is risky business and it hasn't slowed down in spite of the spills, explosions, and marine life devastation. Again, political clout is more powerful than humanity's best interest."

"What's unusual this time?" Ikiku Asu asked.

Cherry pulled her legs up onto the couch, scratched an itch on her right cheek, and replied, "Their monitoring equipment has detected tremors at depths close to twenty thousand feet."

Almost everyone on the call interjected, disturbed by the number they'd just heard.

"I know—it's insane," Cherry said, cutting through the noise. "I've checked the oil rig's website and the extraction depth hasn't been reported. On top of that, the emergency valves haven't been verified at depths below ten thousand feet over the last three months, there are no spare parts for the maintenance submersible, and even then the technicians are afraid to venture down. During a previous attempt, the cables connected to the vehicle inexplicably froze, cutting off power and oxygen. They were pulled out manually, just before they died of asphyxiation."

"Does the email give more details on the data that worries them?" Asu asked again.

"Yes. Toxicity levels are getting higher. This means there's a breach in a nearby natural gas or methane pocket. If the puncture isn't sealed, contaminants from the Gulf could reach the Atlantic Ocean and the coast of Europe. It's only a matter of time before the world's oceans are compromised," Cherry clarified.

"And if we corroborate it with an underground earthquake, the methane could erupt and break through the ocean floor creating a tsunami of unimaginable destruction," Ikiku Asu explained. "Marine life would be wiped-out, oil rigs dismantled, and maritime commerce ravaged. It would make the 2010 BP Deep Water Horizon disaster look like child's play."

The vocal cacophony resumed.

"Let's do our due diligence first." Pilb raised her voice, bringing the noise level back to a mumble. "Ikiku, you have the right contacts in the US to confirm what Cherry shared with us. If proven correct, we'll inform the authorities. Does anyone know what the chances are that underground seismic activity would calm down if the vibrations and disturbances caused by drilling ceased?" Romana Pilb asked almost rhetorically. Drops of perspiration gathered on the fine, blonde hair above her upper lip. Her wide palms and short, thick fingers lay splayed on the desk in front of her.

Seconds later, she asked another question, convinced no one was able to answer the previous one: "Cherry, have you encountered similar critical reports uploaded to the site?"

The younger woman shook her head. "Nothing as critical as this one, mainly anomalies related to water behavior from Africa, Australia, Russia, and China and points in between. I'll ask Josephine to help Pat and I sort through the emails and plug relevant information into the data models we use on project evaluation. We'll look for patterns, triggers, and anything else of significance," Cherry said, providing a plan. "One report is worth mentioning: in the Kalahari Desert, the watering holes should be full at this time of the year, but whenever the locals visit it to collect water during the day, the water's gone in the early morning and only resurfaces at dusk when the villagers can't compete with the thirsty herds of wild animals. It's a cycle that's been observed for the last several weeks. It's as if water's taking care of nature's innocent stock and punishing us. It's consciously avoiding us."

Cherry's disturbing news raised everyone's level of discomfort.

"Have the water restrictions increased in your region?" Pilb asked everyone.

She's trying to assess if the governments are in panic mode, the limnologist thought.

No one answered in the affirmative.

"That's good news, but that doesn't mean that they can't tighten the screw overnight.

"We were also supposed to monitor the crowd's behavior along the two rivers. Any updates? I've personally had no time to check the news online," Pilb stated.

Just then Srinitham Maghatham came online and introduced himself in two jerky sentences, before continuing, "The shores have become permanent camps. No matter the time of day or night, people stare at the flowing water, waiting for miracles. Street vendors have moved closer to the tents since the increased traffic is great for business. Yogis and religious men dot the edge of the Ganges, singing and praying to delight the multitude. They gladly accept offerings of food and money to interpret the signs shown to them by the sacred water of the river."

Srinitham was in the thick of it, dense smoke from open fires and burning incense going up everywhere. Children were yelling, men and women were sitting cross-legged directly on the dust or on narrow, woolen carpets. Distant drumming and chanting surrounded the young man who had decided it easier to show them than explain the situation. The dying sun cast an orange trail on the impromptu gathering as if the Diwali festivities had begun anew. Several rows of tents separated him from the water so no one on the call could see how many people were engaged in the "purification process."

"Are the devotees still dipping in the Ganges?" Pilb asked in a low tone as if afraid that in spite of the background noise some-one else might hear her questions; she'd forgotten Srinitham was wearing earbuds.

"Yes, now more than ever. Let me show you." Srinitham made his way through the labyrinth of tents with barely a narrow passage left between them. He stepped over cords secured to the ground by metal hooks, avoiding a group of young boys fighting over a piece of dirty piece of bread that had already twice escaped their grip. He was ready to step out of the shadow of the last row of tents when a woman covered in orange and red veils bumped into him, and they both lost their balance. Srinitham recovered first and helped her to stand. Without looking at him, she vanished into the maze from which he'd just emerged.

"Are you all right?" Romana's black eyes widened and her upper lip quivered imperceptibly.

"I'm okay," the man assured her. He turned his phone horizontally to get a wider shot of the Ganges.

Srinitham was standing at the edge of the camp. Below his vantage point, stairs of stone extended over the shore and down to the water.

Only the top arc of the sun was visible, its powder-like light dropping down onto the Ganges, its surroundings, and the invisible entities believed to linger on its sacred shores as auras of spiritual cleanliness.

Silence suddenly strangled the human voices along with the wind blowing between the tents. The dissipation of the last ray of celestial light seemed to calm everything and everyone. Only the Ganges, due to its primordial role in the creation process, had the right to vortex its waters, creating playful waves and caressing those immersed in it as they waiting for a blessing. The fires lost their vigor. Birds quieted their chirps. Paddles froze in the water. The peace was profound, something felt even through the phone connection.

A scream bit the silence, then another, and another, joining each other in shrieks of terror. The calm water reflected the flames from the nearby fires and the looks on the devotees' faces. They were the ones shouting, fear and pain engraved on their features.

"Srinitham, what's going on?" Cherry asked, her body tense and leaning forward to distinguish the events in the dim light.

"I don't understand," the young man replied. The image he projected jolted up and down as he tried to get closer. "They're all coming out screaming."

A man in his thirties wearing nothing but a loincloth collapsed beside the WFA representative. Everyone on the call saw the inflammations on his legs, arms, and chest as if he'd bathed in boiling water.

The wailing intensified. A stampede erupted as men and women, young and old, grabbed onto each other, looking desperately for support as the pain from whatever had attacked their flesh made them move as if in slow motion. Few on the shore dared help pull them out. More and more of them dropped to the ground, howling in pain. People moved torches closer to the shore.

Srinitham pointed his phone toward the water again. There, in the knee-deep water, two elders looked around them, puzzled by the commotion. They were also wearing a loincloth, their long, white hair and beards framing their incredibly creased skin, the result, no doubt, of many years of exposure to the sun. The changes to the water hadn't seemed to affect them, and their composure remained calm and serene. As if to convince themselves of their unexpected immunity, they scooped their hands into the waves and poured the water on their backs. The liquid trickled down their bodies and returned to its source without harming them.

The Ganges, the sacred river, protects and punishes at the same time.

Cherry wondered if their age had been a relevant element in their treatment.

Srinitham turned around as loud voices approached him from behind. Tent canvases flew left and right, cut by machetes wielded by policemen. Paramedics followed them, carrying folded stretches—they couldn't have dragged them on the uneven ground, littered with trash, wood from the fires, and the bodies of the exhausted who had no place else to go.

The group passed Srinitham in a hurry, dispersed to soothe those in pain. Trained for crises, they'd been told not to go into the water to rescue those poor, remaining souls still struggling to exit. Instead, the policemen used oars from the boats secured to the wide stone steps as dragging tools.

Overwhelmed by the situation, the WFA representative was unable to his phone steadily. It seemed he'd forgotten he was attending a live call.

Cherry saw the crowd swarming around Srinitham, shoulder-to-shoulder with him, recording the events on their phones or broadcasting live to a wider audience.

A low battery-warning message flashed on the screen, and the man's sweaty face appeared on the camera. Several locks of hair dangled over his eyes that were filled with fear. "I have to go now. I have to help these people," he yelled. Saliva burst from between his thin, dry lips.

"Srinitham, please let the doctors do their job. There's nothing you can do before they know the cause of the reaction," Romana Pilb advised loudly, almost begging him. "We also need you. The WFA counts on you being our eyes and ears when reporting incidents like this one," she went on. "Don't forget that earlier today the water was benign. People bathed in it and prayed for the cleansing of their material attachments and the opening of spiritual channels. What changed in the last few hours?"

With tears in his eyes, the young man looked around at the throng moving chaotically about him. "How can I walk away?" he wailed.

"We need you to stay safe. What I'm going to ask you now is more important than helping those people. You have to secure water samples and take them to the lab ASAP. Please, Srinitham," the woman insisted. She wanted to say something else to dissuade him from acting irresponsibly, but the Varanasi connection died.

Those that remained on the call were void of words. Finally, Cherry crumbled the crust of silence by asking, "Has anyone checked if the feeds are already live?"

Josephine's shrill voice reached them after she disappeared from the video frame. "Yes, it's being broadcast live. It's still chaotic, but more paramedics are on site. They've even brought floodlights for better visibility in the rescue operation.

"There are reports of crazy fishermen putting their boats in the water, tying them together in a straight line, and throwing their nets into the water to catch the bodies before they washed away down stream. I don't think they understand they could also get burns when they touch the wet bodies."

Josephine's child-like face reappeared in the AR projection. She was holding a portable AR device. With the swish of her hand, the nightmarish images from Varanasi shifted to the main conference screen so they could all witness the event.

"Have similar incidents been reported from the Jordan River?" Pilb asked, hope in her voice that the time delay between the two locations might save some lives. "Could the harmless Palmaria Palmata switch to its toxic strain so quickly?"

Josephine had already thought of it. She pushed another live feed onto everyone's screen.

"The occurrences started minutes ago, but only a handful of people had nothing more than minor burns. The Jordan River's a trickle compared to the Ganges. Access to the water is controlled and bathing is done in an orderly fashion. The reports mention the red algae's intensified nuance of red just before people getting hurt," the girl said, nervously shoving a long, black lock of hair behind her ears. "Those for whom faith is beyond existence were protected, and the water didn't burn their flesh … I assume," Josephine added shyly.

"If these people have a strong belief in God or any other divinity, how does the water know about it?" Romana Pilb asked with a puzzled inflection.

Cherry, who was already immersed in the stories of the First Nations, tried to answer. "There's an aspect of water that doesn't surface too often and even those involved in the movement forget about it: water has memory and water communicates. The Ganges washed the bodies that had been immersed for purification and the feedback it got from the water around the faithfuls was positive. Being a believer means to love all of the Creator's children, to be compassionate, and to care about Gaia. All these implicit feelings must've meshed into a protective shield. I personally can't think of another explanation."

"You might be right," Boulanjois said, engaging in the conversation after what had been a long silence. "It's the only commonality so far."

"Guys," Josephine interjected, somewhat alarmed, "alerts are coming from websites about those living along the Yangtze River and the Nile; the effects are spreading fast. The similarities cannot be denied anymore."

"To any naysayers, here's your answer: the water's alive and its actions are retribution for the careless way we've been treating it for far too long," the limnologist mumbled but it was loud enough for all to hear.

Josephine muted the livestreams so they could think quietly about what to do next.

Cherry had her own insight into the latest events.

Corrective measures were needed. Water had provided ample time for redemption, but our inflated egos and feelings of entitlement had blinded us to the necessity of treating water better. How could something or someone so wild and smart ever be chained? Water had witnessed humanity's fall into purposelessness; it had absorbed our anxiety, greed, hate, hostility, addictions, and the negativity that ran at a much higher percentage than love, compassion, and gratitude. Water was fed up with our deluge of irrational decisions that would wipe everyone out in the end.

But water would survive.

She would purify herself of all the memories we'd etched onto her molecular structure.

"I'm suggesting the following," Romana Pilb said. "We contact Srinitham in a couple of hours, which should give him enough time to take the samples to the lab and charge his phone. I'll call him; I want to be sure he's all right.

"Josephine and Pat: take care of the feeds Cherry mentioned earlier.

"Cherry and I will work on a swift, official message. I'll pull in the PR guys as well.

"Let's assume for a moment that water's fighting back for its own survival," she said this while moving her fingers to indicate air quotes around the word 'survival'. "This means that lately, we, as a society—or at least some of us—have acted in a way that tipped the balance of common sense toward stupidity even more than before. Our message should call on governments to revise water-related laws and immediately stop irresponsible extraction.”

“I don’t count on anyone listening, but we can try,” Pat accepted the challenge.

It was a hectic schedule, but one that everyone was ready to take on.

“Should we contact Hayyin?” Boulanjois said. “Maybe he’s uncovered some dirt on the big corporations. Now’s the time to splash it on the net.” Perspiration darkened his red t-shirt around the neck, with more of it trickling down his puffy cheeks.

“That’s a good idea,” Pilb confirmed. He cracked a shy smile. “I’ll let Cherry send the request. Let’s reconvene in three hours.”

• • •

Cherry Mortinger hung up and remained on the couch, holding her knees tightly to her chest. She felt as if every drop of energy had left her body, squashing her will to move, think, or do anything else but remain frozen like a gargoyle on top of a cathedral, watching over the blessed souls praying inside. Varanasi was supposed to have been a safe place, protected by the gods and beliefs unshaken by thousands of years. Jesus and John the Baptist had walked the banks of the Jordan River, imbuing the ether with their own Christ-like energy, removing pain and sin and physical and spiritual deformation.

Why had such a cruel punishment senselessly clobbered the people who had retained the sanctity of these sacred places? It was subtle, yet harsh at the same time. To Cherry, the message was, without a doubt, one of strength as well as a warning of additional repercussions that might follow.

Cherry leaned her chin on her knees. Wandering thoughts came and went as if her mind were stuck in a revolving door. Would Hayyin’s message turn the tide in any way? Had Hayyin really made a difference in the past?

Suddenly, Cherry wasn’t sure anymore, not of the struggle millions of caring people needed to overcome the stubbornness, greed, and myopia of the few.

If the water retreated underground or refused to let herself be tamed again, they were all going to die. Tears dropped on her yoga pants. What could be changed in Hayyin's delivery to take her message to unforeseen depths? Would the carrot be more powerful than the stick? Hayyin shouldn't be afraid to echo the elders' spiritual message about the memory of water, nor should she underestimate her incredible capacity to enact reaction, change, and adaptation to the surrounding environment.

Cherry silently acknowledged how absurd it was for Hayyin to take a spiritual stand, risking a reputation built on exposing undeniable proofs and facts about water rights illegalities. The regular crowd might ridicule her request to pray for water's forgiveness or to manifest a deep love and appreciation for the liquid in which the first embryos of life had developed billions of years ago.

She unwound her legs and walked around the room using small steps while she considered Hayyin's next significant move. Cherry crossed the hallway to her office and stared at the mask hanging on the wall, quiet and shrouded in a mystery not yet unveiled by its existing owner. No answer to her burning question came to her mind. The immobile, wooden face kept a stern expression as if the pain it had endured since its creation made it void of any tenderness.

Cherry held her focus on Hayyin's face as if begging for a hint. Still standing, she brought her palms together near her chest to say a concise, simple prayer. Her ultimate, internal compass had never failed to show her the proper direction.

She invoked her heart. A tender thought imbued her consciousness with hope, delivering, at last, what she'd been looking for. The WFA and not Hayyin should be the one to dispense spiritual guidance to the world as had been publicly explained by Kahuna and Landing Eagle.

Cherry searched within herself, hungry to receive long-term knowledge, but there was nothing else. She gave a short bow to end the invisible communication. Her energy, having doubled with hope, bounced inside of her, generating a pleasant vibration warmed her thin body for several seconds, confident she had the right script for Hayyin.

Cherry went back to the living room where she found a dozen emails had populated her inbox. A quick look at them almost made her enthusiasm from moments before vanish—the latest chemical analysis of the Ganges' water confirmed its healing properties were gone. The bacteria used to destroy cholera had disappeared. Those caught on the water hours earlier displayed symptoms of profusely watery diarrhea, leg cramps, and vomiting. There was no word yet whether the effects extended to the holy men, and she was convinced it hadn't crossed anyone's mind to investigate. Cherry composed a short note for Srinitham and cc'd all committee members.

The next one that drew her attention talked about Mexico City. For almost forty years, the city had sucked its potable water from an aquifer which had depleted at an incredible rate. The air replacing the water had turned the porous, spongy subsoil into a sinkhole to which the government had paid no attention. The structural instability reached its tipping point the night before when a big chunk of the east side—almost twenty square kilometers—took a forty-meter free fall. Tens of thousands died in their sleep and gas pipes burst like fireworks killing even more. It started a chain reaction of destruction that only an earthquake of eight degrees magnitude or higher could have achieved. Online videos showed burning pits like the ones that had been CGIed into the Mountain of Mordor, the flames almost reaching the level of the initial drop. The intervention crews were safe on the other side of the city and had no training for an incident of that scale.

To control the fires, hundreds of drones equipped with remote-controlled containers filled with chemical agents focused on buildings higher than five stories. The strategy differed where the lower structures were concerned: four drones had been hooked to two hundred square-foot, fire-resistant blankets that were to be placed over the houses and secured to the ground with thick nails ejected by the drones. Without oxygen, the blaze would slowly die down, making the terrain more secure for the firefighters to attack hidden, smoldering charcoal.

Cherry couldn't watch the despair of the survivors and rescuers. It took her several minutes before she understood the TV anchors had been calling those lucky enough to still have their homes and offices above ground rather than buried in a sinkhole "survivors." There was no more city hall, nothing left but a physical location which wasn't enough to fill an overwhelmed mayor and his petrified councilors with any semblance of confidence. Their appearance at one of the two remaining TV stations only served to create further chaos—flee the city, they advised, as the underground air pocket was much larger.

She gasped for breath, her mouth dry, a spike of pain coming and going on the left side of her skull. On the way to her kitchen, she glanced at her reflection in the hallway mirror. The blue of her eyes seemed darker, only this time it wasn't due to unchecked fury, but the agony she felt for the citizens of Mexico City.

Cherry turned the water tap on only to be told her daily rations had already been consumed. She didn't swear this time, but took a tiny apple from the fridge, cleaned the skin with a piece of cloth, and bit into it. Her lips, tongue, and taste buds thanked her for the small bit of moisture that soothed her mood momentarily.

I'm alive, she thought.

I have a roof over my head.

I will be able to drink a glass of water tomorrow.

The people on the TV are either dead or have lost everything.

She went back to the living room.

Cherry thought she'd absorbed enough suffering for one day, but then another subject line caught her eye: Venice's future is doomed.

It had been determined thirty years ago that new technologies would allow Venice to raise its unique buildings against the slow but constant rise of water levels on basalt poles, protecting them. Complacency and sometimes indecisiveness as to which palazzo might be saved first had dragged the project into long delays. That it had reached ten percent completion was the most about which officials could brag. The water had risen swiftly overnight, submerging the first story of every building in the city. Chaos ensued. The number of casualties announced by the authorities was below one hundred, but was expected to grow after a door-to-door survey had been concluded.

"What part of the world will collapse under the next water attack?" she said out loud. "Has water been awakened as Landing Eagle predicted?"

She heard a jingle and glanced down at her lit up phone screen. "There you are again!" she exclaimed at the new message from the anonymous donor. "What do you want this time?"

The message was short and had an attachment. "Share this file with your WFA buddies or with a trusted third party," it said. "It has to go out. Don't open it on a device attached to the Net as it could be traceable."

She pulled out her iPad, disabled the Wi-Fi, and opened the file. The report carried Mosamoni's and Narankama' names and she instantly realized how powerful Hayyin's message could be.

CHAPTER 9

Ilanda still couldn't believe she'd agreed to further her research on crystals outside the safe, respected University of Toronto environment. She chalked it up to a moment of scientific weakness. It was sacrilege on her part, biting the hand that had offered her such an exclusive opportunity.

Her lust for knowledge over recognition from the scientific community had drawn out her easy acceptance. She was aware of the WFA's reputation and achievements, but she knew nothing about the people running the organization. Panic wrapped around her like a synthetic fur coat. Adamant speculations of failure clung to her mind, unmoved by her conscience desire for good. Cherry appeared to have been honestly and sincerely devoted to Kahuna's rehabilitation which had persuaded Ilanda to send a comprehensive list of equipment, supplies, and necessities for the lab, but that had been eight weeks ago. Since then, her main goal—and it was a rather unrealistic one at that—was to keep the Hawaiian leader alive and his brain active.

She had listen to Maahes and, when the Hawaiian healer came to the hospital to attend Kahuna, she sealed the room and let no one else inside during the ritual. For the first time ever, she'd experienced a sacred water ceremony, shivers running down her spine as if the water in her body, triggered by the chanting and prayer, was actively participating in the healing process while healing itself as well. She was unable to control her trembling flesh as the fulgent energy passed up and down her body, invigorating her cells.

Aside from the critical medical cases that had seized most of her attention, the world outside of the hospital had climbed to a new level of craziness. She had no interpretation for the irrational behavior of water that had taken place in various regions of the globe. If not for the livestreams being posted all over the Internet, she'd have considered such news nothing more than plain old science fiction.

Whimsical molecular changes, high level fluctuations outside of the moon's gravitational pull, and pigmentation modifications were the most reported incidents which, to her, had no immediate scientific or logical explanation.

As much as she wanted to believe in the coincidences of natural events taking place simultaneously or with minute amounts of time between them, reality threw hard evidence in everyone's face like a lightning strike in the wake of thunder.

Ancient cultures had treated water with reverence, love, and respect. They'd had insight into the complexity and sophistication of its structure and memory. Their prophecies, disregarded by the modern world, had seeped through the seams of history, like bad omens unleashed by broken promises.

Ilanda, whose family had immigrated to Canada from Sweden in the 1960s, grew up immersed in Nordic folklore. Näck, the water spirit, known for playing enchanting songs on the violin, could be either malevolent or harmless, irresponsible or as soft as the wind kissing a willow. In her imagination, the stories conceived a life-giving character. Water pulsed in her veins, in her family's veins, and in the streams surrounding the city her great-grandparents had left behind and followed them to the land of discovery. Water helped them when they were in need and punished them when they were destructive. Water was alive. It had memory, one that could never be erased, and Ilanda intuitively knew it.

Cold crept into her small office like fog rising from a lake on a damp, early morning. She was unable to move from the couch, choosing, instead, to let mid-November's dusk swallow her body and morph it along with the plastic furniture and photographs of New York hanging on the walls into unrecognizable shapes of gray and black. The workday had come to an end, so she should have been excited, filled with adrenaline by the message that had confirmed her dream come true: "The lab is ready for you to visit." The text contained an address on Queen Street East, only minutes from St. Michael's, making it easy to get to by 7:00 p.m. that evening.

Deep down she still wanted to consider it a joke, Cherry and the WFA playing with her transparent ambition about being the first to find practical applications for the crystals' buried potential. If the lab was real, she'd have to keep her promise.

She moved gently, shaking the shadows from her shoulders. Freed from their tight embrace, Ilanda stood, picked up her purse, and changed into a pair of running shoes. From the door, she looked back at the familiar space, the dark pierced by the light from the hallway. She supposed, in a way, she was saying goodbye to the office in which she was likely to spend less and less time.

The streetcar left her steps away from the address, an old school building no longer in the hands of Toronto School Board after being sold to the highest bidder. Over the years, a reduced birth rate meant fewer children in the classrooms, forcing educators to take a different approach. Gone were the days of onsite courses. Many people worked from home which allowed parents of toddlers through to high school kids to choose specific, online courses from a flexible curriculum that was still decided at the provincial level. The teacher, an AI entering everyone's homes through Augmented Reality technology, kept the students engaged and organized. Universities and colleges had shrunk to the bare minimum where personnel was concerned, contracting physical teachers for specialized subjects for which an AI had yet to be developed. The visionaries in the AR industry boldly entered various fields, packaging information, knowledge, teachers, and the environment into over-the-counter modules that were impossible to refuse.

The two-story building was at least sixty years old, rooted in the landscape of the modern city, a vestige of sentimental value for which there was no one fearless enough to propose a facelift. Most of the street-level windows had been boarded up. Some on the second floor were missing panes of glass. The brick wall facing north was stained with grey moss. Stubborn rust slipped through several layers of paint on the poles of the main entrance.

On top of the poles, sheets of flimsy metal were barely secured with screws that had long ago given up their resistance to the bite of determined winds and rains. New scaffolding had been propped against the west side of the building, a sign that renovations might soon begin.

Ilanda tried the metal doors, inset with four squares of thick, yellowish safety glass that distorted the image behind them like funhouse mirrors; they opened easily, without squeaks or screeches reverberated along the dark hallway that followed. She pulled her AR device from her pocket and texted, "I'm here." The dim light shone on the walls, revealing faded graduation photos hanging in dusty frames. On the opposite wall, a glass case still showcased trophies whose glittery sheen was long gone. She heard hurried steps coming from the lower level and a narrow tunnel of light took a turn toward her.

"I'm glad you made it," Cherry said gleefully.

"Hi. It wasn't hard to find."

"Don't be bothered by the dilapidated surroundings. Renovations are scheduled to start next week. It should be awesome. The ground floor will host the administrative offices and the physical recuperation room, while the upper level will host the patients—*your* patients," the limnologist emphasized. "There isn't much to see here, so let's go to where the magic will happen."

They descended the stairs, carefully pacing themselves in the faint light of their devices. At the bottom, Cherry flashed a plastic card in front of two metal doors that opened inward.

"This is your pass. It'll work until your retina and thumbprint scans are set up over the next few days," Cherry clarified. "I've followed all the instructions you sent me: the double air filtration system, the antiseptic process, the lighting requirements, and even the surround sound system."

"And the floor plans we discussed? It's all done?"

"To the letter. The space to the right has been divided into four separate labs with mobile walls. On the left are two operation rooms, able to accommodate a large number of assistants if necessary."

"Good," Ilanda said. Her eyes tried to take in as much as possible, afraid she might never be allowed back again.

They were walking down a wide, well-lit hallway that opened into the spaces mentioned earlier. There were no labels on the doors yet, and Ilanda opened one of them out of curiosity.

"A donor made a recent, significant contribution to the WFA, and he asked that a portion be redirected to complementary water activities," Cherry said, confirming the initial strategy she mentioned at their first meeting. "Until now, I've been the main contact for the contractors and equipment suppliers. Moving forward, that'll be your job. It's your lab; mold it as you wish."

"You want me to handle the remaining work?" Ilanda put her hands on her hips, demanding details.

"Look, on the WFA side, I'll be receiving financial reports on the remaining budget and we'll hire an office manager soon. The position could even be filled by someone you know," Cherry clarified.

The neurosurgeon nodded in disbelief. It was hard to fathom that what she'd thought had been an informal discussion two months ago had materialized into a state-of-the-art research lab, even better equipped than the one from University of Toronto. MRI, PET, MEG, and CT devices lined the walls, still wrapped in their plastic packaging. In another room, she noticed the surgery robots and the headrest system for neurosurgical procedures along with unopened boxes of clamps, retractors, occluders, distractors, and all of the necessary tools she'd need in the event manual intervention was required.

Ilanda felt sure she'd be able to make a real difference there.

Cherry continued bombarding Ilanda with uninteresting details. "The outside brick wall's falling apart, the metal posts alongside the entrance are ridden with rust, but the overall building structure's in good shape. I'll send you the updated architectural and design drawings—if you want to change anything, now's the time."

"Okay...okay," was the only reaction Ilanda could muster.

"As for your assistants," Cherry said, pausing to ensure the neurosurgeon was paying attention, "you have the liberty to post the jobs and go through the resumes yourself. I'll send you a list of names as well, in case you want to shorten the hiring time-frame. Tell the candidates as little as you can about the project for now."

"So how much can I say?"

"List the job as being in the realm of in-depth, crystal-related research, which isn't too far off the mark. You can only divulge more after they sign confidentiality agreements."

"Understood."

"By the way, the WFA took the liberty of negotiating compensation for the names on that list, in case they are hired. Use the same figures for those you select yourself."

"Wow, that really makes my job easier," Ilanda replied, impressed with the efficiency of the organization.

"We focused on young researchers who have published several papers during their university years and those who have displayed an interest in complementary fields. Specialization is good, but having an open mind is even better." She offered Ilanda a large smile. "What do you think?" she asked.

The neurosurgeon didn't reply. She just kept opening doors and looking around corners as if looking for new discoveries. "Are there any software developers on your list?" Ilanda asked.

"No", Cherry replied, flipping through the pages she was holding. "It definitely wasn't on the list you provided," she said, sounding somehow disappointed.

"Sorry. I forgot," Ilanda said, shrugging her shoulders like a dismissive teen.

"We need a magician, one able to understand how code matches the crystal's vibrations."

"I think I have a potential candidate in mind. Could he work remotely, or do you need him on- site?" Cherry enquired. "This guy's quite private."

"On-site, off-site—it doesn't matter much if he's able to do the work. We'll mainly use AR for closer interaction."

"Okay. I'll look into it tomorrow." Cherry browsed through pages again, looking for anything she might've missed.

"The whole place is amazing. How long until the upstairs and exterior are finished?

"Come in tomorrow morning and revise the plans with the contractor. We weren't sure if the rooms required specific facilities. He can give you a final date."

"No serious research can start in here until the building's fully renovated and the crew's gone. The location's convenient, but the outside world's vibrations might impact the crystals. The streetcars, car horns, the bell of the nearby church—anything might create an undesired noise that could interfere with the elements of an experiment," Ilanda explained. She pushed a lock of hair behind her ear and thought about the critical nature of the issue at hand.

"What do you suggest?" Cherry asked.

"The floor needs phonic insulation. It's doable and shouldn't go over the budget."

Cherry didn't argue. "Like I said, now's the time to apply any changes you think might help your work. Oh, and something else: the electronic wallet information will be sent to you through a secured channel. It already has four types of coins you can use to purchase high-quality crystals."

"I hope you don't expect me to handle the financials of this venture," Ilanda replied, a tinge of worry in her voice.

Cherry waved her hands in a definitive no and said, "No, not at all," as if for emphasis. "An accountant had already been hired, but no transaction will be processed without your approval and there are other checks and balances in place to keep the research afloat."

"That's good. Being bogged down by administrative work is the last thing I want," Ilanda confided openly.

She read a couple of labels on the boxes that were stacked in the corner and she clapped her hands in a gesture of joy. "My own lab. I still can't believe it!" She walked over to Cherry and gave her a hug. "Thank you."

"I can't take all the credit for it, Ilanda. This just happened to meet the WFA's interest in saving Kahuna and similar future cases," Cherry said, justifying her success.

Ilanda released the younger woman from her arms. She liked everything about Cherry, from her vibrant presence to her boyish look to her liberated attitude; there was no pretense about her—no falsity lay behind those blue eyes."

"Are you planning to bring Ojani here?" the limnologist asked, curious she hadn't heard any updates as to the joint activities Ilanda had mapped the last time they'd met.

The neurosurgeon's eyes widened for a moment. She put her hands on either side of her neck and tugged on her trapezius muscles in an attempt to release the pressure there, but also to give herself time to find the right answer.

"Yes. His bank of blood samples is unbelievable. When we make headway in finding the right balance between the type of crystals and thickness of the implants, my expectation is the user's experience will increase exponentially and finer details will be forthcoming," Ilanda explained.

"Okay. Be sure he's aware of the security measures we have in place. He's going to benefit from the outcome of this initiative anyway, so any leaks won't help him."

"He's not the type to sign a confidentiality agreement, but he believes in a firm handshake." Ilanda straightened her back and changed the subject.

"Let's aim to have interviews, renovations, and an action plan ready by the end of the year so we can start fresh in 2056!" Ilanda exclaimed before turning to exit the room, followed by Cherry, who turned off the lights.

CHAPTER 10

Ojani—also known as Orange, the nickname used by his friends, customers and employees—gathered everyone into his tiny office on the top floor of Toronto's Royal York Hotel for the morning's pep talk. All seven of them—Ojani included—crammed against the walls and the narrow window facing south toward Lake Ontario, obscured now by the countless glass towers, like an overgrown forest with no room left for breathing. There were four women and two men in total, all of them in their mid-thirties, all of them with families and responsibilities and for whom keeping their jobs was the main focus, no matter how challenging.

Ojani's atypical Jamaican look had encouraged him to keep a certain distance from the community. He was not a mulatto, but a pure breed on whom genetics had played a cruel joke, tinting his skin color with an orange nuance, rather than the dark brown one might have expected. Since his childhood, the teasing had had its ups and downs, the one that stuck with him to the end of high school and bothered him the most was the one about his having been conceived by a lonely sperm lost in a glass of orange juice. A number three haircut replaced the traditional dread-locks, black eyes sparkled on his round face hemmed by a dense, black beard, grown with the purpose of covering skin that developed the cast of a rash for unknown reasons. A scar parted his right eyebrow, the consequence of a defensive gesture in grade three when, in a moment of weakness, he'd tried bullying a girl for her lunch apple. As a teenager, and later as an adult, he didn't flourish into a physical presence that might impose respect, leaving him with the only option of using his smarts to search for opportunities in places or circumstances where everyone else was too afraid or complacent to look.

Ojani's thoughts came back to the present. The daily, morning speech reminded everyone that some clients were about to arrive from their rooms, ready to try—some of them for the first time—a costly experience that would forever be engraved into their consciousness. The business never had important or unimportant clients—they were all treated equally. Employees had to acknowledge this from the first day on the job, as it was Ojani's obsession to offer amazing customer service.

"Today, we'll switch roles—Martin and Julius will be your backup, ladies. One of the customers is an eighteen-year-old girl that has selected the experience of a paragliding pilot who has flown in the French Alps, had to withstand some crazy winds, and almost perished. Lala is her name. She has a heart condition and not even her parents were able to change her mind to choose something milder. Lala's a spoiled brat for whom we need to take special measures. A team of paramedics will be on site. Cara: don't take your eyes off the vital signs monitor. This is a wealthy family that's already come back several times and did a great job of marketing our business," he presented them the toughest challenge of the day.

At age thirty-two, Orange considered himself phenomenally lucky, with the stars having aligned for him at just the right moment to allow him a relatively smooth path in life. The Jamaican community in which he was born had kept him isolated from the outside world until he'd entered grade one. His parents, young and in love and with little life experience, had wondered at his coming. Working two jobs, bombarded with countless restrictions on their personal lives imposed by a failing government, little Ojani slowly turned into more of a burden than a joyous sight at the end of the workday. His grandparents on his father's side had shielded him from outbursts of irrational behavior by his parents ignited by the consumption of Omega 10, a synthetic drug popular with low-income individuals with a quick high that hooked the subconscious with colorful visions. The inhaled crystal crawled its way through the veins, aiming to enhance synaptic activity. People's minds were destroyed faster than their bodies, with the drug's consumers slipping into a vegetative state, leaving, mainly the homeless ones, exposed to merciless organ traffickers who thrived due to the lack of Canadian legislation.

By age ten, Ojani understood his parents would never recognize him, nor were they able to participate in after-school activities like the parents of his peers.

"I suggest she put the oxygen mask on from the beginning. All of the other customers are new and without concerning health issues. Be sure that before they arrive, the rooms have fresh towels, the incense is subtle, and a glass of water is available. If they request more water, add it to the bill but only if they've paid for the basic experience: listening to a book-reading, concert, bird-watching…you know the drill," Orange explained. "I'll be out for a couple of hours to bring more structured water from the temple. Call me only if you need to."

His speech didn't divulge his roots, but there were moments either in elated happiness or brutal despair when he couldn't stop his mind from speaking certain slang that gave pause to those who were listening; he sometimes enjoyed their puzzlement.

Orange measured his employees with one last look before sending them out for a final check of the four rooms he'd rented in the hotel for a hefty monthly rate. Their morale was important to him, as he was aware of how much influence their attitude could have on the customers and the crystals and water with which they came into contact. Their *heartical*[2] had to be in sync with their mind and their *konshens*[3] clean, so he could only accept positivity, gentleness, and a large smile. After so many years in business, he was able to tell if the smile was truly genuine.

Orange dressed his employees in Hawaiian shirts, the golden standard used to mimic the islanders' permanent state of happiness. He followed suit; rarely did he wear a black shirt, though when he did, it hinted at his mood.

Before taking the elevator down, Orange hailed a driverless cab through the Uber application on his cell. Since the explosion

---

[2]   Heartical – from the heart

[3]   Konshens – conscience

almost three weeks ago, the hotel had been under permanent surveillance. The workers involved in the renovations were checked thoroughly, daily. Even Orange himself was not exempt from the painful process, regardless whether his business owner pass would operate from inside the hotel.

The three weeks of cancellations that followed the unfortunate event hadn't hurt him that much financially. The hotel had voided the rent during the shutdown, and the employees' salaries were manageable. He cared more about the blood samples he'd received from all over the world from his network of personalities and ordinary people that had gone through unexpected or intentionally induced experiences. The specially designed receptacles shielded emotions, vibrations, and thoughts from interfering with the sensations that had been recorded by the body of the handler. They lined the shelves in the upstairs storage room like soldiers waiting to be woken for battle. The unaffected building frame hadn't forced him to move his inventory to a safer location.

"Payment on delivery" was his business motto, and profits generated by his cryptocurrency venture—in which he still had a fractional interest—poured into purchasing more samples. He diluted them in structured water and made them available to whoever had the money to pay.

Outside on the street, he jumped in the cab and recited the address of the Riwoche Tibetan Temple. The weekly visit to the oasis of tranquility and beneficial vibrations created by the monks had been, for many years, his way of recharging his mind and body. He was convinced his weekly visit to the temple and the way he'd lingered in its manicured gardens for longer that fateful day had saved his life. Orange had assessed he wouldn't arrive on time for the WFA's introductory speeches and logged onto the webcast. Faith, a word whose meaning had been revealed to him in his teens, had other plans and had kept him away from death or permanent injury.

If it hadn't been for the failure of his parents being involved in his life, he wouldn't have had the chance to befriend Tenzin, a most unusual schoolmate in the form of a tiny Tibetan who had landed in Toronto with his family when he was only six-months-old. His rare visits to Tenzin's house three streets away from his own had become more frequent as the warm atmosphere, the low chanting coming from the upstairs, and the delicious food stirred an echo of familiarity in Ojani. Homework was done in silence and games were played without the exuberance of unchecked yelling and exaggerated gestures. It was a natural act of reverence on their part toward Tenzin's parents who had brought beliefs and spiritual practices with them that they still rigorously followed. There was no enforced meditation or reading schedule, but it was a natural extension of their daily itinerary, an unspoken agreement joining everyone in a magic web weaved by ancient Buddhist culture.

Along with Tenzin, Orange immersed himself in books illustrated with intricate, colorful mandalas and images of Buddha in contemplation surrounded by symbols and messages, the meanings of which countless devotees were still in search of.

By age eleven, he felt reborn through knowledge and spirituality; matured, but also more sensitive to repercussions water challenges and environmental disasters had on his immediate community. He understood the future was bleak and was unable to use Tenzin's family as a surrogate for what he was missing. A combination of stellar marks in school and street smarts erected a bridge over the valley of sorrow into which his parents had almost dragged him. He took coding classes that proved too sparse for his appetite. His fingers danced on the keyboard like a virtuoso playing the piano, creating his own songs, improvising, testing, re-playing the 'notes' in his mind until there was no more room for optimization.

At age fifteen, improving on an open source code for a neural network and using rented processing power, he built a product he could be proud of: a data model able to predict the untapped potential of existing technologies in completely unexpected directions. His fascination with cryptocurrencies—something which had taken off twelve years before he was born—grew fast and wild. His generation was unable to fathom its value beyond the now-defunct paper money. Anarchists and technology seers stated that, twenty years after its inception, the cryptos "were still in the development phase with much room to grow." Volatility was high in the middle and bottom echelons of the coins' hierarchy, and he didn't feel comfortable buying someone else's intellectual property. Better someone buys his, invest in his ideas, and then he would ride the next wave of wealth.

After crunching thousands of coins' mathematical models, market value, offer and demand, and business feasibility, his neural network model spat out a coin no one had ever thought of: space coin 2.0. Leisure space exploration had had a rough start in the 2020s. Nevertheless, dedication, patience, and a stubbornness only visionaries had in abundance had made the short flight to the moon a success.

He'd attended his first crypto-conference in Toronto accompanied by Passang, Tenzin's father, who, even if he wasn't versatile in any particular technology, encouraged the teenager's fascination with it.

This was the platform in which Ojani had tossed himself like a raging fire from booth to booth, drenching himself in block-chain related materials, asking demanding questions just to understand how others had solved similar issues. Not a word on space coin 2.0 had escaped his mouth. He was a minion in a macrocosm of coding celebrities attached to a soaring market capitalization, and most of the time, intellectual egos.

Spotting one of his targeted-companies' CEOs on stage talking about the X-Space program in his attempt to attract security geniuses to work for him, Ojani made an executive decision to pitch him his concept. He felt unexpectedly rewarded after the important man's interest resulted in a formal meeting the next day. They clicked right away and an ICO [4] followed, attracting the main players in the industry along with suppliers, and most importantly, NASA, which, due to the USA government's bankruptcy, had to be sold to a consortium of the largest creditors.

---

[4] ICO – Initial Coin Offering

The Buddhist culture taught people to stay humble and preached non-attachment to physical property, and he respected it. He had the innate desire to prove he was able to surpass his dreadful family experiences and graciously climb, harnessing the gifts bestowed upon him by the Divine Energy. With his grandparents becoming feeble and his parents at the mercy of untrustworthy government social workers, Ojani had to provide for everyone. Karma had pulled him in the right direction, instilling his being with love and compassion for the people around him no matter their social status.

Over the years, the monks at the Riwoche Tibetan Temple had grown fond of Ojani. They had watched as he became a decent human being, inquisitive, and inclined to the gentleness of Buddhist teachings. When in need of a complete disassociation from his hectic daily life, the boy had always found refuge inside the temple.

That was the time when his relationship with the water began. The ignorance most of the world's population had about water had dissipated quickly for him, replaced by knowledge and stout belief. He witnessed sensible ceremonies whose origins were lost on the monks, but not the meaning and the steps that would make the incantations effective. Guttural sounds had alternated with mantras chanted with deep intensity in front of copper bowls filled with water. Beside the bowls had been small, wooden mallets, waiting to awaken the sacred sound of the metal, which made an interesting sight for the young Jamaican who hadn't asked any questions, but who had only watched, fascinated. His silence and black eyes enlarged by curiosity had the monks divulge the essence of the sacred ceremony. "We chant to the water our thanks and the ancient stories that have survived on decrepit scrolls, and above all, the Aum sound which is the primordial vibration of the Divine Mother that has created us all," he'd been told by one of the monks.

"Why?" Ojani had shyly asked, afraid his question might cause the unexpected confession to cease.

Instead, the gentle smile had brightened the old face and warmth had exuded from the tiny man's entire body, covered in saffron robes. "Water is alive, my son. Water is the earth's memory since before all creation. Deciphering the water is finding lost knowledge. We are one of the few that still remembers it," the monk had said. He'd touched Ojani's cheek with thin, scraggly fingers.

The boy had enjoyed the parchment-like skin rubbing against his own.

"Humanity has mistreated the water, showing no reverence, no respect. Our culture teaches differently. We nurture the water, and our chanting changes its structure, charging it with healing powers."

"Healing powers?" the youngster had asked, not getting the meaning of the old man's statement.

"I'll take you to the library tomorrow to show you images of frozen water molecules that have been exposed to chanting, prayer, positive feelings, and other contemporary activities. For now, just imagine that water's structure is adaptive and it can learn new tricks like a child that goes to school. People can develop into loving, positive individuals or sour, glass-half-empty types depending on the environment in which they've been raised. The same principle applies to water: our chanting engraves information that improves the molecular structure. When consumed, the water is beneficial for the body, enhancing, through association, the quality of the water circulating through our internal organs."

The monk hadn't gone any further into the explanation. Instead, he'd crossed his fingers, turned his palms up, and looked at Ojani's lips as if ready to voice another thought.

"What's the purpose of the crystals?" the boy had asked, pointing to the two blue and green, irregularly-shaped stones laying on the pillow in front of the monk by the water bowl. He'd leaned forward while still in the lotus position to hear any hushed words from the elder.

"Crystals are as ageless as water is. They vibrate and resonate with water and their structure is equally fascinating. When I repeat my mantras, I generate a scalar wave field with a geometry able to unlock the information contained in the crystal," the man had explained. He must've sensed Ojani's puzzlement because he'd added, "You learned about the energy field surrounding our bodies."

The boy had nodded.

"This concept is similar, but it pertains to our DNA. Chanting creates a vibration which, in turn, generates a two-way current within our Mobius-shaped DNA."

"I don't understand," Ojani had confessed, his cheeks brightening in embarrassment.

The monk's face had beamed with love. "Do not worry. Just remember that a person can release information recorded in the water and crystals through the proper fluctuation of our voices. Tonality, intensity, and duration are imperative factors in learning how to control such a process," the renunciate had said. He'd picked up the bowl filled with water and rested it on his open palm. Then, he'd grabbed the wooden mallet and hit the edge of the bowl. A muffled sound disturbed the silence that had grown between them for a short moment. The water inside the brass container had gently rippled in a tiny tempest. Ojani had the impression it was talking to him in the cyphered language of vibration. It was one hadn't known how to interpret.

Even as an adult, Orange always remembered those highly-charged learning sessions that had changed his life-perspective into a more acceptable one. Ojani had been seventeen-years-old when his teacher-monk transitioned to the astral plane. The boy had no doubt his future, successful businesses would be under a watchful, graceful eye, and he could only be appreciative of such attention. Renouncing his normal life for the saffron robes had never crossed his mind, nor had he made promises that such a goal would be later reevaluated. His conscience carried no bruises. Further degradation of his parents' mental condition combined with the omnipresent worry of the government suspending their assisted living subsidies forced Orange into an active, "look-out for opportunities" state of mind, and generating income became his number one priority.

The cab pulled over in front of the temple on a dead-end street. Orange swiped the back of his hand on the dashboard scanner to pay for the trip and then stepped out. The red brick, two-story building hadn't changed much. Over the years, the side parking lot had been turned into a garden. A single-person path around the perimeter forced one on a slow, introspective walk while taking in the carefully designed patterns of wild grass and bushes dotting the evenly placed sand and gray stones. A generous donation received ten years prior had allowed the temple to purchase the adjacent building, a tiny structure on a narrow lot that had become the library along with ample storage space.

He would have welcomed the gentle touch of the wind on his face meandering through the adjacent buildings if it hadn't stirred the dust that got into his eyes. Through the extended warm months, the whole city had to endure a thick blanket of annoying particles with which the aged air filtration systems were unable to deal. Protective eyeglasses and face masks had become the norm whenever spending time outdoors.

Orange left his shoes at the entrance and walked toward the front of the room to bow to the six, five-foot, gold-leaf plated statues: the Buddha and masters of the temple's lineage. Incense burning and fruit and flower offerings covered the ledge which was raised off the floor. He kneeled down on a square cushion, bowed, and repeated the mantra in his mind three times. Then he gave thanks for everything he had and for the man he had become. Orange kept his ego subdued, refusing to take his prosperous situation for granted, as much as possible.

To his right, seated on one of the benches in deep silence, was Tenzin, his old school friend, whose calling for the monastic life had overpowered the temptations of an existence of convenience. Tenzin was on a sure path to becoming an important part of the Riwoche Dzogchen Lineage.

Ojani's weekly visits for the blessed water he sold to his clients as a naturopathic product maintained their spiritually strong bonds. The revenue generated by this financial arrangement couldn't have been done by a more trusted party in a world dense with cut-throat individuals. The temple has been conferred an above-average water ration as a result of its religious status, allowing the monks to imbue a certain quantity with healing mantras, potent thoughts, and love. The altered liquid was kept in basalt-made receptacles that would shield it from outside inter-ference that might alter its molecular structure. Only Orange, who was able to control his behavior around such valuable mer-chandise, was able to dilute several drops into tap water which would, in a couple of hours, absorb the imprint, inheriting the same characteristics. The final price also depended on how many liters of liquid had been used for dilution, limiting the number of people that were able to have similar experiences.

Ojani sat beside his friend, his elbow lightly touching Tenzin's, like a code exchanged to acknowledge each other's presence. He calmed his breathing and forcefully removed any negative thoughts with three consecutive deep exhales. His mind drifted into the energy field he identified as protecting the temple with an ozone-like layer, repelling maligning radia-tion. Losing awareness of his body's weight hadn't come naturally lately, due to the worries that had pierced his defensive shell. The world might have seemed inoffensive from behind those walls, but the separation was fragile at best. Appearances might crumble if the existing weather, water, and social crisis met at the tipping point, creating the perfect storm for humanity's devolu-tion to its nomadic and primitive beginnings.

An elevated spiritual path, a goal to which Tenzin was much closer, somehow became unrealistic for Orange who preferred improving upon other people's lives through his one-of-a-kind crystal technology. He'd witnessed the transformation of many of his clients into more conscious human beings, increasing their empathy for those around them. There were, of course, those searching for a jolt of adrenaline that might bring some diversity into their dreary existence. And he had to admit, the bulk of his clients were rich, egotistic, and surrounded by a bubble of false confidence and self-imposed lies that earth was doing just fine and its civilization was still bustling in the right direction.

He charged them insensible amounts in cryptocurrency, silver or gold, and even fractional ownership of hard assets, to com-pensate for the free sessions he offered once a month to patients with addictions, in the late stages of cancer, or with physical disabilities, people who might otherwise never have experienced such exhilarating feelings and sensations. For some, the crystal's vibrations would eliminate pain for a while, and that felt good on his part. He couldn't do much for his parents, yet atonement for their sins was paid forward to strangers through his goodwill.

A soft touch on his cheek jerked him out of the reflections that had disturbed his peace. He opened his eyes and followed Tenzin outside.

"You should move here for a while," the monk said as soon once they could speak in private. His narrow face ended with a sharp, straight chin, lacking any hair. His shaved head exposed two symmetrical, light-colored birthmarks on the sides of his cranium, contrasting with his overall look. Tenzin seemed frail beneath his ochre robes, but Orange knew the image didn't depict the real qualities of his friend: a will of steel, kindness, compassion, and the knack for reading people's characters.

"I'd like to hide for much longer than a week," the Jamaican replied. "Unfortunately, there's no one else I can trust with the business, especially now, when Canada's confidence about being immune to terrorist attacks has been shaken."

They slowly walked the few steps to the adjacent building.

"Sell the business and join me here, at the temple," Tenzin insisted. "There's always a place for you as our brother."

Orange shrugged and caressed his beard with a couple of strokes as if he were considering Tenzin's offer, but he was just buying time to come up with an excuse different than the ones he'd already given in response to previous, similar, well-intentioned requests.

"You know I can't—" he started, but a gesture from his friend stopped him.

"It's fine. I have to try to read your pulse on the subject from time-to-time." He smiled and opened the door for Ojani.

Adopting the life of a renunciate wouldn't have stopped Orange from being responsible for his parents' care. It was the business that had kept him on an excited high. Building the network of VIPs to supply fresh blood samples after each new experience took a lot of his time and energy. No one else would have been capable of handling them and grooming someone else as a replacement wasn't high on his to-do list. The crystal technology developed five years ago was crude and clunky but revenue-generating. This fact hadn't bothered Orange until recently, when he'd realized how complacent he'd become, and how, surely, competitors had been seeping into the market with similar devices and lower prices. Boris, the Russian-born engineer that had helped design the prototype, had long gone to the US for greener pastures and from which he hadn't returned. They didn't keep in touch, so to say, "help was on its way," didn't apply. He felt the urge to be challenged again through intellectual pressure; it was the only need he was willing to accept in his life.

"What else is bothering you?" Orange asked. He saw the shadow of worry sticking to Tenzin's brown eyes which were usually so clear and happy, like those of his parents after each meditation session.

Tenzin didn't answer. He just pointed to three recipients on a low, wooden table containing the water modified through chanting and prayer into structured water for Orange's clients.

"Only three this time? Have the monks increased their chores lately?" he joked, looking for the reason as to why the delivery had suddenly halved. "That's why you're worried?"

The monk nodded. "We've received an official letter from City Hall. They've revoked our special water privileges, plus they've cut the rations even more."

Orange hadn't heard about similar measures being made for the Royal York Hotel. Maybe it was because it would have stopped the trickle of tourists and convention attendees which was still a significant source of revenue for the city.

"We've implemented changes inside the temple already. We have to save every drop of water if we don't want to send any of the monks away. They'd become beggars. This is our last delivery," Tenzin said, the statement justifying his sadness.

Orange opened his backpack and gently put the containers into specially created pockets to keep them straight.

"What if I bring you the water? Will you still pray and chant over it?"

Tenzin touched his rosary as if he were expecting an answer from the sandalwood beads.

"I'll ask Dorja Ripoche, but the payment would have to change, too," he added, almost certain the request would stay firm.

"I'll double the amount I'm paying now," Orange replied calmly. He was prepared to cut into his profits to preserve the business. Or maybe he would have to increase his prices by a small percentage to compensate.

"That won't help. The payment would have to be in water," Tenzin said, embarrassed. He shuffled his feet denoting an uncharacteristic impatience.

"I understand. I can last up to three months on the reserve I have," Ojani confessed without anger.

The deepening water crisis had everyone on edge, turning allies into foes, dividing countries, and shattering communities. A friendship like theirs was invaluable, the Jamaican thought, and he intended to keep it that way.

"At least come for the service. It'll do you good," Tenzin almost begged.

"I'll try."

"The Divine Matrix tells us that water is changing all over the world. It either attacks or hides," the monk disclosed. He exhaled deeply as if he'd just let out a secret that had been bubbling inside him. "There's no turning back unless we shift our mentality, and dramatically at that."

Ojani noticed his friend counting the beads and mentally repeating a mantra as a way of forcing undesirable thoughts out of his mind.

"Water is alive. I heard someone say this at a conference or in an interview, I can't remember where. I didn't pay attention then, but now I believe it. You don't listen to the news, otherwise you'd have heard about the Ganges and Jordan River incidents, about the rising water levels in Venice, and about the underground water rivers and aquifers that have altered their courses away from dams."

"Really?" Tenzin exclaimed.

"It's getting worse by the day. It's payback time for water. I don't see a way out," Orange confessed. He raised his backpack to his chest and held it tightly as if contained his most precious possessions.

No other words had to be spoken. Challenges awaited them in a world that was crumbling with exponential speed. Where would the monks go if the water and food rations were cut again? How long might they last in the city?

Ojani touched his friend's shoulder gently and said, "I'll see you next week. Let's pray for forgiveness."

CHAPTER 11

"What do you make of Hayyin's latest disclosure about Mosamoni's and Narankama's assets in the middle of nowhere?" Romana Pilb asked Cherry and Pat Boulanjois after connecting for a midday, ad-hoc meeting. The WFA's president was in her office looking completely exhausted. Her eyes were bloodshot, and her straight hair entangled as if restless snakes had tried to make a nest of it.

Updates were arriving through multiple channels and monitoring the WFA's on-site teams had become a major priority.

Cherry had decided for Hayyin to deliver his message from a new platform, the Estonian equivalent of the WFA, to confuse the US government entities trying to pinpoint the troublemaker's location. Anonymous provided a secure connection, bouncing it off of three continents. She let Pat Boulanjois speak first, pretending she was making notes on a notepad resting on her knees.

"He might be onto something," the man said, wiping away the perspiration as it ran down his double chin. "Sorry, my air conditioning is broken and I can't afford to fix it. I'd rather save money for additional water rations," he added. His gray t-shirt had dark spots scattered across his shoulders and chest.

"In today's political climate, these corporations won't expand their operations unless they can pick the ripe, low-hanging fruit. The time for long-term business development plans is gone—survival is the main priority," he continued.

From her living room, Cherry spoke slowly, attentive to each word. "I agree with Pat. Purchasing thousands of acres of barren land is business suicide for any CEO, especially if there is no immediate revenue generation associated with it. Hayyin posed the question to the crowd about soil composition…where was that again?" she asked rhetorically and shuffled through several pages. "Ah, I've found it. He mentions ringwood, liquid hydrogen, and silicon dioxide. A geologist or hydrologist might know what this produces. We should find out soon."

She already knew the answer, but challenging and engaging her followers to seek the correct results would bring further exposure to the culprits. The reaction between the two substances in the ringwood layer of the upper mantle generated primary water, water that had never encountered any form of pollution and had never come into contact with information from the earth's normal water cycle. Cherry thought it might be the only liquid without a memory, a pristine imprint of evolutionary rhythm that, if not protected, would be tainted, captured, and sold. She cringed at the thought of how powerless these governments would be against Mosamoni and Narankama to protect such invaluable, underground wealth.

Hayyin had the influence of his supporters from all over the world—this time he would do whatever was necessary to point them in the right direction. With the stakes so high, nothing was off the table, not even the manipulation of people. The corporations needed a strong warning and the crowd would find the solution.

"Hayyin didn't mention if he had a local source feed him the information, or if he could learn more. It's such a remote place with the military contractors controlling the area, I doubt anyone would even try to get close," Pilb said.

Cherry noticed a distinct worry in her voice about the lack of on-the-ground feeds, yet Romana had explained to her, after the Ganges River incident when Srinitham had exposed himself to the dangerous situation there, that she didn't want to feel responsible for anyone's life. In retrospect, not having access to the border region between Mongolia and Kazakhstan was a good thing.

"The government's the only one who can stop them from improperly handling the water if the resources are proven. They have to abide by the existing agreement," Romana Pilb continued.

They won't if the world finds out what they've discovered is primary water. Cherry almost smiling at the thought, not to mention the idea of mobs sieging the headquarters of those corporations and demanding justice for water. For a long time, she'd dreamed of the common conscience awakening around a worthy cause impacting ninety-nine percent of the population, even if the stinky rich, one percent believed themselves untouchable, no matter the crisis.

"I was wondering when Hayyin would make his next public announcement. I was concerned something might've happened to him after the explosion in Toronto," Pat Boulanjois confessed. The perspiration continued to exude from his red face. Behind him, the windows were open, but no breeze pushed in, as if it were afraid of suffocating in the sauna-like room occupied by Pat's large body.

The limnologist kept quiet. She faked taking a sip from the empty mug and waited for the subject to change to another burning affair.

"I assume that digging dirt up on these guys takes time, but Hayyin also has to protect himself. He serves our cause well," Pilb said. She rubbed her eyes under which purple bags hung heavily.

"What's new from India?" Cherry said, steering the discussion to safer ground.

"Oh, yes. That's the main reason I called for the meeting. Sorry for the tangent," the WFA president said apologetically. "Srinitham managed to get blood samples from the old men and processed them in the lab. As some of you have hinted, their blood's molecular structure and the structured water in their bodily composition has a perfect hexagonal shape. It's what protected them against the toxic changes occurring in the river."

"And there's still no evidence behind what's responsible for generating these defensive properties?" Pat asked.

Neither of the women dared answer, even if they had their suppositions.

"It's a combination of faith—strong faith—meditation, and the acknowledgment of one's role or mandate, if you wish, in this existence." Cherry had spoken fast as if she were embarrassed she hadn't bit her tongue and let Romana go first. Her comment was followed by silence. Only Pat's heavy breathing ruptured the dense silence between them.

"Is there a scientific explanation? This is what I meant," the man explained slowly. He continued, "Faith and meditation are intangible goods."

Romana Pilb jumped to defend Cherry, probably more due to female solidarity than conviction.

"Pat, you have to accept all of those studies done years ago and updated only recently, measuring internal changes in states of super-consciousness and deep meditation. Most of them are visible on MRIs or at the energy level."

"Yeah, I read about it," he said, sounding unconvinced the women were right. "Those two old men were active at that moment. How could they be in a stupor state and behave normally at the same time?"

"That was also proven," Cherry said, encouraged by the unexpected help. "I'm not saying the individuals happened to be in a trance, but such cases have been documented." She hoped her explanation wouldn't antagonize Pat.

Silence again. The man had muted himself so he could cough without disturbing his colleagues.

"For now, an empirical explanation is better than no explanation at all," Romana Pilb concluded.

"Can they inject the so-called perfect blood into a different host?" Boulanjois asked. He wasn't talking about a guinea pig, but rather, another human. It was easier said than done.

"Yes, local scientists have thought of that. They've identified an individual with the same blood type and explained the circumstances to him with the goal of finding what might have caused the dramatic changes in the Ganges."

"And?" Pat couldn't contain his curiosity.

"He agreed to the transfusion. His blood had adapted to the imprint, but when asked to step in, the fear of the water took over. The absence of his belief that the sacred river would spare him reversed all of the previous, positive changes."

The president shared the details Srinitham had provided to her earlier in the day.

"So, we close the loop on faith," Cherry said cautiously.

Boulanjois smiled and let the remark go.

"How's the crowd behaving?" the limnologist asked.

Romana Pilb moved her fingers over her tablet and released a video for both of them to see.

"This also came from Srinitham. The situation isn't improving," she said. She bit into a sandwich while Pat and Cherry watched the images.

The date superimposed over the image showed November 12, 2055, three days after the river's changes had occurred. The vantage point was high, maybe a meter or so above the throng of people packed tightly against each other with barely any space to turn around, let alone move in any direction. People of all ages gathered into a silent sea of bodies moving up and down in a wave when some of them raised onto their toes in an attempt to look toward the river for signs or messages they could understand. Children were lifted onto their fathers' shoulders, feeling safe and delighted by the opportunity to allow their innocent to wander farther away than usual; even they respected the silence imposed by the adults. The angle in the video moved slowly, three-hundred-and-sixty degrees so Pat and Cherry could see the ghats to the south and a similarly dense crowd on the other shore.

Television crews from national and local stations had secured the high ground and were broadcasting non-stop though there were no reporters on site yet. The time would come when a miracle, witnessed by so many, would give consent for the silence to be broken. The image froze on a group of older women closer to where Srinitham was recording. Suddenly, one of them—wearing a light blue sari—vanished, as if the ground had opened up to swallow her as payment for allowing the crowd to loiter on the spot.

"Did you see that?" Cherry asked, waiting for the others to confirm the miracle.

"Yeah. She fainted," Pilb clarified, still munching on her sandwich. "The perspective plays nasty tricks."

Moments later they saw two of the men cut a narrow wedge into the crowd from which they pulled out the old woman's inert body. From time-to-time, bottles of juice or coconut water were passed from hand-to-hand to those standing close to the river to keep them hydrated.

Sitting in their homes and offices, in spite of the small discomforts such as broken air conditioning, the three of them sensed solidarity and determination exuding from the images.

When the five minutes of footage ended, Pat Boulanjois said, "It would have been nice to see if anyone else was in the water." He swiveled in his chair and opened the windows wider as if he were still hoping for a cool draft to come in.

"The authorities forbid that. Srinitham confirmed that police boats are patrolling along the shores. I think everyone understands they aren't as holy as they thought they were, and they'd rather not end up in the hospital," Pilb said. She gathered her tangled hair into a ponytail and secured it with a rubber band she'd grabbed off of her desk. "Any other pressing issues?" she asked.

"Other than the fact that massive crowds have followed the Indian example and are gathering along most of the sacred rivers in the world—including the Yamuna, Kshira, Yangtze, Godavari, Yellow River, Zambezi, and the Mekong, for example—the most important thing is to identify how to reverse the process," Cherry said, adding her two cents' worth.

Romana Pilb leaned forward and let her head rest on her open palms in an attempt to transfer some of the pressure to other parts of her body.

"Srinitham has contacts in the government and he will let us know immediately of their findings regarding the water wells in that area. They are being tested for contamination along with samples taken from upstream," the WFA president said. She inhaled hard several times and let the air go with loud sighs.

"Have you heard an official government position on the situation?" she inquired. "France is pretty much under a news quarantine and Internet access is sporadic."

"This time, it seems all politicians have found a common threat and come out with the same declaration, advising the populace to stay indoors and not to go into any rivers, streams, ponds, or bodies of water in general. They're looking into it," the younger woman disclosed.

"The regular bullshit," Pat interpreted in a more direct style.

"Pretty much," Cherry agreed. She massaged the skin on her narrow neck several times and shuffled impatiently in her chair. Her buttocks lost its numbness and she felt thousands of needles poking at her flesh instead.

"Anything else you want to discuss?" she said briskly. "I should go back to the reports streaming in through the website."

Romana Pilb looked grim and strained. She nodded in agreement. "We'll keep everyone updated by email as often as possible," she said, sudden and stern; tiredness had finally caught up with her.

They were about to hang up when Boulanjois called, "Wait! Wait!"

"What now, Pat?"

"The crowd's answered Hayyin's question. They've identified what could be generated in a ringwood layer from the mixture of liquid hydrogen and silicon dioxide."

"What's that?" Cherry snapped, still playing her role.

"It's…it's primary water," the man said, slowly reading the words off his screen to let their meaning sink in."

"I'll be damned!" the limnologist shouted. "That explains why the water didn't show up on any satellite images. It runs very, very deep."

"That's huge," Romana added, sounding reinvigorated by the news. "That explains the secrecy. All of the known primary water vents have been stripped and pillaged. No new sources of primary water have been identified in more than ten years."

Pat Boulanjois stood up, cackled gleefully, and moved around the room, unable to hide his emotions.

"This is gold to these companies. No wonder they'd try to smuggle it without sharing a single drop. Hayyin has to lead this fight," the man declaimed, powered by a newfound energy.

It was Cherry's turn to show elation. She walked around the couch several times to let her legs regain blood circulation, without saying a word as she waited for Romana's reaction, a crisp smile plastered on her high-cheekbone, tiny face.

"This is the bread and butter of the Primary Water Institute," Pilb said. "Has there been any reaction from Hayyin?"

"Not yet," Boulanjois confirmed, dropping himself back into the chair. He'd decided to wrap a piece of cloth around his thick forehead to stop the sweat from dripping down his skull.

"The Institute just released a statement," Cherry said, jumping back in. "They're sending their people over to Mongolia and expect the government's full support in obtaining more information from Mosamoni and Narankama. That should be interesting. Why don't you join the team?" the limnologist suggested to Pilb. "There is no other way for us to have a local presence."

The president straightened her back and stared directly at the AR projection, assessing the suggestion. "I agree. The only hurdle I see is about perception: both organizations are US-based, which might not be well-accepted among anti-American sympathizers in the region. And there are plenty of them."

"But at the same time, we're known as tough and objective advocates. We've exposed a lot of US companies who conduct shady, offshore deals. We have a good reputation," Cherry said as a counter argument.

"I can hear the knives sharpening," Boulanjois responded.

"What do you mean?" Romana Pilb asked.

"Here's the basic assessment of the political implications, and believe me, I love to come up with these types of scenarios. If either Kazakhstan or Mongolia—both of which are backed by Russia and China respectively—block Mosamoni and Narankama from milking this source of primary water, the US government, under the pretense of protecting American businesses, would start another war. World War Three, to be precise." He wasn't smiling anymore.

"You have to go," Cherry almost begged Pilb. "We need diplomacy now more than ever."

Romana still looked undecided. Her frozen pose hadn't changed, and Cherry wondered why she was hesitating.

"I'll contact my counterpart at the Institute," Pilb finally said. "I might be unreachable while I'm there. Keep in contact with everyone else. Inform the board of any significant developments."

Cherry and Pat wished her good luck at the same time.

CHAPTER 12

Orange returned to his office inside of the Royal York Hotel, carrying a gloomy attitude. Acquiring additional liters of water to replace the quantity the monks couldn't supply anymore was doable, but the request for payment made in the same currency worried him.

Diluting the structured water in lesser volumes meant higher prices, which would narrow his clientele to the one percent of the one percent. It crossed his mind he could apply the same model and charge some of them the equivalent in water as they'd most likely have the black market connections to acquire it and the means to transport it over tight borders using the VIP luxury of personal jets. A handful of them were close enough for him to approach to offer such deal.

He walked into his office, waited for the retina scan's confirmation, and opened the door to the storage room. Ceiling-high shelves took up almost all of the space, leaving a narrow path in between them. His skinny frame allowed him to turn in the tight area, but anyone else with a prominent belly would have had a problem.

Orange used a black marker from a plastic holder on the wall to write the date on each of the three containers that had been blessed by Tenzin and the monks and placed them toward the end of the room where the temperature was a controlled fifteen degrees Celsius.

The quantity of water imbued with winter-related experiences was low, and Orange knew he wouldn't get any more samples unless the weather patterns changed overnight to what they used to be around the time he was born. Proper winter had ceased to exist the moment snow ceased to materialize as a heavy, white, protective, and enjoyable coat. What the Northern

Hemisphere received instead was a reddish slush with an ephemeral duration on the ground, amazing people rather than stirring in them a desire to spend more time outdoors. It wasn't the scientifically known, watermelon snow found in the summer in the alpine and coastal polar regions but something totally different.

Scientists had issued a quick explanation for its strange and disturbing hue: the atmosphere was charged with microscopic copper particles that inserted themselves into the hydrogen-oxygen combination forming snowflakes. A Canadian weatherman had even joked on the subject, hypothesizing that a portal from another dimension had opened onto our universe as soon as winter approached, dumping copper residue with it; we were, in effect, someone else's garbage bin. The statement had been made on April 1, so he got to keep his job.

Orange looked around, assessing the demand for remaining experiences and how long they might last without replenishment. "Eighteen months, tops, at full capacity. Maybe twenty-six otherwise," he mumbled to himself. The week before he'd had several cancellations for upcoming slots and there had been no alternative bookings as of yet. "It's getting tougher for everyone. It doesn't matter how rich one is."

He shuffled his feet as if scratching a lottery ticket on the floor and he hoped it might reveal novel ideas as to how to procure more water. A shiver spiked through his body in the low temperature of the room so he hurried out.

Maybe Tenzin could write to the network of monasteries in Tibet. At that altitude there was no government control. Over there, the resources were responsibly used and equally shared. "I could arrange transportation," he said to himself. He smiled and almost patted himself on the back. "We'll see."

The monitor on the left side of his desk displayed the number of his employees quietly waiting in the staging area for their sessions to end. They'd disconnect the clients from the sensors attached to the crystals upon which the structured water had been dropped. After helping them to another room where they could spend some time recollecting the experience, the staff would sanitize the chair, read the next client's profile for any special requirements, and be ready to welcome them. It was a straightforward process that had worked well for Orange so far. It was both a cash cow for him and at the same time, a way of enhancing potentials people didn't know they had. Most of them came out of the experience changed and grateful for it.

If Orange had political power, he imagined he'd make the procedure mandatory, but what government wished to lead awakened citizens able to see through their lies, thievery, and corruption, and who would hold them responsible? It would be a utopia, he knew, but he enjoyed plotting these implausible scenarios in his mind, nevertheless.

Even if he'd wanted to pack up and leave the city for a remote location, he'd fail to reach internal peace as long as his parents were still around. Only his weekly visits assured him they were getting the care for which he'd paid. Skipping that permanence would have raised justifiable worries in his mind that otherwise needed soothing.

He checked his email—there were three more cancellations for November, and two in December already. The sheik from Qatar, scheduled for the last month of the year, was sending his son to experience the life of an Inuk. The session would last several days and include such adventures as hunting, ice fishing, igloo building, lovemaking, trenching a seal, and training sleigh dogs. There was a whole lifecycle stored in those potent drops of blood mixed with structured water and translated by the crystal's sensitivity into vibratory feelings. The memory of the water would release its stories, moods, and images, projected into the minds of a lucky few.

The international news feed was constantly updating. Ojani clicked on the follow-up article to the Venice story. It wasn't about the raised water levels anymore but about the molecular changes that had made the submerged, wooden pillars decay, a process that shouldn't have occurred in the oxygen-poor conditions that had existed for centuries. The hydrologist interviewed on a local TV station was explaining that in the past, harsh toxic conditions had forced the water molecule to adapt to the heavy concentrations of methane, alkalinity, and acid in mine drainage in a way that could still sustain life. What had happened in Venice followed the reverse process, where the water had become corrosive to the point where it had "eaten" into the basalt pillars that had once been considered safe. The level of such toxicity was most intense beneath the buildings. Water was displaying a conscious, self-organized process, "in a self-defense approach," the man had explained. The effects were visible on a couple of structures that had borrowed the same angle of inclination as the Tower of Pisa. The water had worked its way through the wood at a fast rate, placing the entire city in jeopardy. Evacuation plans were being debated and all road entries had been blocked by *carabinieri*. Supply trucks carrying daily necessities were the only ones allowed access within the city limits. Not everyone wanted to leave, especially not those whose houses were resting on the safer, basalt stilts. At least, that's what they'd thought so far.

"There's no guarantee the water level won't continue to rise. Please don't choose to sink with the ship," the mayor implored the citizens, his face red from the effort of trying to convince them to value their lives more than four brick walls. "The government has already confirmed new accommodations. You can take whatever you want with you. There are no restrictions."

Multiple voices yelled back at him, but there was no translation of the cacophony, and Orange muted the sound while looking for another feed.

Hayyin surfaced again for the first time since the explosion had targeted the WFA. He had facts on Mosamoni and Narankama that didn't initially make much sense, at least, not until the crowd had figured out the hidden motive behind the corporations setting up shop in such a remote and unlikely place on earth—they'd found a source of primary water.

It was a nice catch that could have turned into a nightmare. The Net was buzzing with activist groups calling for their supporters to fly to either Mongolia or Kazakhstan and take a stand. He made the selection to receive any new information on the subject and moved his attention to the next batch of clients.

Catrina Gold, a seventy-two-year-old woman based in Miami, Florida, had expected his greetings as usual. She'd been one of his first patrons, back when he still wasn't sure how much he should charge for such a novelty. Having had the experience of generating billions from negotiating deals, she'd guided the then young Orange to the right price point. She didn't do it for a discount, but Ojani always waited for her with flowers and offered her a healthy dinner during which she'd detail her experience. Not many were willing to share, and he appreciated it. Maybe she'd be will to bring him water as payment. There was also Binji, the Kenyan magnate who had built his wealth on commodities such as salt, zinc, and limestone. He could bend the rules, too.

He put a smile on his face and walked out of his office to say hi to Catrina Gold before the prep work for the session.

• • •

"There's a former client at the reception desk asking to see you: Ilanda Mazandir. Should I tell them to bring her up?" Martin, one of Orange's employees, asked from the door to his office.

"She's downstairs without an appointment?"

"Uh-huh," the stocky man confirmed and shrugged his shoulders for lack of a better explanation.

"Hold on a second," Orange said. He quickly tapped his iPad screen to retrieve the file he had on her. "She's a big-wig at St. Michael's Hospital. Been here once last year to experience climbing to Mt. Kilimanjaro. Nothing unusual," the Jamaican said. "Maybe she wants something more special this time, and she's shy to make the reservation online." He puckered his lips. "Yes, bring her upstairs," he said

Martin turned around and vanished. Hotel management's rule was that only guests who had purchased an experience would have access to his floor. Anyone else had to be escorted. Since the explosion, the rules had been enforced without exception.

He adjusted his colorful shirt on his wide shoulders, brought the window shades down a bit to block the light falling on the chair on the other side of his desk where Ilanda Mazandir would sit.

Ojani didn't know what to expect of the visit even if he'd joked about it minutes earlier. It had been the first time a client had shown up unannounced. He glanced at the monitors with images of Catrina Gold and another client being hooked up to the crystals and enjoying experiences they would never have been able to experience in their real lives.

Ilanda Mazandir filled the door frame with her imposing stature. "Hello, Ojani," she said. "Not much has changed in here since my previous visit," she observed. Ilanda was almost one head taller than the man and a bit bulkier.

Orange put his hand out to shake Ilanda's. The prospect of filling one of his vacant slots using minimal effort emboldened his attitude.

"What an unexpected pleasure. You bring a ray of sunshine to a monotonous day," he said, trying to be charming until he was able to gauge the reason for her visit. "Please, have a seat. What can I offer you: a fruit, a snack? Tea or coffee isn't possible; I hope you understand."

The woman sat down, dropped her tiny leather bag onto the carpet, and smiled back at him. She crossed her long legs covered with a pair of lime-colored pants, keeping her back straight while sitting on the edge of the armchair. Her sleeveless blouse, cut deep on her chest, gave the right balance to her blonde hair which had been gathered in a short ponytail.

"I'm quite fine. I know you're busy, so I'll get to the point."

Ojani stepped back to his seat.

"Can you please shut the door?" she said when she'd noticed the man who had brought her in had left the door open.

He complied without making any comments, even more intrigued by what she had to say.

"How can I help you? Are you looking for a specific experience? I'll do my best to find it for you," he said, starting his sales pitch.

Her smile broadened. "I'm here to help you," Ilanda said. She laughed openly when she saw Ojani's reaction.

"Really? It's been a long time since anybody wanted to give me their assistance," the man confessed. He leaned back, much more relaxed. He knew that no sale would be made that day with Ilanda Mazandir.

"What you do in here is unique and what I consider to be a necessary service."

Ojani nodded and let her continue.

"Unfortunately, it's a service that few can afford and those that can do not always use it for the right reasons."

Ilanda leaned forward, elbows on her knees as if she was ready to plead with Ojani to accept whatever she was about to say next. "I'm intrigued by the fact that you understand the potential of crystals on decoding the brain's wavelengths and the messages encrypted in water."

"Thank you," he replied at the compliment.

"You know what I do for a living: I dig into people's heads trying to repair their sensitive plumbing, but I'm also fascinated by crystals, by their beautiful structure, resonance, and overall beneficial properties to our spiritual forms encased in our phys-ical bodies." She spoke slowly, but passionately, as if building up the momentum for her request.

"You said you wanted to get right to the point," Ojani said a bit sarcastically. He let out a hefty laugh.

She joined him. "I'll be blunt. Your technology is rough and hasn't been improved since its inception."

"I know," the man replied, noticing surprise on Ilanda's features. "I couldn't find anyone trustworthy enough to look 'under-the-hood' and enhance it. It runs on cruise-control. I don't know for how much longer, given the turmoil in the world, but I'll milk it until something better comes along. What about this is blunt?" he said, turning halfway toward the window. Heat filtered through the UV panes fell on his shoulders, but he didn't mind.

"I started my own crystal research several years ago and was recently given my own lab. I have access to quality crystals, lasers, specialized assistants, and patients willing to be the first to undergo the implant surgery, however, I lack your bank of diverse blood samples and I don't want to reinvent the wheel. Plus, you already have an established network of blood donors," she said, finally declaring the scope of her visit.

"You want to permanently embed crystals?" he asked.

"Yes. This is the only way for the experience to last longer and sink into one's consciousness. I know what I'm talking about—that's why I became your client. I'm convinced all the fine details of an experience would be enhanced by this strategy."

Ojani looked through her for several moments and thought that maybe the time had come for him to let go of his attachment to yet another venture. He'd checked Ilanda's reputation in the medical community after she'd submitted her online application and he'd been unable to find any blemishes, not that he'd care—he was there to provide a service, not to judge people.

"I want this procedure to be done in a safe environment. Too many crooks call themselves neurosurgeons." She pushed forward as if she were afraid Ojani might consider the financial downfall as a consequence of the partnership she proposed. "The ramifications of developing a portable version of this technology are great. I'll share more with you if you're on board."

The man refocused his gaze on her, touched the scar over his right eye as if to reassure himself that it was still there, and said, "Life's been generous with me. The Divine Mother has given me everything I need, except for present and engaged parents." He forced a sad smile, his pearly teeth hidden behind his wide, dark lips. "At the same time, it's offered me the means of taking care of those near and dear to me—what else I could ask for?"

"Let's do some good together," Ilanda said, stepping in as the man had paused to gather his thoughts.

"You're the pushy type, aren't you?"

The woman clasped her hands and arched her eyebrows in a gesture of admittance.

"What do you have in mind if I accept?" Ojani asked, listening intently to the plan she was about to reveal.

• • •

Later that day, while winding down for the night, Orange checked the news one more time and his heart froze with panic.

He never thought something like this might happen, no matter how strained the political and environmental situation had become—monks and priests had been kidnapped in China, the US, Russia, and a couple more Eastern European countries. Strong words had been used to draw their attention. Their simultaneous disappearances didn't stand on real proof, but rather, on assumptions—they'd been taken to bless the water of the rich in private setting. Either that or pray for the water to return to lands once heavy with crops but which were now deserted.

Is the sacred space of a temple no longer safe? Is Tenzin in danger? These disturbing thoughts and more crossed his mind. The holy men were praying for the earth's betterment—why put strenuous and unnecessary pressure on them? Ask them kindly and they will continue to serve humanity. It's their mandate. How much longer would people be able to move around the globe before a partial or complete shutdown might be instated? It seemed the possibility was getting much closer. Purchasing a piece of land, even now, at the eleventh hour, was a sensitive option. A place where his life could be extended for a while if he'd manage to grow any food on it, which, given his practical skills, was very unlikely.

CHAPTER 13

"Octana, how familiar are you with my research on crystals?" Ilanda asked the woman sitting on the other side of the camera. It was the first interview scheduled to select her assistants.

"Not to brag," the young woman started, her thin brown hair cut shoulder length waving from side to side with the energy of her words, "but without even knowing about the job posting, I read all of the peer-review articles and your research published in the *Journal of Neurosurgery* along with videos available online." She paused for a moment looking down, maybe at a piece of paper on which she'd written the main points of her speech. "My father's a geologist," she continued. "Our house is full of stone and crystal samples and all sorts of oddities he dug up all over the world. When I was young, he used to tell me stories about the rough but wonderful creations of the earth. He was quite good at it." She giggled and flashed her pearly teeth.

Ilanda fancied the woman's bubbly attitude and hoped she knew when to bottle it up.

"By age twelve, I knew that crystals could heal through their vibrations. I also knew the best source of these crystals, and I even knew a bit about how shamans used them in their healing processes." Octana sounded humbled yet somehow proud of what she'd learned from her father. "I've also studied Edgar Cayce's readings on stones and colors."

"And how have you used this knowledge so far?" Ilanda asked.

"During my third year at university, I obtained a grant to study the refraction of sound traveling through quartz and peptides, but also to see the effect of the resulting vibrations and resonance in human subjects. Knowing there were no possible side effects to such exposure, it wasn't hard to find willing bodies for my research."

"And?"

"Eighty-two percent success rate in diminishing malignant tumors and—"

"Wow!" the older woman said, interrupting Octana. "What happened to the paper I assume you wrote on it?"

The interviewee shrugged her shoulders. "Never wrote one. The funds came from pharma conglomerates who shut me down as soon as they saw my intermediary results—everything belongs to them as per contract."

"How nasty!" was all Ilanda could think to say, aware of how she'd kept up the pretense that there were no naturopathic alternatives to the recovery drugs she'd to recommend to her patients.

"It happened soon after that horrific media campaign against that traditional healer started."

"I remember that," Ilanda said. "A friend of mine—an energy channeler—had to leave New York for New Mexico. The national brainwash against them was effective."

"Pharma has the dough. They can block any information that doesn't suit their agenda."

"I assume you still have the data?" the neurosurgeon asked. She leaned forward, hoping for a positive answer.

"Of course. The non-disclosure agreement's valid for two more years, though, but that doesn't mean we can't use it as our starting point for whatever your project's all about," Octana confessed. The statement reminded Ilanda how vague the job posting had actually been, and she hoped the selected candidates would make their decision based solely on the salary and their desire to work alongside her.

Cherry—or to be more precise, the funder that had used Cherry as a conduit—had sent her a list of candidate requirements, confirming what the limnologist had mentioned to her at their first discussion on the subject: candidates shouldn't be actively engaged with either the university or the hospital, have a clean criminal record, and not have connections to xenophobic organizations. She had the liberty to post the job on any website she felt met her own professional requirements. While Ilanda understood the secrecy and confidentiality surrounding her work, she hated getting acquainted with new people, learning their strengths and weaknesses, and going through the lengthy human resources process.

Everything written on the resumes qualified the applicants as experienced, valuable, and trustworthy scientists, even if two of them were half her age. She also needed people who were simple-minded, free not only from scientific preconceptions but with tame characters that would follow her guidance while handling the crystals. Two of them—who happened to be locals—had been selected to do just that.

In the end, Octana and two other researchers that Ilanda selected made their way to Toronto from Montreal, Halifax and Victoria. After much deliberation, the neurosurgeon didn't go with Cherry's recommendation for the software developer and wound up using the job posting site, too.

Those hired gathered in the former teachers' office that had been converted to a conference room, furnished with a long table made of solid plastic simulating dark wood, metal chairs, a file cabinet that matched the table, and an AR projector which hung from the ceiling. The renovations were almost done on the upper level where the medically equipped rooms would be, but 2056 had started out on the right foot, with the research floor being fully functional and ready for the new bodies to breathe some life into it.

Ilanda had already greeted the new hires the day before at a dinner arranged at the Beer Bistro on King Street East, not far from the office. Even before they'd reached Toronto, she'd encouraged them to rent apartments downtown and within walking distance, if possible. Commuting had become an unbearable hassle, and she'd wanted to eliminate any additional stress that might impact their focus.

"I hope you enjoyed the get-together last night," the neurosurgeon said.

"Oh, yes! Definitely! Great beer," everyone agreed.

"Good. There won't be another one until we get some tangible results," she continued seriously.

Their faces froze, unsure how to react.

"Just kidding!"

They laughed again and relaxed in their chairs.

"Everyone: I'm a neurosurgeon, and I need your help. I'm in the process of becoming a crystal specialist. I don't have the time and the patience to get involved with infighting or personal issues. There's only a handful of us, so we have to get along and make our research the main priority. Communicate and bring forward all concerns, no festering resentment. Understood?"

They all nodded in agreement.

"Another important administrative task: I've sent the request to City Hall for your water rations to be transferred to Toronto. Even if this location has a new designation, there's a grandfather clause that gives us a pretty good water allocation. You still have to scan your chip when you use it so we can avoid any waste.

"Now, let's chat about more important stuff.

"You all got acquainted last night, and the conclusion is that Octana and Mark have extensive, practical experience with crystals. Nanette," Ilanda said, addressing the woman with indigenous features who straightened her back right away, fully aware of the discussion, "is our sound specialist. She'll run a baseline for Octana's data. The next steps for her are related to all of the known, harmful, Hertz values and assess if crystal interaction might reverse their impact."

"Is this a countermeasure to the rumors that governments are sinisterly exposing large sports and entertainment gatherings to sublevel sounds that affect people at the molecular level?" Mark Sarafian asked. He was short with a wide frame and well-built chest. His Armenian genes seemed undiluted in spite of his mother's family who had spent fifteen generations in Canada. He had a blocky face with the permanent shadow of a beard and long, black locks of hair, parted in the middle of his head which served to give him an overall frazzled look.

"Yes, and seldom is there smoke without a fire. These vibrations, if they're real, are meant to breakdown cells and weaken the immune system. People will seek out medications and the endless cycle of getting better will begin again," Ilanda replied.

They furled their eyebrows at the remark. It was awkward for such a statement to have come from a doctor who had been one of the leeches in the system.

"Another important avenue we're going to focus on and which had generated this initiative," she gestured at her surroundings, "is how the combination of crystals and water can sustain optimal mental and physical levels of patients in deep comas. This is the first stage. The second stage is about how we can bring them back safely with their memory still intact."

"That's very interesting!" Octana exclaimed. "What, exactly, do you expect to happen in phase one?"

"Brain stimulation through structured water, decoded by crystals," the neurosurgeon replied. She opened the tablet in front of her, touched its screen a couple of times, and the AR projector turned on. Then, with a brusque gesture, she pushed out 3D pictures of Kahuna. "Here's our first patient," she said.

"Oh, the big man." Nanette had recognized him immediately.

"I thought he didn't make it," Mark said, confirming, once again, how easily today's news was forgotten by the public if it wasn't brought to the forefront ad nauseam.

"It was the Landing Eagle whose body wasn't able to sustain his wounds," Ilanda clarified. "Here are his MRI scans before and after he was treated with Hawaiian holy water. One of the tribe's elders came over for a healing session. For months now, Kahuna has been getting transfusions with structured water so his cells won't be deprived of the DNA information keeping his internal processes on autopilot, but the process can't go on much longer."

"That's a big improvement," Raman, who had kept quiet up until that moment, observed. His skills in developing blockchain technology and other highly encrypted banking protocols along with sophisticated modules for the gaming industry was what had gotten him hired. Cherry had done the grunt work for the initiative and Ilanda couldn't have been more grateful. Nevertheless, her involvement would soon end, and the neurosurgeon would have to provide milestone updates directly to the funders through a secure channel whose coordinates she'd already received. Cherry would go back to her WFA work, teaching classes, and fulfilling the occasional limnology-related contracts.

"As I said, feeding Kahuna with structured water isn't a sustainable solution," Ilanda said, emphasizing her earlier statement.

"I assume that once the crystal implant is embedded, it will remain inside Kahuna, even after he'd fully recovered," Octana said.

"That's my intention, of course," Ilanda confirmed. She absent-mindedly combed a lock of her hair behind her ears.

"Is this a long-term strategy for whatever technology or approach we're going to develop?" Raman said, jumping in, his blue eyes enlarged with wonder.

They all looked at their new boss who didn't seem in a hurry to answer.

"I'd say we should have a short-term strategy for brain enhancement in mind," she said slowly, carefully choosing her words. "We shouldn't focus on medically challenged cases alone, but also on those interesting in having the implant."

"Are you referring to the handful of incidents in which people have died during improperly performed surgeries for such implants?" Nanette asked.

"Maybe only a handful of them have been reported by the media, but I know of more cases than that, all of them failures," Ilanda replied, saddened.

"Officially, there's no institution or organization that does what we intend to do. My work at the U. of T. had restrictions and limitations, so I doubt that any research performed in a similar environment would make significant strides," she explained as she shuffled in her chair.

"When these individuals were brought to the hospital, did they have any record as to the types of crystal and colors that fit their bodies' vibrations?" Octana asked. The girl shook her head quickly, her fluffy hair, seemingly electrified by the static electricity of the sweater she was wearing, created a funny aura about her. They all smiled at her, but no one dared crack a joke.

"I wish," was all Ilanda could think of to reply.

"So, how did the neurosurgeons performing the operation hope to successfully embed the crystal?" Octana asked rhetorically. "It's not possible."

"Of course, it's not possible," the older woman said, "but the victims were faced with the enticing option of brain enhancement. The small print was never presented to them." Ilanda stood up and walked along the wall, disturbed by the images of those she couldn't save from other doctors' malpractices.

"The partial database of crystals and their corresponding vibrations and colors aren't enough to cover a wide spectrum of medical patients. We'll need to work on that, too," she said, a bit ticked off.

"Edgar Cayce's readings on the subject should be our starting point," Octana suggested. Her background indicated she was already familiar with the psychic's legacy where crystals were concerned. "We can also deepen our efforts into the connections he made between crystals and the body's main glands which, when imbalanced, immediately reverberate throughout our bodies."

"I agree," Ilanda said, still pacing back and forth, her arms crossed over her chest. "This is what initiated my research at university, anyway."

"What crystals have you played with so far?" Nanette inquired. She readied herself to take notes.

"Low-grade lapis lazuli and ruby; funds were limited."

"Any such restrictions here?" Nanette said.

"Not for now. I've sent a request to a South African source. I also know a couple of people in New Mexico who could help. The transactions should happen quickly, as long as the terms are agreed upon."

"That gives us the time to come up with a plan," the young woman concluded. She scribbled some words in her notepad.

"Yes, about that," Ilanda sat down and she embraced everyone at the table with a look, "I'm still needed at the hospital two full days a week, so you'll be pretty much on your own. For now, as a team, decide on which crystals we're going to use first, create test cases and their durations, and assess which off-the-shelf software application might be used to record the data. Use Raman for any code customization that might be needed," the neurosurgeon instructed.

The early morning wave of energy that had pushed her spirits high had washed away, and the woman felt suddenly old and decrepit in the presence of youth. Her body, still in good shape, seemed to weigh tons on her large frame, keeping her pinned to the chair.

A random thought about Maahes, who had sent her an email from the Middle East, brushed at her mind, distracting her even more. Recently, his visits to that part of the world had become more frequent and barely planned. *I've got something important to discuss when I'm back,'* he'd said laconically. When was he going to understand the world had changed, and he was still frozen in an outdated business model and life scenario? Selling water was more important to him than anything else—until the day came when there was nothing left to sell.

"Please present me with a draft in three to four days," she said, coming back to reality. "And get ready to welcome Big Kahuna in less than two weeks."

"I can't wait to see him in person." Nanette clapped her hands and smiled widely.

Ilanda paid no attention to the outburst. She continued, "After we settle him in and hook him to the monitoring equipment, I want you to confirm that agate is the type of crystal most likely to match his physical makeup. He's born in May so agate should be the right choice."

"No problem," Octana assured. "Do you expect the crystals to have arrived by then?"

Ilanda thought for a moment, mentally counting dates. "Yes, they should be here by then."

"And after that?" Octana insisted as if she'd sensed her boss' suggestion was a prerequisite for the plan she'd asked them to work on.

"After you determine which crystal would be the best fit, load the room with as many of them as possible. If necessary, we'll order more."

The earlier heaviness she'd felt tugged at her confidence again. Fear had inserted into her mind the clear message of failure, dissolution, and the efficiency of such research. She shook her head vigorously, not noticing the glances her assistants exchanged.

"Are we going to accept more patients after Kahuna?" Mark Sarafian asked.

"Not immediately. At least, no one in a comatose state. He needs our complete attention until the data's more consistent and showing some improvement in his mental activity," Ilanda replied.

"Octana, you might want to share the procedure you used in your university research with everyone. Expand on it to work with a larger variety of crystals. Start with your colleagues as human subjects," the neurosurgeon suggested, and she stood up ready to leave. "If we successfully develop this enhanced technology, you guys can be the first to try it, if you're interested," she continued. "I can think of at least one man who'd be willing to stick a crystal in his brain tomorrow." She thought of Maahes.

She walked toward the door but turned to add: "Our funder's dead serious about keeping a lid on what we're going to do in here: no documents, notes, or emails will be sent to unauthorized individuals. Understood?"

Heads nodded.

"See you tomorrow," Ilanda said. She stepped out leaving the door open behind her.

CHAPTER 14

The necessity for Hayyin to address the public was first and foremost in Cherry's mind. Not only would her secret identity fuel the agitated crowd that had already organized itself and were flying to Mongolia in steady streams, but she also wanted to protect the representatives of water-related organizations heading there by acknowledging them by name.

This time she opted for a recording rather than a livestream. She chose the same Estonian entity as a delivery venue to make the broadcast harder to trace.

In her windowless office, Cherry dimmed the light and strapped on Hayyin's face. She was wearing a baggy, black shirt and had mittens resting on her lap. A tiny, half-full glass of water on the corner of the desk in front of her—it was no more than three healthy sips of her daily ration.

"Dear friends," she began, "our common front against a greedy enemy had proven very effective today. Our determination helped us identify Mosamoni and Narankama's nefarious activities in countries in which water regulations have loopholes in favor of such corporations. The fact that they surround themselves with armies of mercenaries speaks volumes to the illegality of what they plan to do with this new found source of primary water."

Cherry's voice raised as usual when talking about water-related injustices. She grabbed her knees to keep her hands still and avoid having to put on the mittens. The reflection on her iPad's screen displayed a somber image—not an immobile, wooden mask, but a vivid face with dark, red tears pulsating to the rhythm of her breathing. Her vision, blurred by the drops of perspiration dripping from her eyebrows, gave the impression that bubbles of water were pouring out of the barely open mouth whose full lips did not move as it delivered the spoken words.

"In the past, the underground resources would be theirs to mine and use. We are not living in such a world anymore. It's not business as usual. Rationed water is the new normal, and it's been like that for a while. We have ended up in this situation because corporations like these couldn't be stopped from pillaging the earth's resources, be they water, oil, or similar commodities. Nature is punishing us every single day. Unexpected events related to water the world over keep warning us that the worst is yet to come, but we still don't take it seriously."

Cherry forgot about the fine cracks that had appeared on her lips due to poor hydration. She licked them, stirring a sharp pain. Cherry almost swore at her ineptitude, and she paused the recording, untied the mask, and emptied the glass of water.

She put the mask back on. "For those going to either Kazakhstan or Mongolia, take care of each other. Don't let the mercenaries provoke you. Representatives from the Primary Water Institute, Water For All, Water Is, and many more are on site and have opened direct communication channels with these governments.

"We have to convince everyone that any new primary water vent is untouchable, and there is no ownership of such a resource. Let it run free and pristine. It has no memory of any of our sins and it hasn't absorbed the collective consciousness of nature's cycle. It's a pure, righteous being. Elusive, yet impetuous. Entrapping this vent will only temporarily solve our water problems, but it will do more to aggravate our relationship with water. Political leaders, CEOs, businessmen—please, wizen up."

That was all she could say. She saved the recording, encrypted it, and used the secure channel Anonymous had provided for her to send it out.

"One less thing to worry about."

Cherry didn't have any predictions as to how the herd of humans traveling to Kazakhstan and Mongolia would behave. Rumors, fake news, or infiltrated agents of chaos, those whom she called paid agitators, could spark an exaggerated reaction, trigger the intervention of authorities, and shift the focus from the real reason behind the protest. People would end up in jail, at the mercy of corrupt judges, to decide upon the gravity of their charges.

The golden hue coming from the setting sun bathing the living room soothed her lingering gaze, and she suddenly realized how much she'd missed her daily introspection. Her flight or fight attitude over the last couple of weeks had distorted her reality, blending days together, folding them into a pattern of putting out fires, reading emails, teaching classes three times a week, and swearing late in the evening when she ran out of water.

Her schedule succumbed to the immediate actions required by the deepening world crisis. Free time had become a luxury. Cherry sat on the couch, letting the warm shimmering rays embrace her body in a gesture of healing. She imaged a huge crystal filtering the light, emanating an iridescent calm. Her mind and senses opened to the liberating feeling that had urged her inner-self to trace and reinstate her balance. In the softness of the moment, all of her daily hurdles vanished, and an indistinguishable calmness overcame her. Layer after layer of anxiety and fear peeled away, exposing her soul to the Divine Energy, awakened, transcendent, and willing to purify an open mind.

Cherry's inner entropy couldn't, however, be entirely restrained. A murky thought pierced the tranquility, spilling disruption: We are the cancer of the earth. With the right approach, we can heal ourselves, but what if the earth applies the same principle of healing itself by getting rid of us? Water is but one of its many tools to achieve that end.

She cringed at the idea of humankind as a tumor, when, in fact, it had been established that we were spiritual beings trapped in physical bodies. Cherry urged her mind to submit to her previous thoughts. A glimpse of darkness emanating from her subconscious once more interfered with her attempt to have a quiet moment.

"Hard to relax!" she muttered, and she picked up her iPad to check the news feeds.

"What the hell?

"'Tibetan temples in Toronto protected by devotees and a small number of police,'" she read out loud. "Oh, it's a follow-up story on the kidnapped monks. Kidnapped monks!" Cherry repeated, unwilling to believe the news was real. "How could I have missed this one?"

Similar events had taken place in other cities around the globe. Those who perceived spirituality as a way out of the dire situation, or at least as a way to improve it, were fighting to protect the last bastions of pure consciousness.

"How can we keep track of this madness?"

Predicting micro- and macro-human reactions connected to changes in the water's behavior had become impossible. Cherry was baffled, and she had a hard time projecting Hayyin's sermons in the right directions. She sorted the news by the word 'water' and browsed the results. There had been hundreds of videos uploaded by eyewitnesses along the banks of the sacred rivers displaying huge gatherings praying, meditating, or contemplating in an effort to revert the water's behavior to the previously safe status.

The recordings were full of hushed comments regarding ongoing water sample tests in an effort to confirm any positive changes. Researchers engaged in the purifying of lakes through prayer had achieved tangible results that had been documented and reviewed by their peers. This time, the number of believers didn't make a difference—the toxicity levels remained high.

"Water has no intention of backing off," she muttered again, "unless we prove that we take its threats seriously and reverse— or at least stop—our stupid actions."

There were no reports of finding dead fish in any of the rivers. It was almost as if the water had created safety bubbles for its natural life forms.

Cherry switched her focus to the news about Mexico City. International aid pouring in did little to change the situation on the ground. The smoldering pit was still unsafe for rescue crews. Authorities didn't have to enforce the evacuation of the suburbs neighboring the crater; everyone had moved out on their own accord, carrying with them as much clothing that would fit into a backpack. Ad-hoc camps formed at the fringes of the city, where the army was busy putting up tents and connecting containers equipped with solar panels, small windmills, and medical units. The remnants of the aquifer were gone, without even a trickle of water left behind to trace. Instead, drones had been sent in carrying infrared scanners with which to search for survivors, but they found Mayan ruins instead, small-scale pyramids that were flat at the tops. It had been a remarkable discovery, but no one had any interest in ancient history or archeology anymore.

Several breezeless days in late November had maintained a thick layer of dust over the area, and the smell of burnt flesh had caused incessant coughing, red eyes, and people walking around in a permanent state of nausea. Medical masks and goggles were in high demand on the black market that always seemed to function better in times of crisis. Plans were put forward for the potential cleanup of debris to uncover any remaining lucky survivors. Dropping heavy equipment into the pit was a tough challenge that only a few companies were willing to undertake.

Cherry's mind wandered from the scenes which reminded her of the trailer for an apocalyptic movie. She wanted to find her internal balance so easily disturbed these days by the human suffering going on. With her eyes closed, the woman relaxed her body and mentally opened to the energy surrounding her, without controlling or interfering in the delivery process of any knowledge she might receive.

Foamy waves seemed to splash against the inside of her skull. An inhalation of air tickled her nostrils with the salty smell of water and seaweed. Her awareness shifted toward her heart which lit up with love as soon as her subconscious had decoded the subtle, energetic impulse. The message seemed familiar and enforced a feeling of gratitude within her. Concentric vibrational waves enveloped first her neighborhood, then the province, followed by the entire country, eventually spreading across the planet. She remained transfixed by what her mind envisioned: her arms extended around a tiny earth, holding it tightly as she pulled it from its orbit and placed it into her heart. The cosmic balance, undisturbed by such a bold gesture, gave her confidence the Divine Matrix would provide ample time before the earth's tumors would undergo an irreversible healing process. She cried tears of gratitude that she had been given the honor of such an intense vision in which the gravitational force of her heart would keep the planet spinning slowly, and her fierce love would clean the oceans and the air, bringing back extinct species. When the earth's rotation had stopped, she intuitively knew she had to put it back on its axis. Content with her achievement, she did just that, tears still streaming down her cheeks.

It was a vision that proved beyond any doubt that if each person living on earth shrouded it in a veil of appreciation, the tide of pollution and decay would be reversed and nature's balance restored.

Hayyin's mandate was to broadcast this message tirelessly until clusters of Lightworkers[5] would stick together in crowds forming a critical mass large enough to influence global-level environmental policies.

Cherry checked her email one more time, anxious for news from Romana Pilb, who had confirmed two days ago she'd safely arrived in Mongolia. A handful of videos had been uploaded by local reporters using their newspaper's Internet access. Everyone else's videos were choppy by comparison, and rumors of the government's having put pressure on Internet providers had begun to float around.

"Tens of thousands have landed in Ulaanbaatar in the last week, forcing the authorities to restrict international flights that could swell the number of protesters even more. Main roads leading to the border with Kazakhstan are blocked by army units, preventing NGO representatives and water activists from reaching Narankama's land, where private security guards are well-armed and ready for engagement," the *UB Post* reported live. "Everyone expects a standoff between these two forces with better odds for the army. Neither Mosamoni nor Narankama have made statements denying the existence of a primary water vent

---

[5]   Lightworker – person working towards a spiritual goal

under their control. Their respective websites have been shut down due to inconceivable amounts of traffic leaving obscene comments that we cannot print here," the article continued. "As major US-based news channel has pointed out in the last several days that geopolitical pressure in the region might escalate if these two American companies aren't allowed to exploit the underground resource. At this point, all information is based on assumptions. Only an official statement followed by an inspection of the site will have the power to calm the tension."

"It's as if they'd read Paul Boulanjois' mind," Cherry said to herself after having read the article. She scrolled the page looking for any links that might point to similar news but found none. She returned to the main page, only to notice the latest news by the *UB Post*: "Mongolian legislators to discuss additions to the existing water regulations, retroactively applied to sources of primary water."

"They want to tighten the screws; too late," Cherry muttered, almost convinced the move would spark an aggressive reaction from the US government under the pretense of protecting its own citizens on foreign land.

"Is there anything of significance Mongolia could be blackmailed with?"

She had no idea and didn't have the strength to begin another investigation with Siri. Her gaze focused on the large, shiny screen of her AR device on the wall. Hayyin's wooden face stared back at her, scrutinizing her actions, deep thoughts, and fears in an attempt to decrypt the meaning behind her next online appearance.

She smiled, knowing her identity was Cherry Mortinger. To prove it, she ran her hands over her face and checked her reflection. Hayyin remained stubbornly in place. A chill made her hair stand on the back of her neck. She was surprised at how hard it had become distinguishing her actual identity from the one she'd created.

Hayyin's personality carried with it a certain heaviness, including the responsibility of his actions influencing many of his followers. Cherry wasn't sure how much longer she'd be able to live in Hayyin's skin and play this dangerous game against the multi-nationals. Water activists relied on Hayyin to uncover shady deals, illegalities, and corruption high in the government in an attempt to drain a system that had been so clogged, not even the forgiving earth was willing to accept. The unrelenting water offensive that had resulted was seen by many as humanity's wake-up call. But for those directly affected financially, water's stand-off was nothing more than evanescent behavior that was unable to match the might of man. While her revelations—most of them having come from Anonymous—had been meant to accomplish results, only lately had she realized that the ensuing, collective chaos could be an outcome over which she would have no control.

Would her protector divulge her identity in the eventuality of her refusal to continue Hayyin's mission, or would they just find another zealot willing to carry the burden? she wondered.

Cherry let her body slide down on the couch, giving in to the slumber that had made her eyelids grow heavy. From the shadows of her mind, Romana Pilb waved at her happily, extinguishing Cherry's worries about her safety. The encouraging message helped her drift into a dreamless sleep.

CHAPTER 15

Daily reports on production issues from various offshore locations no longer elevated his blood pressure, nor did it make him lose his temper. Maahes had adopted a new life perspective, the carefree attitude of letting things go. It was something he'd lost many years ago when the difference between his personal and his corporate activities had merged. It was then he'd started squandering the only stable and significant human connection in his life before he became an empty shell, avidly searching for physical enrichment and power.

In the past, he'd scoffed at Ilanda's warnings, somehow assured of her presence in his life due to the deep love she'd always felt for him.

Maahes looked around at his spacious, corner office. The high-quality couch; the expensive, Italian cherry wood desk and chairs; the wall-embedded bookshelves hosting volumes he barely had time to browse, let alone read entirely; the two original Group of Seven paintings—these things no longer kindled warm feelings of achievement for him. A burst of unexpected awareness had transformed him into a rational being, revealing the meaning of what life could become once he'd affected an attitude of non-attachment.

The attainment of such a conclusion dispelled the darkness veiling his mind, offering him a second chance. The random thoughts that had started fluttering through his mind's eye three years ago had revealed a potentially ineffable existence, absorbed by meaningful things such as love, care, and compassion for others.

There had been no coherence in his life up to that moment, only a string of soulless corporate events along with other power-hungry, feeling-starved individuals.

He swiveled in his chair to see the tall windows facing Lake Ontario. A plane was about to land at Billy Bishop Airport, while a ferry—full to the brim with passengers—pushed its way to Toronto Island, a fifteen-minute trip one way.

The initial worldwide fright that all of the water on the planet might turn toxic had subsided in Toronto after two weeks of daily monitoring and chemical analysis turned out negative. If Ilanda and all the research being done on water having been influenced by human behavior was correct, then the mélange of cultures and lack of conflict in his cosmopolitan city should keep the lake indefinitely inoffensive.

"Maybe quantum water entanglement doesn't apply to us," Maahes reflected in an expression he found himself making quite often of late. "We promise to be respectful in how we handle water and acknowledge its importance in our lives," was the new mantra said every morning in schools along with the opening prayer and national anthem.

He turned his attention to his AR device which had blinked twice, announcing a new message. He tapped it and a 3D recording of his lawyer popped up.

"Maahes, I hope you made it back safely. As instructed, here is your updated will for Ilanda's eyes only. I need your fingerprint in the highlighted fields on every single page. At the end, hit Save and Return to Sender. Let me know if there is anything else I can do for you."

An entire life had been captured on the forty pages of the detailed will, carefully drafted so no individual or legal entity would be able to challenge it. The apartment in downtown Toronto was the only asset still carrying his name as half-owner, and he didn't expect there to be any claims on it from those who might have felt unjustly treated by his decision to re-align the company's long-term position vis-à-vis water.

Maahes pressed his thumb on the shimmering image on the first page, then flipped to the next and repeated the gesture until every page had his authentication. He saved the file and sent it back as requested; one less worry before playing dead.

If his physical disappearance wasn't likely to generate significant market capitalization losses, the leaked news about the re-possession of key water-related properties would. The company might crumble from within faster than anyone could predict. Because ethics didn't apply to a "dead man," Maahes had instructed his stockbroker to short the company's shares and make a killing in the process.

He'd chosen Egypt as the place for his bereavement, not only because it was easier to fabricate one's death and supporting legal documents, but symbolically, because he wanted to close the loop of his life on the same grounds as his mother had.

His new identity had been obtained through low-level contacts for which money was more important than having annoying questions answered. He also grew a rebel's beard, altering his otherwise sharp look. A private plane—paid for in advance— would take him to Costa Rica along with a handful of former marines as his security detail.

With Marian's help, offshore bank accounts had been opened and a fake credit history created for the fictitious persona. Maahes' intention was to keep a low profile with only one major goal: Ilanda's success in crystal technology. Their casual conversation on the subject had stirred his interest as to how much capacity and processing power might be added to his brain, but she was more interested in using crystals as a decoding tool for the brain than enhancing thinking and storage capacity. If water's rebellion continued indefinitely, dehydration could become the leading factor of human deaths, surpassing cancer, heart attacks, and every other disease in number.

Without the necessary fluids, the body's cells would dry-out, shut off, and leave behind an empty shell. What if her undeclared goal had been to identify the *perfect resonance* of crystals able to keep a person's cells in a *happy state*, conveying the impression of a self-sustained structured environment? Maybe a mouthful of water per day or per week would then do the trick, allowing the organs to adapt accordingly. It was a crazy thought that was more than a little scary.

Everyone he cared for would share what little cash had been left in his bank account. He had no doubt his Egyptian relatives would survive the even harsher times that would follow in the wake of water's unpredictable behavior. For them, he would continue to provide financial support, paying for their ongoing water rations. It was a gesture that should temporarily relieve their parching thirst.

The unofficial stash of cash would also provide him with a constant source of water from one of Costa Rica's Pacific shoreline desalinization plants that Maahes would soon live nearby.

• • •

The call from Maahes's lawyer reached Ilanda at the hospital while she was resting in her office between surgeries. To be sure she'd be able to take his AR call, he'd send a recorded message letting her know of the follow up an hour later.

After he'd introduced himself, Joseph Maninov kept an official tone in his voice and a somber look on his narrow face. His brown hair touched his shoulders seeming too thick for a man of his age. He wore it parted a little off-center on his wide forehead, framing his pointy nose and piercing black eyes.

"Mrs. Mazandir, I'm calling you on behalf of my client, Maahes."

"Is he all right?"

The man stared at her. He swallowed several times to lubricate his dry mouth before continuing his prepared speech. "No, he's not. In fact, he passed away in Cairo this morning," he announced abruptly.

Ilanda smiled, stood up from behind her desk and got closer to Joseph Maninov's virtual image.

"How is that possible?" she asked incredulously. "He emailed me two days ago. He was coming home."

She crossed her hands over her chest defiantly, waiting to see if the lawyer would crack a smile and divulge the real reason behind him contacting her.

"It seems impossible, I know. I didn't believe it either until I received this photo from the triage doctor that cared for him."

The lawyer swiped up in the air with his fingers and an image of a lifeless Maahes on a morgue table, half-covered with a white sheet appeared on the screen. There was no sign of a concussion or violence on his pale skin and the serene features of his face told the story of a painless death. Only then did Ilanda walk the two steps to the couch and drop onto it, hands covering her mouth.

"Before calling you, I reached out to Dr. Timberlane at Princess Margaret Hospital. He treated Maahes five weeks ago, checking him in for several days to perform some tests. He couldn't give me more details due to doctor-patient confidentiality. You, of all people, should understand that." Maninov explained why his inquiry had fallen short of producing concrete information.

"What caused his death?" Ilanda finally asked, her face a depiction of misery.

"I stopped the autopsy until I had your permission. I've invoked a fictitious clause stating that a spouse has a say in making this decision, but it won't hold water for too long. Dr. Timberlane did tell Maahes that any additional stress or extended trips were not recommended," the man said. He squinted his eyes to convey to Ilanda his helplessness when it came to Maahes' strong will.

"I want them to send his body back to Canada," she said, sounding harsh. "No autopsy. Just send him back," the neurosurgeon repeated herself, reinforcing a request for which she didn't expect to receive a negative answer.

That is, however, exactly what Joseph Maninov delivered. "Mrs. Mazandir, I have no legal authority in that part of the world. They have stringent laws when it comes to such circumstances. Additionally, Maahes still has close family ties in Egypt and they have a say, too. We might get back his belongings, but nothing more," the lawyer said.

"We'll hire a local lawyer. He should know what to do," Ilanda pushed back with a fierce gaze, expressing her anger that the guy in front of her would be willing to give up so easily.

"I've already done more than that. I called the Canadian Embassy in Cairo, but no one wants a diplomatic conflict in today's volatile environment."

"So?"

"They reached out to their counterparts, but as I said: it's complicated. Maahes had dual citizenship, so he can't be treated as a foreigner."

"What the fuck?" the woman hid her head in both hands and leaned forward, almost touching her knees.

Without waiting for another question, Maninov offered an explanation. "I assume it was a request from his mother before she passed, for his Egyptian citizenship to take precedence over his Canadian one."

"Fuck, fuck, fuck!" Ilanda leaned back on the couch, wiped her tears, and then asked: "So why the fuck are you asking for my permission for the autopsy? If I can't have him back I don't give a rat's ass if they cut him open or not."

The lawyer nodded his narrow head, a movement that seemed totally disengaged from the rest of his body, but said nothing.

"Will we get the results at least?" she asked, hopeful.

"This is a concession they might make. I'll push for it at the diplomatic level," he replied gently but reassuringly.

"Anything else?" She had a glacial tone as if she wanted to get rid of Joseph Maninov so she could mourn Maahes freely.

Before the man could answer, a pre-recorded video message appeared at the door, asking her to come to the operating room for the next surgery. "Cancel it!" she bellowed using air from deep inside her lungs.

The message repeated, ignoring her command. She launched herself toward the shimmering image, punched the Decline icon, and said, "Cancel the surgery or find a replacement doctor. I feel sick."

The lawyer conceded how she might not be able to think straight and keep a steady hand. She didn't sit again, but paced back and forth agitatedly.

"There is something else," Maninov said, undisturbed by the interruption.

Ilanda stopped and fixed her gaze on him.

"Maahes's will. It was updated after his release from the hospital."

"I'm not interested," she snapped back. "I'm a doctor and his wife, for God's sake! Why didn't he come to me? I could have helped." She seemed unable to let go of the thought that Maahes had perished away from home, away from her, and somehow in secrecy.

The death of Maahes, the CEO of the Vivus Water Inc.—the third-largest water bottling company on the planet—wouldn't go unnoticed. Nor would it pass without affecting the industry.

"You're the main beneficiary of his estate. I'll wait until you're ready to deal with it."

She scoffed and turned her back at him, facing the enlarged photos of New York on the wall. Though the enormity of the loss she'd just suffered had seeped slowly through her body, her attitude didn't falter again in front of the lawyer.

"I appreciate your effort in getting everything in place per Maahes's request."

She turned to look at him, her hands plunged firmly into her pockets. "And obtaining the autopsy results would be quite an achievement. I really want to understand why he didn't trust me on this one."

Maninov smiled for the first time, a light extension of his lips to the side as if he were afraid her suddenly mellow demeanor might shift again.

"I'll let the Canadian Embassy take a firm stand on this issue. They might have to grease some pockets, but it will be done," he said confidently.

Ilanda walked to her chair behind the desk. "About the will: who else is a beneficiary?" she asked.

"His relatives in Egypt and a non-profit, *Water For All*."

He scrutinized her still tense face for any sign of objection, then continued, "It's a very unusual decision for someone in his position."

"How much?"

"A quarter of a bitcoin."

"What's going to happen with his shares in the company?"

"I don't know. There's no mention of it in the will," Maninov replied.

"Did he sell everything ahead of time?" Ilanda asked. "Can you find out?"

"Only if I receive a written request from you. As Maahes's wife, you have the right to inquire. Maybe it was a company buy-back or maybe he sold them on the open market in small chunks. Regardless of what he did, the money's gone," the lawyer said, disclosing his assumptions.

"Have you informed the board yet?"

"He instructed to call you first so you wouldn't be taken by surprise if they reached out to you."

"I was very thoughtful of him," Ilanda said, scoffing sarcastically.

"It will be quite the shocker for everyone. I can't tell if you are going to attract any media attention, and while I understand the importance of what you do on a daily basis, I'd suggest taking a vacation for a little while," Joseph Maninov said. He motioned with his hands to the space in front of him as if pointing her to the direction of the nearest airport.

Ilanda kept quiet, a subtle smirk appearing on her face.

"The relevance of this news won't exceed four weeks," the lawyer said pushing forward, having sensed the woman had begun to unwind after the initial shock of the news.

As if in slow motion, Ilanda opened the drawer to her right and took out an already open box of biscuits. She bit into one while staring absent-mindedly at Maninov who, with a quick gesture, pressed a hand to the side of his head. His hair shifted slightly, and he hoped Ilanda hadn't noticed he was wearing a wig. "I'll listen to your advice," she said. "If anyone asks, I'm out of town."

"Really?"

"Yes. Contact me only when you have the information we talked about. Let's keep these encounters to a minimum."

"Understood. Maybe next time we'll also settle the will."

"Maybe. Goodbye, Joseph, and thank you," she said, disconnecting from the call.

• • •

Left by herself, Ilanda couldn't move. She felt pain in her mouth, a thick slime that hurt her tongue and gums. It was an excruciating pain that she instinctively knew had been generated by the trauma of losing Maahes. Their strained marital relationship had still given them the sense of belonging to a place to call home, even if had been empty most of the time. She loved him, and he loved her back. It was more out of care and compassion than a carnal attraction that had waned down as the years had passed them by.

Strenuous work hours and the desire to be the best had kept her away not only from Maahes but from her family, too. Loneliness would characterize her life moving forward since she couldn't picture herself building new sentimental connections, especially not when her crystal research was her number one priority. Professional distance had to be maintained where her team was concerned, as well.

She had to harness the pain, resentment, and disappointment with the shortcomings of her personal life to create an embodiment of achievements that would elevate her name not only as a neurosurgeon but as a scientist as well.

Ilanda often prayed for a comeback of the world's saintliness in spite of the volatility of daily events that stubbornly tried to shatter such hopes. Shortages of all kind, from water to grains to energy, splattered the daily news incessantly, reminding everyone of their frailty against an All Mighty energy that wouldn't stop badgering humanity until a natural balance was restored.

Humankind's defiance had no limits, not even when self-destruction was the end result. She didn't want her work to be in vain. Pushing forward on the rough path of brain enhancement through crystal implants was the obvious choice for her, contrary to the better judgment that any erroneous stride could ruin her reputation. She had nothing else to lose now, her reputation being the least of her worries.

Darkness buried her under a thick cloak, pinning her down in her chair and forcing her overwhelmed mind to be more introspective of the moments she'd shared with Maahes in their life together.

She tapped the back of her right hand to display her remaining water rations for the day: one glass left, but as a neurosurgeon, through the hospital, she was entitled to an additional two hundred and fifty milliliters. The effort required to pull herself up and reach for water dispenser in the hallway implied a strength she didn't think she had. Instead, she let herself melt into the furniture, hiding under a crust of sorrow and sudden indifference to the world's challenges. Her optimism sagged against her afflictions and the feelings and circumstances she'd assumed had been firmly anchored on her life's path. Lofty dreams and achievements she'd worked diligently toward might stop her short, hindered by unexpected events she couldn't control.

An image of Maahes' funny, swaggering walk lulled her into a dreamless sleep.

CHAPTER 16

"Let's look at the results," Cherry said, addressing her students after everyone had ordered their drinks and food at a terrace restaurant near the University of Toronto.

The server scanned the chips on the backs of their hands and the daily rations of only seven of them had been exhausted. "Bring extra empty glasses," Cherry told the server. "We'll share."

It was the end of November, and the balmy weather had urged Cherry's wild side to move the day's class outdoors to review the field trip's outcome while they breathed in some relatively fresh air. They'd pushed five tables together to accommodate the class of twenty-five, with Cherry presiding at one end. Copies of the report had already been opened on their iPads and portable devices.

"Thank you, again, for joining my annual scavenging trip through mud puddles, rivulets, and rivers," the teacher said.

Everyone laughed. They raised their glasses.

"As you've all noticed, water hasn't punished us in any way yet. I'm convinced our positive intentions have contributed to our safety." The statement had stirred more laughter. She smiled along with them, but she was glad her initial doubts about possible major molecular changes in the lakes and rivers of Ontario hadn't occurred. It seemed as if an invisible field of energy had kept the country safe, an exemption to the entanglement every scientist and news anchor mentioned daily. Based on the findings of previous years, Cherry didn't expect any improvement in the quality of water they had sampled. It was hard for her to witness the slow but undeniable degradation, and the pain of it nagged at her on the inside. She found the justification to endure the self-inflicted agony, using it mostly as a teaching tool against the baseline she'd initiated soon after she'd graduated as a limnologist. Over time, she had learnt that exposing a new generation of environmentalists to the crude reality of water's molecular degradation had a powerful impact on just how seriously they would treat their future jobs.

"Let's hear the results of the Lake Ontario samples we rushed to the lab directly from the site," Cherry said.

A red-haired guy with freckles covering his hollow cheeks and a pronounced stutter started first. "Th-th-these s-s-samples didn't come into physical contact with any of us so we sh-sh-shouldn't have caused any s-s-struct-t-tural alteration. Compared to previous years, th-th-the molecular s-s-structure is quite s-s-similar. In t-t-terms of chemical compos-s-sition th-th-the s-s-situat-t-tion s-s-sucks." He looked around the table to see if anyone else wanted to pick up the conversation, but no one did.

He continued, "Th-th-the concent-t-tration of heavy metals has doubled. A quick invest-t-tigation along th-th-the main tributaries hasn't revealed any changes in th-th-the t-t-terrain; th-th-there are buffer zones bet-t-tween th-th-these areas and urban clusters, and th-th-there is no industrial bus-s-siness presence."

"So, there's no logical explanation?" Cherry inquired. She sipped nonchalantly from a glass of orange juice.

This time, Zanice, the girl with the shaved head, jumped in. "I can share my assumption as to why there's been such a drastic increase over the matter of a year."

"Go ahead," Cherry said, encouraging her.

"I think the type of entanglement happening in Ontario is that the water's sucking heavy metals from the lakebed, making the water purification process for human consumption more difficult, and at times, unfeasible. The Municipality of Toronto is the only official entity that can confirm my assumption, but I doubt that they'll do that. It won't do any good for the morale of the citizens," she said, ended with a note of sarcasm.

"Are there any other opinions?" Cherry asked. She sat cross-legged in the plastic chair, leaning back so the sunset brightened her red t-shirt and alabaster skin.

Opanah, a mahogany-skinned man, chimed in. "I think the higher concentrations of heavy metals is a natural process we don't know how to interpret yet. And while I do buy into the entanglement concept affecting water all over the world, I'd expect a much harsher reaction here, in Ontario."

"Why's that?" asked another student, a Chinese girl whose name Cherry couldn't recall. "You don't believe that our attitude of inclusiveness has an effect on water's benign behavior?"

"No, I don't. Ontario-based businesses are spread out all over the world. Don't tell me none of them are bending the rules of environment protection to generate a profit. If it affects the earth, the punishment, in my opinion, should not only be applied locally, but through entanglement in the companies' countries of origin. If we accept the premise that water is intelligent and alive, then it's the same everywhere," Opanah concluded. He smiled largely, displaying his crooked teeth.

"In other words, you don't have an explanation as to why the water's still inoffensive in Ontario," Cherry stated.

"Correct. Oil sands have been a dark spot on the country's environmental reputation for decades. They've depleted enormous underground water resources, contaminating the soil with cyanides, and damaging completely fertile soil. Let alone the fact there's been no consideration for Native rights. Is this list not comprehensive enough to force the erratic attitude of water?" Opanah asked maliciously.

Cherry liked Opanah's combative style, even if it was sometimes a little too aggressive for her liking. "I got your point," she agreed. "Wherever one looks, there's damage done at different levels of impact, whether it's been done consciously or not.

"And we all agree this has to change, starting with each of us? We talked in class about this aspect of human behavior: it's not a switch we can simply turn on and off, consciously or unconsciously. It's a battle that might take years to overcome." The teacher in her always yearned to present concepts beyond the field of limnology as a step to hasten their mental maturity.

"Let's move along," Cherry suggested.

The guy with the freckles took the initiative again. "It was-s-s…dis-s-sappointing th-th-this year to discover a drastic reduction in th-th-the cultures of micro-organisms and algae in Lake Ont-t-tario. We visited th-th-the s-s-same locations in order to have consistency." When speaking quickly, he made a visible effort to keep his voice steady. Try as he might, it didn't work.

"Th-th-the s-s-same findings are consistent upstream Humber River with unexpected results for th-th-the fauna bordering th-th-the body of water."

"What's that?" Cherry asked, still sitting relaxed, eyes closed.

"Th-th-the banks are becoming deserted. It's like th-th-the plants sense th-th-the changes th-th-the water is going th-th-through and won't t-t-touch it. They'd rather perish," freckles said, almost whispering the last words as if he was afraid of being laughed at.

No one made any comment. They were too busy playing with the few drops left at the bottom of their water glasses.

"I consider it a normal defensive reaction that one who searches intently would find in nature," the professor said, sharing her opinion. "Nevertheless, I won't rule out a much closer correlation between the water's poor quality and the plants' behavior. What else?"

Zanice, who had analyzed the samples collected from the highest point upstream during the trip, jumped back in. "There's a specific characteristic that really bothers us, and we don't know how to interpret it: the viscosity gradient is way higher than it should normally be. It's a one hundred percent increase from last year. If this trend continues at the same rate, I predict a visible change in the water's fluidity in less than two years." The girl slurped noisily from the bottom of her glass and glanced around for reactions.

"Are you saying that water could soon have the viscosity of molasses?" one of her colleagues asked.

"It's possible," Zanice replied. "It could also be another form of quantum water entanglement. We have to watch for similar reports online."

Cherry straightened herself in her chair, interested in this unexpected development.

• • •

Cherry let her students go and lingered for a while in her chair, absent-mindedly staring at the empty glasses. She remembered the stories told by her parents who had used to meet friends to go out drinking. There were no restrictions on beverages of any kind, and water with ice was, in fact, the first to be brought to the customers by the servers. Tap water had no price tag. It was an invisible item seldom used and taken for granted since everyone desired fine wine, eccentric beer, or strong spirits imported from the other side of the world.

In 2055, water was priceless. Having observed the events unfolding everywhere, she knew it was only a matter of time before atrocious wars would burn whatever was left of humanity to a crisp.

The hour-long walk to her place would help to clear her mind of the anxiety caused by the recent lab results. Cherry picked up her backpack and left. She crossed Yonge Street toward the east side of the city, zig-zagging across the short streets hidden by countless condominiums until she reached the Prince Edward Viaduct, linking Bloor Street to Danforth Avenue. She paused at the middle of the bridge, glancing down at the Don River Valley through the thick metal wires installed to prevent jumpers from ending their lives.

The panoramic, impressive from both directions but especially from the south due to the protruding tip of CN Tower, always stirred in her the contentment of living in a cosmopolitan city that valued the environment. The present Don Valley River, a shadow of its once lush forest and tumultuous, meandering water, only infused despair now. She had no confidence the brittle ground would ever retain enough humidity to spark life once more into the dying brush whose treeline was continually receding from the trickling river.

She pulled out her phone to immortalize the landscape as part of her year-to-year comparison and started to walk again.

Thunder fractured the city's noise pollution. The sun's light, even though it was mellow, didn't indicate a storm or precipitation, which would have been very unusual for the late fall. She glanced to the south toward Lake Ontario which was only a few kilometers away to see a dense blackness gathered in a vertical pillar, emitting the madness of death, swirling its way straight to the core of downtown. It seemed the glass towers, tiny and fragile, would topple like the sticks of a child's Jenga game. A small plane ready for landing had nowhere to go. It hit the ground before being slurped into the ferocious combination of wind and water. The threatening column wavered left and right, gaining speed and bit the plane's tail violently.

Cherry couldn't see anything else. Panic seized her instantly, and she looked around for a cab that might drop her home in minutes. She hailed one with the free sign on. Before jumping in, she glanced once more to the south to assess how quickly the tornado would touch down in her neighborhood, but there was no longer any sign of atmospheric turbulence; the sky was clear.

She wondered if it had all been in her imagination, worried that what had just happened to her might have been another one of her day-dreaming incidents that had recently increased their occurrence. While in the car, it hadn't crossed her mind to turn the radio on. She just wanted to get home fast, frightened that whatever nightmares Hayyin's mask had witnessed in Africa since its inception had soaked into her psyche and had taken over her rational thought.

"All that pain and injustice has seeped into me. No way I'll survive the awareness of such ordeals," she muttered, scanning the back of her hand to pay the fare before getting out in front of her house. Inside, she rushed into the kitchen, gasping for water.

If it were a dream, she reflected, she should have unlimited tap water. She placed her hand under the sensor attached to the faucet, smiling at the reading instead of releasing her usual bout of foul language. Half a glass was left on her daily ration, telling her she was still living in reality.

Next, she turned on the news. The CBC's breaking news confirmed the bizarre natural weather phenomenon had lasted less than two minutes before disappearing as enigmatically as it had formed.

"We are waiting for confirmation as to how many people had been on that plane and their identities. We should receive this information any minute now," the anchor said. "There are no casualties or damage to downtown Toronto and no other airplane at the Billy Bishop Airport has been affected."

Cherry dropped onto the couch, transfixed at the TV screen.

"We have on the line Larry Husband from Environment Canada. Thank you for joining us on such a short notice, Mr. Husband." The man nodded and waited quietly for the questions the anchor had prepared for him.

"How can you explain this phenomenon, sir? Have you seen anything like it before?" The anchor seemed to love acting, and he was pushing past his dramatic limits.

"Hmm. The same phenomenon, yes, but it only rarely occurs in Ontario. It's mainly seen in the mid-west USA. What's unusual is its almost instantaneous appearance and disappearance. A tornado of that magnitude needs special meteorological conditions and enough runway in order to gather speed and force. Neither of these conditions were present today, so—"

"Thank you, Mr. Husband. Sorry to interrupt, but we've just received the identities of those that have perished in the crash."

A list of six names appeared on the screen.

"We can confirm, now, that everyone on board had been attending the annual oil and gas conference at the Metro Toronto Convention Center. They were the CEOs of several industry leaders who were flying in from New York for the weekend."

Cherry muted the sound. Her mind raised a frightening thought she wished would vanish: oil and gas were the main polluters of water and the earth—was this a coincidence or payback? "Water entanglement…water entanglement…water entanglement…" she repeated it like a mantra, wanting to appease the unstoppable, daunting force of nature. Then, almost involuntarily, her subconscious connected the previous purging events with what she'd just witnessed.

The anchor changed the subject, and she unmuted the TV.

"November 26, 2055 will go down in history as the day with the highest number of CEO casualties. Maahes Mazandir, CEO of Vivus Water Inc., the third largest water-bottling company in the world, has also been reported dead during a business trip to Egypt. Inside sources have confirmed the news. Health issues were mentioned as the cause of death, but no other details were given."

"Oh, my God!" Without hesitation, Cherry picked up her cell phone and dialed Ilanda. She realized she must be swamped with similar calls when she got the neurosurgeon's voicemail.

"Ilanda, it's me, Cherry. I just heard about Maahes. I'm really sorry." She didn't know what else to say, so she repeated the banal statement, "Call me if you need to talk," and hung up. Her gut told her the turbulence she'd witnessed had an innate, vengeful, and terrifying intelligence. Water had turned itself into a tool of death, scalable and relentless.

"Two more planes fell out of the sky in Saudi Arabia and China," the anchor continued. "Similar atmospheric turbulences were formed at thirty thousand feet. The captains had time to report the imminent danger before communication was cut off. While airlines can't release the full list of passengers, they will run an internal crosscheck to determine if any other CEOs or decision-makers were on these flights."

"I'll run my own," Cherry said out loud. She lowered the TV's volume. "Siri, identify problematic offshore projects of companies run by CEOs who died today. Get their names from online newsfeeds."

"Checking now," the soothing voice assured her.

Cherry kept her eyes glued to the images from the Chinese crash. The one in Saudi Arabia had happened over the ocean, and a rescue mission was about to commence.

"There are four recent entries for Banaris Geological, Dinaris Prospecting, Fabianer, and Potomac Investments. The first two are involved in offshore oil and gas exploration. Serious leaks were reported back in August 2055. Previous similar incidents took place in 2037, 2041, 2042—"

"Okay, okay," the woman interjected. "What about the other two?"

"They own oil pipelines. Most of them run over Native American lands. Spills contaminating multiple natural habitats in North and South Dakota ignited a standoff the companies squashed with government help."

"Is that the one from two years ago?"

"Confirmed. Very little was done to clean up the polluted areas."

"That explains the airplane crash," Cherry said.

"I do not understand the command," Siri replied unfazed.

"Never mind. Thank you, Siri."

The strident sound of her cell phone ringing startled her. It was from an unknown number and had no AR options, but she answered it anyway. "Yes?"

"Hey, Cherry, it's Romana Pilb," a hoarse voice said.

"Romana, how unexpected! Are you okay? I didn't recognize your voice."

"I have a bad cold. The conditions here aren't very welcoming," the WFA president explained. "Is everyone safe?"

"Oh, yes! We were worried about you. The worldwide craziness has reached a new level. Did you hear about the plane incident in Toronto?"

Cherry heard only crackling and background noise in reply.

"Romana! Romana!"

"Sorry. It's a borrowed connection, not very reliable. The government's blocking most of the outgoing traffic. What did you ask?"

"About the unusual tornado that appeared in Toronto this afternoon, crashing a plane. Several CEOs of oil and gas corporations died."

"Oh, my God! No, I didn't know."

"Romana, this is no coincidence. All these companies are heavy polluters. Water killed them."

Cherry stood up, excited she had someone with which to share her theory. "And there were other, similar incidents on the same day."

"I don't know what to say, Cherry. Here the army and mercenaries hired by Mosamoni and Narankama are at a standoff, but there are rumors the army's offensive is imminent."

There was a pause and then some coughing and sneezing.

"Romana, were there any negotiations? Are Mosamoni and Narankama willing to preserve the vent? Their stubbornness will destroy them and could start a war."

After reading more about the political sensitivities in that region and the implications of those countries succumbing to US powers, Cherry had realized how fragile the balance between peace and war really was.

"We met with government officials and they assured us that the vent wouldn't be touched. They aren't going to give into the US's pressure."

Cherry smiled at how the intent of her thoughts had reached Romana Pilb. "That's good news, isn't it?"

"Not yet, Cherry. The support offered by China, Russia, Japan, and most of the Asian countries is still unofficial. Documents are being drafted. A common front will block any US blackmail attempt, which is the main concern right now."

"How soon will it be signed?"

"In a week, maybe two. There's a lot of bureaucratic red tape. Parliaments have to gather behind closed door sessions to approve it."

Cherry kept silent, thinking of what else could be done.

"Cherry, are you still there?"

"Yes, I'm here. When are you coming back?"

Again, the crackle, and Romana's voice broke off. "Not before these agreements are in place. Only then will the US stand down, I think."

"Romana, have you thought of presenting a resolution in front of the UN?"

The woman walked around the couch, unable to contain her frustration with how slowly the decision-making factions acted, even now, after there had been tangible proof water had begun to react to injustices. "You're the president of UN-Water. They'll listen to you," Cherry insisted.

Romana's answer was barely audible, and the limnologist increased the volume to maximum.

"I agree. I've been thinking lately that this could be another solution. I'll ask my colleagues to prepare a draft. Cherry, please send my assistant any ideas you might have.

"I have to go now. Take care," Pilb said, and the connection cut off.

"There is still hope," Cherry said, pretending the WFA's president could hear her.

Cherry rushed into her office, opened her laptop, and feverishly typed clauses to be included in the UN resolution draft.

"Governments will agree to the following:

- to hold, effective immediately, all oil- and gas-drilling operations performed by either national or international companies;

- to hold, effective immediately, all the mining operations in areas that were once declared natural safety zones or in close proximity to such sensitive zones;

- to hold, effective immediately, any manufacturing operations that, intentionally or not, dump chemical residues into rivers, lakes, or coastal areas;

- to hold, effective immediately, any water harvesting from underground or above-ground sources. All existing explorations must be monitored by international teams of experts and specific quotas should be put in place;

- the above restrictions will be kept in place indefinitely.

"What else…what else?" she asked herself, aware of the huge demand, especially for developed countries. "Everyone will complain, so they need something in return. Nothing else will keep them quiet and content other than money, so let's give it to them."

She added another line: "Loss of profit will be assessed on a case-by-case basis. Monetary compensation will be provided for the transition to complementary and sustainable industries. Barter transaction to be considered first." *They might like going back to the basics*, she thought amused.

Cherry read all the points one more time. "Not bad. They can add as much legal verbiage around it as they want, but the meaning has to stay."

She squinted her eyes, thinking hard at what else might be required to kick off the discussion at such a high level. Cherry gave up after several moments. The email for Romana Pilb's assistant was ready. She hit send, then went to the kitchen to prepare herself dinner.

CHAPTER 17

"Kahuna is ready." Nanette addressed Ilanda who was sitting with Marinka on a couch in her office, giving the healer's daughter assurances about the success of the surgery.

"Dr. Roppocone is an amazing ophthalmologist and my equal as a surgeon. This isn't the part I'm worried about," Ilanda said, gently touching the other woman's hands. Her skin was soft and warm. For a second, she lost her train of thought, disoriented by the deep green of the Hawaiian's eyes, the color of a Mexican cenote.

While taking care of Kahuna, Ilanda had grown fond of Marinka, her siblings, and the inclusive island community. The gentle talk, the profound understanding for the environment, and the strong spiritual foundation shepherding the islanders' lives, impressed her more than she was willing to admit.

"The agate crystal we purchased for your father is of the highest purity possible. Its cut is flawless and it will fit his pupil like a glove."

"Thank you for all you've done for him, and also for letting me stay here with him." Marinka's eyes leaked tears that almost found their way down her chocolate milk colored cheeks, but she wiped them quickly away. "He can't transition yet. I'm not ready to take his place. You have to bring him back."

She released her nervousness by grabbing her long hair in a brusque gesture and brought it over one shoulder, where she continued to caress it slowly.

Ilanda couldn't commit to more words of encouragement. She had no clue as to how Kahuna's body would react when the structured water flowing into his veins through the perfusion would be gradually decreased.

"Ask the entire community to pray for him. He's strong and his spirit will continue to fight."

Ilanda couldn't believe the words that had just come from her mouth. It felt as if she'd been spiritually radicalized without her consent or the awareness of when the transformation had occurred.

"You can watch on the monitor, if you wish," she said and walked out.

"Dr. Roppocone is waiting for you," Nanette confirmed as soon as she saw Ilanda coming down the corridor to the operation room.

Ilanda joined the ophthalmologist in the small area adjacent to the one where Kahuna lay in a comatose state as he was being prepared for crystal insertion.

"Sorry for the delay. I had to ward off some of his daughter's concerns."

"I hope you didn't make unnecessary promises," the man replied in a sober tone.

His build reminded her of Maahes. Part of his mouth twitched when saying certain words, but he totally lacked Maahes's sense of humor.

"I told her what we both know: that the biggest hurdle is the recovery."

"That's good. I don't want any hysterical nonsense in case the outcome isn't a happy ending," he replied, content he wouldn't be held responsible. "If the crystal doesn't vibrate as expected or if the information contained in the water is somehow corrupted and doesn't diffuse properly, there's nothing we can do."

"Yes, I explained that very clearly to her."

"Let's not delay it any further. I've entered his face's coordinates into the computer. The crystal was cleared, too."

"Good luck to us," Ilanda said and watched Dr. Roppocone hit "Enter" on the digital markings displayed on the thick pane of glass separating them from the operation room.

Almost immediately, the robotic arm positioned above Kahuna's head shifted slightly to the right and picked up one of the two tiny crystals from the glass tray. When it got closer to the man's right eye, a part like a think finger extended from the robotic arm to pull up the eyelid. With one smooth motion, it placed the crystal on Kahuna's pupil, leaving only the iris exposed through a specially cut hole. Several drops of liquid escaped from a tube attached to the finger that was still holding the eyelid.

"One down, one more to go," Dr. Roppocone said without taking his gaze off of the monitor. "His vitals are good. We should be done in no time."

Ilanda showed him her crossed fingers but made no comment. She was tense and not willing to count a defeat on the first attempt.

"How long before we can see the crystal's vibrations?" the ophthalmologist asked.

Ilanda had an irrational urge to swear to release the pressure that had built up from all of the unknowns surrounding their research.

"Minimum within the hour, but it might take longer," she replied as seriously as she could. She resisted taking her eyes from the robotic arm which had just finished with the second implant.

Dr. Roppocone hadn't noticed the tinge of sarcasm in her voice, and she remained focused on the closing steps of the intervention. He touched the "Activate nanobots" key on the glass and only then did he turn toward Ilanda with a satisfied smirk on his face.

"There's no going back now. Those little buggers will mark the path to the pineal gland. It's a permanent mark. Any stimuli that touches the crystals will hit it right away."

Ilanda stared at Kahuna as if expecting him to open his eyes, move his arms, and get up from the immaculate table and dance around the room under the loving protection of his ancestors, against all odds.

"It's only permanent until we develop a new coding routine able to divert the informational flux to other parts of the brain for different types of processing," she clarified.

"Yes, of course," the man agreed. "Your code developer did a great job; he's an artist."

Ilanda enjoyed the praise and returned the smirk.

"Did I understand correctly that his daughter's next in line for a similar implant?"

The neurosurgeon nodded, then replied, "In about a week. I want to see Kahuna's reaction first. A positive response will, of course, be the determining factor to her getting it. We hope her father's knowledge will be transferred to her after being decoded by the crystal."

"You're optimistic." Dr. Roppocone looked as if he wanted to say something else, but changed his mind.

"I'll be sending you daily updates on his status," Ilanda assured him. "Thank you again."

"No problem," he said and left the room. His assignment for the day at the research facility was finally over.

Hypnotized by the nanobots' fluorescent path inside Kahuna's brain, the woman couldn't move.

"Kahuna, please, don't join your ancestors yet. There's so much work left for you here. We all need you. Please!" Ilanda murmured.

She gathered her thoughts from stretching further into the abyss of desperation by touching them with a flutter of positivity. Losing Maahes so unexpectedly had affected her emotionally, making her spirit lay shallow, incapable of picking itself up and moving on. It had been hidden under the debris of crumbled feelings and memories, scoffing at her attempts to resuscitate it.

Executing Maahes's will proved to be easier than she'd thought and only when she'd received his belongings from the Canadian Embassy did she let a deluge of tears soak her entirely, releasing the self-imposed shackles that had guarded her emotions so well until then.

She didn't want Kahuna's death to follow so soon and extend an agony that already had drained her limited emotional bank.

Ilanda heard the door open behind her. "Sorry to interrupt," Nanette said. "Marinka's waiting for you. She's worried. She wants to hear directly from you that the implant went okay."

Without turning her head, Ilanda replied, "I'm coming. Everything's fine. Everything's just fine." She followed the younger woman out of the room.

• • •

The email invitation to attend the UN session for the proposed resolution scaling back on any type of exploration, drilling, and manufacturing with a high and visible environmental impact arrived only hours before Romana Pilb had called Cherry to let her know she was back in New York, safe and sound.

"I'll tell you stories you won't believe," she confessed. "Just come over, and I promise that after the resolution is presented, whether it's passed or not, we'll spend some quality time together."

"Okay, I'll be there," Cherry assured her. "Any hint at how the countries most affected might react?"

"Not a clue. There's significant groaning, as you predicted, but that's normal for any resolution the UN brings forward. This time, what we propose affects everyone evenly. We have to obey the same rules."

Cherry giggled. She liked the humbling circumstances their neighbor to the south had to endure.

She was sitting on one of the balconies on the right side of the assembly room, along other special guests. She took in the atmosphere of the enormous hall that had witnessed so many historical decisions. Some of them had been more political than others, generating division instead of cohesion. Cherry felt like she was sitting inside a time capsule. The photos lining the walls up to the main door of the assembly room revealed little to no change in furniture and the room's overall look. The most visible change she noticed had been a new type of flooring, a kinetic energy surface that absorbed the impact of their steps and used it to power the room. In addition, they'd replaced the shiny UN logo with a huge display at the front of the room on which simultaneous translations of the discussions scrolled continuously; the jobs of translators had been taken over by AI.

Cherry pulled a small bag of pretzels—the perk given to all guests—from her purse. She opened it and started chewing on them, one by one, as if she were preparing to watch a movie.

The UN president, originally from India, approached the microphone. He hummed a couple of times, then spoke. "Please, take your seats. We'll start shortly."

The people still standing shuffled in and out of the rows. Knowing the stakes of the gathering, Cherry expected the meeting to drag on into stiflingly long hours, interrupted by many breaks.

"Hello, ladies and gentlemen," the UN President began. "Thank you for attending such an essential meeting. It means that my name still carries some influence with all of you." His remark raised a wave of laughter. Cherry had never met the president in person, but she was accustomed with his fragile appearance and the baritone voice.

The meeting was being broadcast live, an event that was only be matched in importance by the announcement of an unexpected Third Degree Encounter. Cherry smiled at the thought. She knew such disclosure should have taken place decades ago, even during her childhood, no matter how advanced the civilization was. A common language existed, a bridge of understanding could be laid over the difference between universes. Her mind formulated the parallel association to bring forth the uniqueness of water. What vocabulary might be required to fill the evolutionary gap between us and water? She switched her attention back to the discourse.

"As always, I'll be blunt with my introductory speech, no double meanings or political correctness. Now, more than ever, is the time to dispel the ignorance that we have all pulled over our awareness as an easy excuse to deny the reality of our social, environmental, and spiritual degradation."

Several coughs followed his pause. Not disrespectful ones, Cherry thought—from where she was sitting she was able to grasp the body language of those who had done it.

"Mrs. Romana Pilb, the UN-Water president, sent me a very unusual resolution to present to the assembly." He sipped slowly from a small glass of water before continuing. "If the gravity of the irregular events of past months haven't convinced you and your governments of the dire situation we're in, I don't know what else will. I'll let Mrs. Pilb instill more fear into the non-believers," the president said and muted his microphone.

A handful of the attendees giggled, but immediately hushed. Cherry was also ready for the somber prospects about to be delivered by her friend.

"I'll follow in Mr. President's footsteps regarding the bluntness of my message. I'm not going to use storytelling as a means to mellow your decisions, which are probably already made," she said in a harsh tone, "but let's not be presumptuous. I recently returned from Mongolia after weeks spent shoulder-to-shoulder with water and environmental activists from all over the world. Our determination has convinced the government to stand up to US corporations that have tried to harvest a primary water vent. We—and I mean everyone involved in this movement—thinks that certain industries and multi-nationals in general have no understanding of what has caused water's erratic behavior. They still deny what has been explained with undeniable scientific proof: water is alive. Water has awakened and is now aware of the entire history of abuse we have put it through over thousands of years but especially over the last two centuries."

She paused and watched the audience. Still faces that were silent participants in a poker game looked back at her. Only a few displayed some empathy.

"There's no point in listing all of the incidents that have shattered our daily lives. How many people have to die before countermeasures are applied and taken into effect?"

Locks of her hair came down over half of her face, and she tucked them behind her right ear. Hot blood colored her cheeks, and her large palms grabbed the sides of the podium. "The maritime Silk Road is at a standstill. This is the latest news I've received before coming here today. Did you know that? I'll bet it was kept confidential. In the Strait of Malacca and in the Red Sea, the viscosity gradient of water is comparable to that of honey. Ships are barely moving, increasing their burnt fuel rate and the time to get to their destination. In the last several weeks, four offshore drilling platforms have inexplicably sank. No one onboard could be saved.

"Is this coincidence? Sabotage? I don't think so."

From her seat on high, Cherry gasped for air. Her students' findings in Lake Ontario had spread at a faster rate than anticipated.

"Airplanes are falling from the sky like flies.

"For God's sake, you still don't get it?" Romana Pilb showed them she had no more consideration to keep a prestigious function if she couldn't do her job properly.

"The desalinized water has suffered structural modifications, as well, and is less and less reliable. After one month of using such water, consumers have reported stomach cramps and blurry vision. The salt is still present at the molecular level, affecting us internally, which means it will harm our crops, too.

"I beg you to vote in favor of this resolution. None of the clauses benefits one country over another as was the case in previous instances. We've recommend a total shutdown of the main polluters in all industries. Small and sustainable businesses will have room to thrive.

"Don't get me wrong: I'm looking out for all of humanity's interest. The Earth will survive long after we are gone. Thank you."

The moment she stopped talking, the majority of the ambassadors erupted like small volcanoes of noise, forgetting etiquette and place. "This is part of the Earth's natural cycle! We can't shut down whole industries! What game are you playing?"

Cherry couldn't stand to watch them bark like a pack of wild dogs. Earth would eventually have all of its energy sucked out of it and the human race would be extirpated and discarded like a rotten tooth. She went outside to the hallway to clear her head.

Cherry hadn't noticed the woman approaching her. "Enjoying the show or crying for your money? "Benny Hertz from The Primary Water Institute," she introduced herself after a short pause and extended her hand. "We met a couple of years ago at one of the WFA workshops organized here by Geanina Botha, God bless her soul."

Sorry, I don't remember," the limnologist said, trying not to pretend.

"No worries. It was a quick encounter." The sagging skin on her neck and hollow cheeks couldn't hide that she was in her late sixties. The color of her hair had been dyed to a shade that only added to her grandmotherly air.

"I met Romana Pilb in Mongolia. She's tough," Benny remarked, looking at the images displayed on the AR devices as to how the president had resolved to restore order.

"She told me how close she was to getting into trouble several times when the government's goons raided her hotel and the activists camp near Narankama's property. I convinced her to go. I couldn't forgive myself if—" Cherry's tears shyly emerged.

The older woman touched her arm consolingly. "We have each other's back. As you can see," she nodded toward the assembly room, "they are on fire because the resolution put forward by UN-Water is backed by the agreement signed by the Asian nations."

"Yes, it was worth going there to put pressure on the government."

"What's amazing is the fact that old-standing US allies have signed it. They didn't submit to blackmail."

Cherry smirked. Her dry lips couldn't afford a full-blown smile.

"Here comes China," Benny announced.

The Chinese ambassador spoke quietly as they read the captions. "Over the last five decades, we, the People's Republic of China, have tried to look the other way when pollution levels reached unprecedented highs. Production output and healthy returns were our soaring goals. Our citizens are dying at an unprecedented rate, and young couples are not considering the newly-incentivized birth policy. Children are not desired anymore in a society that cannot provide the basic elements of life."

The tall man had dark bags under his eyes. Cherry had the impression that a tremor had convulsed his right hand. "We know what China has decided, but will the USA, Australia, and the few remaining European countries follow suit?" the limnologist asked loudly.

"They will. If they continue on this path, no one will trade with them or consider any other dealings. Isolation is a powerful punishment. It will be a first for the US," Benny answered.

"They have one night to sleep on it," Cherry said.

She noticed Romana slipping from the room. "Benny, it was great seeing you again, I have to go now. If all goes well, I promise to visit you at the Institute."

"No worries," the older woman repeated what seemed to be her favorite reply. "Everything is going to be just fine," she added confidentially, surprising Cherry with her demeanor.

• • •

"Are you going to be further involved in negotiating compensations?" Cherry asked Romana while mulling over a tiny cup of coffee at a terrace near the UN building. Romana had lost some weight, and her head seemed a bit oversized for her slender body.

"I've opted out. That's the consulting firms' bread and butter. I'm back with you guys, monitoring water's reaction to our first measures of scaling back," she replied.

Cherry loved her. Romana could have been an older sister—much older—but someone she could potentially rely on in times of need, nevertheless. "It's healthy to be out of that bureaucratic quagmire. It drains you and keeps you away from meaningful action," the limnologist said.

The WFA president kept quiet.

"What's on your mind?"

Romana raised her gaze from her fingers which had been folding a paper napkin into various shapes.

"I expect the scale back to hit us within a week—less oversea traffic, fewer imported goods, and higher prices on locally produced ones."

"That's it? No mobs on the streets? No destruction of private and public property?" Cherry asked, laughing as if she were enquiring about a potential brawl at a frat party.

Romana placed a saucer on top of the napkin so the wind wouldn't blow it away. She slowly massaged her temples.

"It can't be worse than what I witnessed in Mongolia, and I don't think full-scale mobs are our main worry."

Cherry couldn't understand her friend's point-of-view. "Why's that?"

"Who, in the past, have been the main puppeteers generating the majority of the so-called political and economic frictions between nations?"

Cherry thought for a long moment. "Politicians," she said.

"Correct! They stood in front of the cameras and looked brave, ethical, and dedicated to their countries and constituents, but the next day, they'd act completely contradictory to their previous statements."

A server approached their table. "Can I bring you anything else?" she asked.

"Another chocolate cupcake, please," Romana replied. "This'll buy us another half hour to bask in the sun." She addressed her friend, "You look confused—let me explain. The common front formed by the presidents, ambassadors, army generals, and most of the Fortune 1000 CEOs shuns any political, opportunistic statements. Anyone who attempts it will be laughed at and ostracized. It's suicidal."

Cherry had to admit that she hadn't been thinking globally.

"I'll be flying back to Toronto tomorrow. This might be my last trip south for a while. As you've said, restrictions will be imposed soon, confining us to smaller areas."

The shadow cast by the office building standing at the entrance to the alley crept toward them, touching the tips of their shoes. Men in suits passed by talking loudly about another ten percent drop in the stock market. Money still seemed their main focus; it wouldn't be for much longer.

"We'll be swallowed up soon," Romana Pilb remarked. She pointed her chin toward the twisted shade that had already crawled up her ankle.

"It would be an easy end for all of us." Cherry couldn't stop herself from making a sarcastic comment in the tense situation.

"Consensus always brings positivity and hope. If I've learned anything by being the UN-Water president in this pit of snakes it's that consensus is a rare gem, and I'm thankful for what's been achieved thus far."

The cupcake arrived, and Romana cut it in half. Cherry picked up her share and bit into it. Crumbs fell into her cupped left hand. They smiled at each other as they enjoyed the chocolate melting in their mouths.

"Water's safe for the time being," Romana said, "but the fight's not over yet."

The shadow of the building tightened its grip on the lower parts of their bodies, creeping up faster. The alley fell silent, distant car horns reached them through the thickness of a multitude of universes, muffled and misplaced. The table vibrated under the sudden buzz of Cherry's cell. She dropped the crumbs from her hand onto the plate in front of her, then touched the screen.

Found who planned the explosion in Toronto!!! Bonus in your inbox. But does it matter now?

Anonymous was cryptic as usual. They'd given her good news but asked a troubling rhetorical question.

"Everything okay?" Romana inquired.

Cherry swallowed the remaining bit of cupcake, wiped her hands on a napkin, and looked straight at her friend.

"Let me ask you something." At this point in time she could only guess at what Anonymous had meant by *Does it matter anymore?* "Should we, as a movement, still pursue those companies and individuals that have caused so much damage, or should we consider yesterday's vote as a peace offering, a reset for all of their wrongdoings?"

Romana Pilb removed her eyeglasses and put them on the table. She placed the empty cup of coffee on her plate and pushed it away from her. "This fresh start should have a strong, trusting foundation. I don't expect one hundred percent compliance, but the number of fakers will be small and we'll root them out."

"So, should we let go of revenge in the name of those who died in Toronto?" Inside her, Hayyin was struggling with the concept of letting go. Justice should prevail no matter the consequences.

"I can't condone an act that caused so many deaths. I've mourned several friends, too, but I'm willing to forgive. Why carry such baggage instead of looking forward?" Intense heat engulfed Cherry's chest. She took it as a sign from her intuition that Romana was right—why mull over a tainted past whose wounds were still infested with pestilence? She waved at the server for the bill.

"I'll update you on any changes in Kahuna's health. The other day, I got an email from his neurosurgeon. For the last eight months, she's been working on a technology that could bring him back. She has high hopes."

Romana Pilb stood up and leaned over to hug her friend. "I'll dedicate my prayers to him tonight. I'll see you around." She threw her bag over her shoulder and walked away, back to the UN building, ready to continue the fight.

CHAPTER 18

Ilanda greeted Cherry as she entered her office in the newly renovated school on King Street. "There you are!" The last-minute architectural design changes requested by the neurosurgeon had turned both the interior and the exterior into a much more pleasant and practical environment.

Ilanda came around her desk to hug her friend and introduce her to a dark-skinned man lying on the couch. His colorful shirt brought a unique aura to the man's appearance.

"Ojani, this is Cherry Mortinger, the WFA activist I mentioned to you. She's the one who helped secure the funds to buy this location and turn it into a top-notch research facility."

The man stood up and extended his hand, a large smile plastered on his face. Cherry sensed a tinge of cinnamon and another spice whose name escaped her. "How are you?"

"I'm fine, thank you. How are you?" she replied, shaking his hand.

"Cherry, Ojani is the only person I know that runs a crystal-based business. His concept, developed several years ago, is the closest to what we want to achieve through our own research."

Ojani waved his right hand in a gesture of humility. "I'm small potatoes compared to Ilanda's vision."

"He's a visionary, too," the doctor emphasized, "and being modest is not always the best approach. Ojani has a wealth of blood samples he uses for enhanced experiences."

"Is this the same as the Kilimanjaro climb you mentioned to me?" Cherry asked.

"Yes, it is." Ilanda went back to her chair and gestured for her guests to sit on the couch. "My initial, unshakable belief about the intimate relation between water and crystals was correct. Not that I didn't trust all the smarter people before me who had the same conviction, but reaching the same conclusion myself was much more rewarding."

Ojani shuffled his slim body against the armrest. Cherry read the admiration he had for Ilanda in his eyes.

"You haven't heard from me in a while because I didn't want to share partial results," the neurosurgeon said, addressing Cherry. "The last three months have been so intense, I've barely made it home to change my clothes.

I've resigned from my position at St. Michael's, by the way," she said as an afterthought, winking at her friend.

"What? Why?"

"I just told you: I couldn't keep my head on straight. This new field is much more interesting if you delve completely in."

"Not even part-time?"

Ilanda shook her head. "At least not for a while." Exhilaration seemed to exude from the doctor's rough features. She appeared genuinely happy and fulfilled by the experience. Maahes' hovering memory kept its distance from Ilanda's daily activities, infusing her with renewed energy.

"You guys should see the beauty of these molecular structures. They're divinely created. The higher their purity, the better their internal pattern is. It's flawless—"

"Is it practical or not?" Cherry said, interrupting Ilanda's discourse.

Ojani giggled at the activist's impatience, giving the impression he had already been aware of what the doctor had meant to communicate by her lengthy introduction. He crossed his legs, pulled an imaginary zipper across his lips, and threw the key away.

"Very much so. The crystals can be sliced horizontally and loaded up with code routines that can use the crystal's vibration to encode information, store data, and make it easily accessible later on with the right thought-command. The code can also unlock certain areas in the brain."

"More than the known five or ten percent?" Cherry asked.

Ilanda smirked and glanced at Ojani, giving him the nod to intervene.

"I suggest we walk and talk." He stood up and made an invitational gesture toward the door. Cherry left first, then Ilanda, followed by Ojani. They turned right at the stairs to the second floor.

"The symbiosis of water and crystals opens up new research territory," Ojani said, walking beside the activist. "When I started my business, I had a limited understanding of the real potential of what could be done. I just wanted my patrons to receive a unique experience that was so freakishly good they'd come back and spread the word."

Cherry kept her head down while walking but listened attentively.

"But some of them—for reasons I can't explain—went beyond the levels filtered by the crystal to feel an expansion of their minds beyond comprehension. And these people weren't the meditative type—certain sensitivities had been triggered from within."

"When did you find out about it?" the limnologist asked.

"Not immediately. It took months for some of them to honestly admit the profound feelings that had been ignited by the process."

They reached the upper floor and Ilanda led them to one of the recovery rooms. She opened the door and stepped in. Cherry couldn't see past her due to the doctor's wide frame, but she could hear Marinka's voice greeting them. She rushed to the Hawaiian woman and hugged her, feeling her tight, reciprocal embrace.

"I'm sorry I haven't visited the hospital in the last couple of months—I've been extremely busy," she said in an attempt to justify her behavior.

"We've been in good hands. Besides, Ilanda forbade me from updating you on the status of my father's health. She wanted to surprise everyone with the outcome of the surgery."

Marinka's demeanor had improved and the sparkle in her eyes had returned; she seemed to radiate an ambience of happiness.

"You already did it?" Cherry almost screamed. She turned to Ilanda who appeared to be smiling through each of her pores.

Marinka nodded to the doctor and moved to the side. Behind her, lying propped upon pillows, was Kahuna, watching the conversation.

"Kahuna Lapa'au," Cherry said, feeling a rush of energy embolden her to step forward. She took his hand and squeezed it gently, transferring as much gratefulness as she could muster. She glanced back at her companions.

"Nice surprise, isn't it?" Ojani said.

"It was hard to contain myself from not sharing this miracle with the world. We wanted you to see my father only after he returned from his astral wanderings."

Cherry couldn't help but stare at the amber-like crystals looking back at her through Kahuna's transformed eyes. Marinka moved to the other side of the bed. There were no tubes attached to Kahuna's body, save a clear, nasal cannula in his nose to provide him with additional oxygen. His head and face tattoos were gone, replaced with new skin that had been harvested from his back. He looked like a different person, but the size of his head still left a powerful impression on Cherry, even if, under the gown, his body seemed less imposing than before. He was also freshly shaved, and his overall look was indicative of his improved health.

"His eyes follow us everywhere," Marinka told Cherry. She patted her father's hand with confidence. "That's a good sign." Marinka glanced to where Ilanda and Ojani were standing.

"Yes, indeed. All of his vitals are stable," Ilanda confirmed. "The nanobots have cut a path into his brain that has already started to develop new neural patterns. His recovery curve should visibly progress within the week."

Cherry prized Ilanda's poised tone after the incertitude of the past months.

"When are we planning to make the announcement?"

The other two women exchanged a quick glance as if they already knew the answer and Cherry was the last to learn about it.

"As soon as my father is able to stand on his own and without any tubes attached to his body. That'll be a powerful statement. When those who planned the explosion see him, I want them to read defiance in his attitude."

Cherry's hypnotized gaze couldn't break away from the waves of color and hues sparkling in the playful rays from the sun coming through the window.

"His locomotor functions are back, but his muscles need significant therapy. The area of his brain that communicates with his vocal cords was the only one we couldn't recuperate," Ilanda said.

"Next week, he's scheduled for another intervention: a speech synthesizer loaded with the latest AI, able to respond to multiple stimuli. All of the information he needs to access will be stored on the crystals and semantically linked with anything else previously downloaded or available on the Internet. He might become the first known technologically-enhanced human being."

This was one of the few instances since Cherry had met Ilanda that the doctor had bragged about her achievements. She returned an encouraging smile and said a heartfelt, "Thank you."

Following Romana Pilb's indirect advice, Cherry kept the names of those responsible for the WFA explosion in Toronto to herself. They had been multi-nationals with dealings in Hawaii whom Kahuna had opposed in their attempts to maintain the islands as outdoor laboratories. In time, their harmful chemicals would have annihilated the birthing strength of a land that had once been blessed and protected by spirits.

They used the conference to eliminate Kahuna and point a finger at the water industry, Anonymous' message had read. *Conniving bastards!*

Cherry let go of the Hawaiian's hand and moved away from the bed.

"Is he aware of what's happening in the world right now?" she asked the three of them. "Or what has happened to him?"

Ojani remained silent.

Marinka sat on a folding chair. She pulled her hair over one shoulder, and replied, almost in a whisper, "Not yet. An emotional shock might trigger a neurotransmitter and other chemical imbalances. His body is slowly coming back to normal on its own terms without the use of fake signals."

"It was an unanimous decision," Ilanda said. She sat on an armchair by the window. "He has to first come to terms with the transformation he's going through. There is a learning curve as to how to handle the embedded AI and software features developed for the crystal. If, up until now, he's had a conscious connection with the astral plane, we can't predict how that might change."

Cherry leaned against the door frame so she could see everyone from her vantage point. "Could the crystal diminish his sensitivities and shut down such communication channels?" she asked.

They looked at Kahuna at the same time, as if expecting him to answer the question, but he only stared back at them calmly, as if reassuring his visitors of his untapped inner-resources for handling the technological add-ons.

"Father, do you feel any different than before? Blink once for yes and twice for no."

Kahuna did none of that. Instead, he gazed intently and chose a third option. "I'm not sure yet."

"We put a mirror in front of him," Ojani said, breaking the extended silence. "He made a funny guttural sound. I'm convinced that, initially, he didn't recognize himself. The implants became the focus of his appearance and they drew everyone in. It happened to you, as well," he said to Cherry.

"Ojani, you told me earlier that you'd offered some water and diluted blood samples for Ilanda's experiments," the limnologist said.

"Yes."

"Which one did you use on Kahuna?"

The man scratched an itch behind his left ear, then answered. "He received the ones blessed by the monks. That's what brought Kahuna back. The vibration of the crystal was almost palpable. It was like watching someone blowing on embers hidden under quiet ash."

"That's powerful stuff," Cherry commented.

"His brain jolted as if under a massive electrical surge. Whatever the monks did to the water was exponentially enhanced by the crystal," Ilanda added. "His MRI matched that of a person in a high state of consciousness."

"This is what you wanted to achieve, isn't it?" Cherry said. The leg holding her weight went numb. She massaged her left calf several times, needles screaming, disturbed by the deep touch.

"We're only three weeks in, and I'm already blown away by how fast it worked," Ilanda replied. She masked a healthy yawn with the back of her palm, then continued, "Our initial vision just got broader. Imagine these crystals connected wirelessly, exchanging information, offering solutions at thought-speed. We can add a conscious layer of action to our unconscious mind while we physically rest."

Marinka giggled. "Let's turn ourselves into organic computers," she said as though she were amused by the prospect of becoming one herself.

"Your wish will turn to reality in less than a month," the doctor confirmed.

"Really?" Cherry couldn't hide her puzzlement.

"Together, they'll make a formidable pair," Ilanda reiterated.

None of them spoke for several long moments. Kahuna's breathing through the tube and the dim hallway discussions lulled them into their own thoughts.

"How did the Hawaiian community react to the news?" Cherry asked. "Do they consider Kahuna to be the same person?" She aimed her gaze at Marinka.

The Hawaiian woman peeked at her father. His encrusted eyes stared back vividly and hungry for her assessment.

"He *is* the same person," she replied passionately. Taking him back to the island would only serve to strengthen him. Pele[6] will welcome him with open arms. I can finish my training now."

---

[6]   Pele – In the **Hawaiian** religion is the goddess of fire, lightning, wind and volcanoes and the creator of the **Hawaiian** Islands

Cherry remembered her friend's concerns about filling in for her father before the knowledge had been completely passed onto her. With a sudden burst of energy, Cherry pushed herself forward against the door frame. The abrupt action made her lightheaded and she momentarily faltered.

"Are you all right?" the other three asked at the same time.

She grabbed the door frame for balance. "I need to get go now. I'm so very happy Kahuna's safe."

The image of the respected healer looking like a wizard from a video game didn't resonate with her. She felt awkward in his presence, and the thought of Marinka going through the same process disturbed her even more. If they were all going to have crystal eyes, why didn't they all just choose their avatar names now? Cherry thought, grabbing her bag from the floor.

"One question before you leave," Ilanda said.

"Yes?"

"We've all heard about the global agreement signed under the umbrella of the UN—it's a big win for everyone, but what's the next step? Do we implement what the resolution states, or is there more?"

Cherry thought for a second, not sure to what Ilanda had referred.

"'Effective immediately' doesn't mean that the affected corporations will automatically shut their operations down tomorrow morning. They'll most likely drag their feet while figuring out where to relocate employees, take proper measures to secure sites, and so on and so forth," the doctor explained. "Don't give me that look. I had to listen to Maahes' tirades when his company had been forced out, several times, by nationalization."

"I still don't understand what you mean by 'is there more'. I'm not aware of any Plan B; this is it!"

Her voice pitched from the frustration that her friend had little confidence in the agreed-upon procedure. At the same time, she might have assumed that most of the bureaucratic red tape would still be in place, causing delays.

"Water doesn't know about our good intentions yet. She'll keep hammering us on the ground and in the air until we find a way of communicating with her."

Ilanda shrugged her shoulders and tilted her head as if indicating her amazement that Cherry hadn't though to fan alternative option.

"I said it before: there is an evolutionary gap between us and water. We need a common language. Connecting with water at a deeper level is the key."

Cherry stepped back until she felt the reassuring firmness of the door frame and leaned back against it once more. "Give me a moment, please." She wasn't sure if her mind was searching for an answer or an excuse for a quick retreat.

The phrase, 'communicate with water' resonated in her psyche, making her freeze. She had a vision of a beautifully-colored, hardcover book with the front cover open. It was stuck in the mud. Intuitively, she knew that no physical effort would liberate it from its sticky embrace. She didn't understand the marks and scribbling on the pages. Cherry tried harder, but the lines floated swiftly off the cream-colored surface and rearranged themselves into intelligible words she could read, but the page shuffled by too quickly to reveal the one following. Similar inscriptions in bright red and green, and pyramids and cones suffered transformations when touched by the vibrations of her intent. Page by page she freed them from the mud's dirty vise, breaking the code into known language. She felt as if she was pulling herself up from the mud, shedding unnecessary emotional baggage, but it was more than that.

"Communicate with water," she repeated mentally.

The answer dropped on her as suddenly as a predator on a grazing gazelle: Masaru Emoto had translated words into images representing the feelings of water. He gave us the first letters of the alphabet. He showed us the way, but we stopped there, incapable of understanding his message.

"Yes, a common language with water is necessary," she said. The others looked at her, uncertain after her long silence. "You work with crystals and water. Encode a message about our new intentions, and release it into the oceans. The water's entanglement should do the rest."

No one reacted to her wacky statement, so she added, "At the same time, you can complete the vocabulary we'll use when communicating with water." Then, she turned around and left, still haunted by Kahuna's sparkly eyes.

ACKNOWLEDGMENTS

Any literary creation needs nurturing and focused attention in order to come out clear, concise and captivating. It was no different with *Water Entanglement*.

Many thanks to my older son, Theodore, who was the fist reader of the manuscript. His feedback on ideas and writing style were invaluable.

Thank you to my editor, Elise Abram.

Thank you to all of the beta readers: Anamaria Negrila, Isabela Gilcescu, Pawan Sharma, Gabriela Casineanu, Ted Mahr and Carly Nudday.

Thank you to those who were so kind as to provide testimonials: Rainey Marie Highley, Susan Ksiezopolski, Nina Munteanu and Gabriela Casineanu. Your kindness and enthusiasm are greatly appreciated, and I know that only blessed water is flowing through you.

To everyone else that gave a word of encouragement during the writing process, I wish that you become a friend of water, if you aren't already one. Nurture it, pray with it, make your own tribe aware of what water really is, and fight those that deny others' access to clean water.

BIBLIOGRAPHY

Campbell, Dan. 1989. *Edgar Cayce on the Power of Color, Stones, and Crystals*. Grand Central Publishing. 228pp

Dispenza, Joe. 2012. *Breaking the Habit of Being Yourself*. Hay House. 342pp

Emoto, Masaru. 2004. *The Hidden Messages in Water*. Beyond Worlds Publishing.168pp

Highley, Rainey Marie. 2012. *Water Code*. Divine Macroverse LLC. 238pp

Munteanu, Nina. 2016. *Water Is … The Meaning of Water*. Pixl Press, Vancouver, B.C. 584pp

Nuday, Carly. 2014. *The Water Codes*. Water Ink California. 288pp

ABOUT THE AUTHOR

Claudiu Murgan is an engineer with a deep yearning for writing with a meaningful message. Originally from Romania, he started writing Sci-Fi at 11-years old and was involved in the Romanian fandom until 1997 when he decided to immigrate to Canada.

Inspiration resurfaced within Claudiu after nineteen years of a creative drought. The result of that blessing from God was "The Decadence of Our Souls", a Fantasy novel touching on spirituality. The journey that culminated with the book mentioned above taught Claudiu that Love, Gratitude and Compassion are necessary life companions that should open one's sensibilities to the Divine Creator.

Writing "Water Entanglement" was a blissful joy that transported Claudiu into the fascinating world of water and crystals. This new book is the author's way of making people aware about the importance of water in our daily lives.

Claudiu lives with his wife and two boys in Richmond Hill, Ontario.

Connect at ClaudiuMurgan.com

Please leave your testimonials at Amazon.com and Goodreads.com